RULE BREAKER

LAS VEGAS VIPERS BOOK THREE

STACEY LYNN

Rule Breaker

Las Vegas Vipers Series

Book Three

Stacey Lynn

Copyright © 2022 Stacey Lynn

Content Editing: My Brother's Editor

Proofreading: Virginia Tesi Carey

Cover Design: Shanoff Designs

Rule Breaker is a work of fiction. Names, characters, places, trademarks, and incidents are used fictitiously or are the product of the author's imagination.

All rights reserved. No part of this work may be reprinted, reproduced, or transmitted in any form without written permission of the author, except by a reviewer who may quote brief passages for review passages only.

This purchased material is for personal use only and NOT to be shared. Thank you so much for respecting the author's wishes.

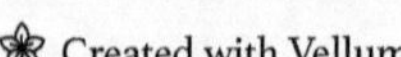 Created with Vellum

1

DOMINICK

The judge peered down at me through thick, black-framed glasses that looked way too small on his round face and balding head. He appeared less happy to be sitting on the bench than I was to be standing across from it.

Didn't really blame the guy. Probably sucked to have to be at work, dealing with assholes like me, the day after Christmas.

As for me, spending thirty-six hours in the county jail lock-up wasn't exactly a great holiday, but I'd also had worse.

I tugged on the cuff links at my wrists, straightening my dress shirt neatly pressed beneath my seven-thousand-dollar gray pinstripe suit, and awaited his verdict while he sniffed into a tissue and pretended like he was reading my file for the first time.

"All assault charges against the woman have been dropped," he muttered, loud enough for everyone in the courtroom to hear, but that wasn't a surprise.

Like I'd drug, kidnap, and sexually assault my *sister* for fuck's sake, but the media liked to spin the tale of me being the bad guy. The bar brawl I got into on Christmas Eve was merely more fodder for their entertainment. I didn't care enough to correct them, and having a sister was a secret I'd kept for long enough.

"And it appears it's your lucky day that the victim of your physical attack is also refusing to press charges." The judge sneered at me over the rim of those glasses.

He probably figured I was some rich prick, a professional athlete who could get away with murder. He wasn't altogether wrong, but that was only because the kind of men I'd ever considered murdering were the men who kept my sister and mom hooked on drugs and sold their flesh for payment.

Chad Attler, also known as *Crank* to those who knew his street name, wouldn't press charges against me, but he was first on my hit list. Had he died the other night, I wouldn't have lost any sleep over it.

"However, the club you destroyed during your tantrum has not been so understanding. For your charge of disturbing the peace, you will face sixty hours of community service. You will also pay for the damages accrued, totaling seventy-two thousand, three hundred and twenty-six dollars..." He glanced down at the paper in his hand and looked back up at me. "And thirty-nine cents."

I scoffed, unable to help it. Thirty-nine cents? They couldn't have rounded?

Next to me, my attorney shoved his elbow into my arm. "Shut up, Masters."

The judge glared. "Is something amusing to you, defendant?"

"No, Your Honor."

Except for the fact that for me, seventy-two thousand dollars wasn't much of a hardship even if I suspected the total wasn't nearly that high. On top of the fine I'd assuredly receive from the hockey league and my team's general manager, the other night's fiasco would end up costing me a pretty penny.

Every penny absolutely worth it to feel Crank's bones shatter beneath my fists and ribs break under my feet.

Fucking asshole.

The judge kept talking. I responded when necessary. Once his gavel pounded and he announced "case dismissed" I turned to my lawyer. "Thanks, man."

I shook his hand as he rolled his eyes. "Stay out of trouble until this community service is done or you'll be spending more than a day and a half in jail."

I didn't make promises I couldn't keep.

I'd do anything to keep my sister as safe as I possibly could. "See you around, Banks."

Jordan Banks was a great lawyer and had my respect. He'd helped me out of more than one jam and had even ensured my sister wasn't stuck with a public defender after she got picked up on a possession charge one night. He'd also helped me get her an emergency bed in one of the best rehab facilities in the state while I was locked up.

For now, and hopefully for the next ninety days, Lucy was safe. That was all that mattered.

I spun on my heels, walked down the small aisle and pushed open the doors leading me out of the courtroom, only to pull to an abrupt stop as Gabby Taylor and her husband—and my teammate—Joey, jumped to their feet.

She rushed to me, hands going to my biceps as she frantically scanned my face. "You were hurt."

I flinched from the contact of her hands on me before relaxing and brushed my finger over the gash on my cheekbone. The one hit Crank had gotten in. Hurt like a bitch due to the rings he wore, but I'd made him pay for that, too.

"I'm fine. Just a cut. Had worse during games. What are you two doing here?"

Joey's brows tugged in and he shook his head. "Didn't want you to come out of here alone."

"I insisted. We didn't realize the hearing would be closed though," Gabby said. "Are you okay? The other night..."

"Was nothing." I gently shook her off. For some damn reason, I was drawn to this woman. Not in the way that made me an asshole, but from the first night Gabby slid into a booth across from me at the bar Joey owned where the team tended to hang out, she'd made it her mission to include me. She was so damn nice, I'd actually felt bad being a dick to her.

She took my effort not to be a dick as me being a good guy. She was wrong, but she had some crazy magic ability to make the world seem less shitty. Somehow, I'd become friends with both of them over the last few months. Not in a hang out every week or anything, but neither of them irritated me as much as others, so I didn't mind their occasional company.

That they were there, though, was surprising.

When was the last time someone ever showed up for me? Definitely not since I was in college a decade ago.

I grabbed my keys from my pocket and flipped the ring around my thumb. "I need to get to the team's offices. Meeting with Coach and Pete in an hour."

"We know," Joey said. "We're taking you."

"Not necessary." I started walking for the exit, keys in hand, when Joey called out from behind me.

"Where's your car, asshole?"

Shit. I dropped my head and stared at the floor as his chuckle grew closer. His hand slapped my shoulder and gave me a quick shake. "That's what I thought. We're taking you. The team should know we're behind you. Whatever's going on, we support you."

Fuck, that felt good. Almost wiped away the embarrassment that I'd forgotten I didn't have a *fucking car* here because I'd come straight from holding to the courthouse, the suit brought to me by my lawyer's assistant. Hell. That meant my car was still parked near the club where I'd found Lucy. Probably hocked for parts by now.

Something else to add to the bill of this shitty holiday season. Why.... why they always had to fall apart around Christmas was an answer I would never receive.

"Thanks, Joey."

"Thank Gabby. It was all her idea."

"Of course it was," I muttered.

He played it off like he wasn't being a good guy, a good friend, probably because he knew not to push me too far. I'd told him once I had problems with my family, but he'd never asked for more information. He wasn't going to get it that day either, even if I saw the questions lingering behind his eyes still focused on me.

A smile twisted his lips and he shrugged. "Come on. Let's go hear the rest of the damage and then figure out how to move on from it."

Oh, if only the shit in my life was that easy. I'd have done it years ago. Unfortunately, my shit had followed me my entire life, literally from Detroit to Las Vegas, and the hits kept coming.

There was no way this was the end of anything.

I'd never be able to move on from the filth that clung to me.

But whatever, I'd let Joey and Gabby think this was a one-off.

No sense dragging them down with me.

"We'll be right here and can take you home when you're done."

Joey's tone left no room for argument. Gabby stood next to him, her hand curled around his arm and rested on his forearm. The two of them stood in front of the elevator we'd just exited like they'd physically prevent me from leaving without their help.

I had bigger things on my mind than arguing with them.

"Fine. Any chance we can swing by and see if my car is where I left it first?" I shoved a hand through my dark black hair and cringed. I needed a cut before it got too much longer, but it was never a priority during the season.

Assuming I'd have much of a season left after the other night.

"Of course we can. Good luck." Gabby grinned softly, worried eyes narrowing on me as she rested her head against Joey's bicep.

He slid his arm around his wife and nodded. "It'll all work out."

Right. Of course he'd think that. As much as I actually

respected Joey, he came from the iconic Taylor family, where everything for them, and people like them, always seemed to work out. Hell, he'd woken up married to Gabby, not remembering a damn thing, and within months they knew they were supposed to be together.

Not that I planned on ever being shackled to a human with a lifetime commitment, but life didn't work that smoothly for me.

Current predicament being the perfect example.

I headed toward the general manager's office, already knowing how this conversation would go—not great would be putting it mildly.

Coach Viktor, the team's head coach and a man who had always had my back, opened the door and stood in the doorway as I approached. He was the only person in my life who knew the truth about my circumstances. He was a hard coach, a guy who didn't care about anything other than hockey, but he'd been there for me in ways other people couldn't possibly understand. I owed him my life, literally, and the concern tightening his features made me fight down the urge to apologize for disappointing him.

"Had to be done," I said instead.

"There's always another choice," he replied.

Yeah, yeah. He'd think so. He'd been telling me I had another choice since the first time I ended up in jail.

He stepped back, gesturing for me to enter first and I wasn't the least bit surprised to find Pete Garner sitting behind his large black desk, hands clasped together, forearms resting on it, head tilted to one side. He wore a superior smirk I would relish punching off his face if ever given the chance.

My hands clenched into fists at his smug appraisal of me, a tic in his jaw as he caught my glare while I took my seat on the other side.

"Do you have anything to say?"

I smoothly kicked my ankle over my other knee and brushed non-existent lint off my suit while keeping my gaze trained on him. "I figured you'd have enough to say for the both of us."

With a heavy sigh, Pete continued. "I was able to speak with the judge and was given permission to assign your community service."

Huh. That wasn't what I was expecting.

Paid in more ways than one to be a famous movie star, I supposed. That it'd been twenty years since his face had been on a big screen didn't matter. Not that I didn't know how privileged I was now. But I slugged through generational filth to get to where I was.

This guy had been acting since he was ten. His mama acted. Her dad acted. Now he waved his status as owner and GM in all our faces. He was born to a former Canadian player who married his movie-star mom, but I didn't think Pete had ever swung a stick longer than the six inches tucked in his Tom Ford or Gucci dress pants.

Besides, he hated me. If I wasn't the best damn defenseman in the league, my ass would have been gone a long time ago. There was no doubt. Coach Vik had come between us about ready to blow our fuses more times than I could count.

His chin dipped, blue eyes narrowed on me. "So, do you want to explain what happened this time?"

He hated the attention I brought to the team off the ice. Not that I blamed him for that one. Too bad you couldn't choose your family —or their drama.

"Nope." I clasped my hands together and set them in my lap. Was I being a dick? Yeah.

Did I care? Not particularly. As long as my community service wasn't picking up trash left on the Strip in the middle of spring break week so it'd be mixed with vomit and other bodily fluids, I didn't care what this guy thought of me.

Even if I did tell him, he wouldn't understand.

He shot a glare to my coach, who was standing at my back, silently supporting me even if he wanted to reach out and wring my neck, and sighed again.

"All right." Pete slid a thin file in my direction. "Here are the details. As I'm sure you know, the success of our team over the last several years, particularly last season, has brought a renewed interest in the sport of hockey. The youth league registrations doubled this year and we're in need of a new coach. Season started a couple weeks ago but the dad who was the head coach took a job in another state."

"Coach," I deadpanned. Sweeping up vomit didn't sound so disgusting anymore.

"Who would have thought, huh? You can thank Vik for this one. Let's say my idea wasn't going to be so... fulfilling."

God, if only I could smack off his smirk.

"Fine." I grabbed the file and flipped it open and couldn't stop my jaw from dropping, brows raising. I couldn't school my expression in any way. "You want me to coach the Squirt division?"

What in the hell would I do with a bunch of nine and ten-year-olds?

A hand clasped down on my shoulder and gave me a gentle shake. *Of course. Of-fucking-course.*

"It'll be good for you, Dom. Those kids need someone to look up to."

Exactly like he figured I needed all those years ago. I hadn't been ten, but the age didn't matter much.

Fuck. My. Life.

I bit down on my tongue.

"Not my first choice," Pete reiterated. "Or my second. But remember, for some damn reason, these kids look up to you, so don't fuck it up."

"Right," I muttered and glanced back down at the spreadsheet. Ages and weight of kids with jersey sizes and numbers. Addresses. Emails and phone numbers. Babysitting a bunch of kids would be painful. They could have at least given me the Bantam division. A few fourteen-year-old teenage assholes would be easier to handle. But *kids?*

Pete kept talking like I wasn't internally freaking out. At ten, I'd only been playing for a couple of years. At eight, I was a late starter to youth hockey, especially in Michigan. Those first few years were a struggle, mostly for attention since my sister had been born a year earlier. I skated with a chip on my shoulder, a need to be seen, a desperation to please the only person in my life who had ever selflessly loved me.

And Coach Vik knew it all.

"Two days a week... three to five. You'll get your workouts in other times. I talked to the youth league commissioner, and we readjusted their game schedule around most of our away games so you won't miss much time with them."

It wasn't even a slap on the wrist. It would still be hell on Earth.

For me—and the kids who had to deal with me.

2

HOLLY

"**B**en! Come on! Get your shoes on and grab your water from the fridge!"

Muffled thumps and grunts came from his bedroom at the top of the stairs while I glanced again at my watch.

We were going to be late.

Again.

I *hated* being late. Especially on the days Evan noticed. Fortunately, at least for today, he was out of town, but he'd know somehow.

He always knew when I screwed up.

A groan sprung from my throat as my chest tightened. *It's just a practice. He's only ten.* I inhaled deep for a count of four and exhaled, panic still growing in my chest.

"Ben!"

"What!" he shouted, grinning at me at the top of the stairs. Shoes on. Hockey gear, at least what he could already wear, on. "I'm right here."

"Come on, kiddo. We're late."

His messy mop of blond hair in dire need of a haircut I kept procrastinating bounced as he jogged down the stairs.

His gear was in the back of my SUV, unwashed since we'd forgotten to take it out of my trunk after last Tuesday's practice. Then Christmas hit. My first Christmas Day I hadn't spent with him since the day he was born. The fact he was right next door—because yeah—my ex moved into the woman's house he was having an affair with—our neighbor and my now ex-friend two days after I caught them cheating, didn't matter. I hadn't gotten to see his face light up with excitement when he saw what Santa brought him. I'd had to feign the excitement on Christmas Eve. It wasn't the same.

Fortunately for me, right after Christmas, Evan took Kristi on a two-week trip to Hawaii, so Ben was all mine. At least for now.

As for me, I was struggling to be a single mom even if I'd always essentially been one during my marriage. But finding out your husband was screwing your best friend, and they'd been doing it for a while and you hadn't been smart enough to catch signs?

That was pretty damn humiliating.

So was having to see them on an almost daily basis.

I swore they made out harder and longer in their driveway when I pulled into mine just to prove their point.

Which I still wasn't sure what it was—that they were cheating assholes?

As much as I tried not to let it bother me. It did. Hell on Earth was having to live next door to your ex-husband because you couldn't afford to sell the home he'd bought at the top of the market that had since crashed and you'd listened to him since you were nineteen and pregnant and had dropped out of school, so now the only work you were qualified to do wasn't nearly enough to keep your son in the life he'd always been used to.

I blew out a breath, and opened the doors to my Aviator, my one splurge once I was awarded child support and alimony. If I had to watch Evan and Kristi ram their tongues down each other's throats, they could watch me drive a brand new, top-of-the-line, sixty-five-thousand-dollar vehicle. Did I need the extravagance? Nope.

Did I enjoy seeing Evan's jaw lock every time he saw it?

Yep.

Was I bitter and petty?

Definitely.

A heavy sigh left me as I climbed into the car.

"Wait!"

I jumped at his shout. "What, Ben?"

"My water. I forgot it."

My head hit the headrest. "Go get it. But hurry!" I called out as he was already taking off and running toward the front door. It took him forever to punch in our security code and then he was back, closing the door and rushing out to the SUV.

"Door!" I called out and he almost fell off our porch as he jogged back to hit the lock button.

The SUV shook and rattled as he slammed the door and mumbled a sorry.

"Don't slam—"

"The door. I know. I said I was sorry."

Two more days until he was back in school. Two more days until he was back in school.

But then I wouldn't get to see him. The story of every mother. Your kids drove you to the edge of insanity and then you went even more crazy when you didn't get to see them all the time.

"Hey." I turned and looked at him over my shoulder as I backed out. "How about if after practice tonight we go out to eat instead of me cooking?"

"Really?"

"Yeah." Because he'd been through a hell of a lot in the last year and none of it was his fault. I could get my shit together for him for a night. The haircut could wait.

Again.

"Dave and Buster's?"

I playfully glared at him. "Only if you *promise* not to whine when I say it's time to leave."

His mouth opened to speak but I cut him off.

"But I *promise* you can play for one hour."

His lips pursed. Pushed to one side. Gave me such a flashback to his father I had to hide my flinch. "Deal."

He held out his fist and I tapped my knuckles back at him.

He was ten and his main form of communication was fist bumps instead of hugs and cuddles. Damn, I missed those.

I WAS CONVINCED there had to be a special place in heaven for parents who sat through their child's sporting event practices. I wasn't even sure the sport mattered. They all had their negatives, but up near the top had to be sitting your butt on a metal bleacher in an ice-cold arena when outside the temperature was in the mid-sixties. I sat for two hours, twice a week wrapped in a winter coat no Nevadian should have ever owned, thick fur-lined gloves and hat on while clutching a hot chocolate or coffee—let's be real, normally it was coffee, and fought cringing at how absolutely uncoordinated my child was on skates.

It was akin to watching a giraffe slip across the ice. Part of that was because Ben got his dad's height. He was always one of the tallest kids in his class, and while he possessed an average set of athletic skills, once he was strapped into skates and wearing ten pounds of gear, he lost all sense of hand to eye to foot coordination.

He swung at the puck, slipped and crashed into the boards on his knees. Again. My own legs locked, fighting the urge to run to him to make sure he was okay. It wasn't the first or second time he'd wiped out. Closer to the twelfth, this practice alone. Despite the amount of time he spent practicing, despite the open skate hours we attended so he could improve because he *really wanted to make Dad happy*, I'd yet to see any sign of said improvement.

The coach, a new guy who skated so effortlessly it appeared he'd been born on skates, slid to a stop in front of Ben and offered him his hand. He pulled him to his feet, said a few words, and the entire time he spoke, my kid gazed up at the guy like he was a god among mortals.

"What the hell?" I muttered and glanced around at the nearby parents to check if anyone else had noticed him. None of the other moms seemed to be paying attention to anything other than the book in their hands or their cell phones.

I'd never seen this guy before, although an email had gone out yesterday alerting us to the change in schedule plans for practices —because that was so quick to rearrange—so I knew we had a new coach after the last dad had a transfer in his job, but this guy didn't at all look like any kind of dad I'd ever seen.

His thick, black dark hair fell around his ears, brushed at his shoulders as he continued talking to Ben. Ben nodded. The guy pointed to his skates, gestured with his hands like how he should use his hockey stick. Ben was enraptured by him, and yet this guy looked like he wanted to take the puck and chuck it into the glass.

Pissed didn't bring to describe his face. Every visible muscle on this guy, and there were a lot of them despite the fact he had on black athletic pants and a tight-fitted, long sleeve gray shirt with the Vipers logo at his chest, radiated irritation.

But he reached out, playfully patted Ben on the helmet and I dragged my gaze off the guy to my son, who wobble-skated away, glancing back to the coach with a tremulous look on his face.

"Poor kid," I muttered.

His dad played hockey growing up, he played in high school and college in Wisconsin. He'd hung up his skates after his sophomore year, but to hear Evan say it, he was forced into quitting because his coach hated how awesome he was and didn't appreciate Evan's talent. Essentially, he'd gotten cut, lost his scholarship, and had to move back home to finish his business degree. We'd met when he'd moved back home. I was working on my nursing degree at a community college. He was going to the local university.

Six months later, I was pregnant.

Both our parents *fuh-reaked* to put it mildly. We were married three months later.

Ben was born six months later and when he was two, Evan got a job in a northern suburb of Vegas working for a pharmaceutical sales company. Not a bad gig, and he worked hard.

The problem with Evan was he always thought he was the best at everything, and especially hockey which meant regardless of what sport Ben tried and didn't *excel* in, his dad was always right there, *Hockey's gotta be your thing. You could be great like your dad once was. You gotta try hockey.*

Two weeks after his dad moved out and into our next door neighbor's house, Ben came to me and demanded I put him in hockey.

He absolutely sucked at it. Every time Evan came to a game it ended in a shitshow. Evan frustrated at Ben for not listening, despite Evan's demands being different from the coaches. Ben was usually in, or very near, tears.

No one ever lived up to Evan's expectations—least of all his ex-wife or his son.

A whistle was blown signaling the end of practice. The kids skated off the rink, stumbling at the door, and then there was the smacking of sticks and skates on the floor as they jostled and rushed to the locker rooms. It'd take Ben another ten to fifteen minutes to change out of his gear, which would give me a few minutes to talk to the new coach.

What were the chances he had any hope of improving before their next game, scheduled for the day after Evan and Kristi returned?

Evan somehow always found a way to get out of helping with shuttling Ben to any after-school activity or sports practice, but he rarely missed a game.

Funny how that worked.

I tried to tamp down my irritation at my ex-husband so I didn't take it out on the coach. He'd removed the goals from their posts on the ice and was lazily skating in my direction where I stood at the door that would take him to the locker rooms.

His scowl was still firmly etched in place and as he skated closer and I could take in that scowl in a closer way, swear to God I forgot the English language.

He was so... damn... a god among mortals. I'd nailed it from sixty yards away in the stands. He was just....

Staring at me with a question in his double arched, thick black brows.

Further scrambled my senses too, which meant when I opened my mouth, what came out wasn't a question or an introduction, it was, "My kid sucks."

Those brows jumped. He scanned the empty rink like he was trying to figure out which kid would have been mine and then shuttered any expression on his face.

My chest squeezed. Because he didn't just shutter his expression. It was closed down. Where for a moment I saw surprise, or maybe amusement at my blunder, there was now nothing good. Only a void of dark, cold nothing that somehow sent a blast of heat all straight down to my iced and frozen toes in my Ugg boots.

"Which one is yours?" he finally asked.

"Ben."

He gave me a blank stare.

Of course he didn't know anyone's names. It was his first day coaching.

"The one who spent more time sliding into the boards than he did on his feet."

"Right." He shoved his tongue to the side of his cheeks. "He, um..." Those brows furrowed as he sought for the words, making me roll my lips together. If he was trying to not be offensive, I was the one who brought it up. "He has a lot of heart and a great attitude."

I laughed and then covered my mouth with my gloved hands to hide it as he once again got a confused look. "I'm not paying you to tell you what I already know about my own kid. What I wanted to ask was, is there any hope he can get better?"

For a moment, I swore the guy was amused, and then that too was wiped away. "Anyone can get better if they want it hard enough."

"By the next game?"

"Why?"

I chewed my lip. Coach Lors had understood my predicament. He'd known because he knew Evan. He knew because his wife and I used to do playdates together and she knew all about why Evan left me, mostly because she'd been at my house several times with Kristi. We might have grown apart when the boys went to different elementary schools, but Dave Lors had still known what worried me.

"His dad... um... used to play hockey. Was good, too. But he well..."

"Needs Ben to be even better."

Yeah. This guy got it, too. "Right."

"Can't promise anything before the next game. Can't even promise anything with me as the coach. This isn't exactly my normal gig, you know?"

"It's not?" Now it was my turn to be confused. If he wasn't a dad and didn't volunteer to coach the team, who the hell was he?

"Uh. No." He scratched at his beard, black and thick and dark like the rest of him and that one move, maybe nerves? Well, there was another rush of heat sparking in my toes all over again except this time it traveled north. What would a beard like that feel like...

"I'll see what we can do," he said, and the fantasy that'd been blooming popped like a balloon.

This was some kid's *dad*. He was Ben's coach.

I had no right thinking anything about him.

"Right. Thanks. Then, I'll just..." Be disappearing before he saw the lust blossoming all over my cheeks. Something I hadn't felt in a *long* time. I shoved my thumb behind me and stepped back right as Ben rushed out of the locker room.

"Mom," he called, a bright grin on his pink cheeks.

"Thanks, Mr. Masters. I'll do better next time, I swear it."

"Like I said, you'll get there. And it's Coach. Not Mr. anything."

"By next practice," Ben assured him. I'd seen that stubborn press of his jaw before.

Shit. He so badly wanted to make his dad happy.

"We'll get there," Mr. Masters repeated. "See you later."

He lifted his hand and Ben high-fived it. "You're awesome! Bye!" He turned to me, grinning like a maniac. "Let's go to Buster's!"

"—ARRESTED or something but now he's coaching and he's just the coolest and he was kind of rude or maybe just rough, but he wasn't mean even if we could tell he didn't really want to be there but he was cool. Especially when Steve shoved me to the ice again. He made *him* do laps because that wasn't cool team play."

Woah. Wait a minute. What?

"Arrested?"

"Yeah. Last week or something I don't know. Geez, Mom, it was on the news like *everywhere.*"

What in the hell was Ben talking about?

In my defense, he'd been rambling about hockey practice from the time I took his gear bag and tossed it into the back of my SUV and he hadn't stopped. I'd zoned him out approximately three minutes later because that was sometimes the only way I could withstand the constant chatter from my back seat. Ben took the volume on the radio as a sign to only speak louder and faster, so I'd already turned that down and was zipping through the streets on autopilot.

Until he said the word arrested.

I pulled into a parking spot in front of Dave & Buster's and turned around to face him in the back seat. "Who was arrested?"

"Have you been listening to me at all?"

Shit. "Sorry, bud. Must have zoned out. So tell me, who was arrested?"

"My coach. Dominick Masters." He gave me a *what the hell how can you not listen to me* look before it was replaced with that earlier sense of wonder. "I mean, can you believe it? We have a real life Viper coaching us. Isn't it awesome? He's so cool, he's like the best D-line guy in the league. Dad freaking *loves him* because he's so mean and doesn't let any other team get even close to their goalie Dubiak. He's like..."

"A god?" I asked.

And slowly, pieces were clicking into place. Why he skated so effortlessly. Why he'd said this wasn't his thing. Why he was so... intense.

"Yeah. Like that. He's like some hockey god. And as a defenseman, he has more goals than any other defensive player, like *ever* and he does it every year. And he's my *coach*. Isn't that so cool? Our team is going to *have* to be awesome now. Dad's going to lose his mind. And Mr. Masters is going to turn me into the best player, like, ever, too. Hey, can I call Dad tonight and tell him?"

When Ben got excited, he sounded like a video playing at two times the normal speed.

Today it was closer to five times. He was talking so fast he almost sounded like a squirrel on speed so it took me a moment to catch on to everything.

"Why was he arrested?" I went back to where the story had caught my attention and frankly, the *only* part of what Ben had said.

"Dunno." He shrugged. "Happened like right before or after Christmas though. Spent a night in jail or something too. I mean, he's so mean he's been to *jail*. My friends are totally going to freak when I tell them."

Jail. Arrested. And they had him now coaching *youth* hockey?

Alarm bells rang in my ears making Ben's chatter blur to the background.

"So can I call him? Dad?"

The bells screeched to a stop. Ugh. How I would have loved to say no to that. Phone calls never went well.

"Yeah, Ben. We'll check the time difference, but when we're done here, we'll try to call Dad."

"Awesome," he breathed. And then those lips pushed to the side. "It'll make him happy, right?"

I *fucking hated* Evan and his narcissistic, unrealistic expectations. "I'm sure you'll always make your dad proud of you," I said, which wasn't exactly what he asked, but the best I could hope for. Even then, it wasn't really the truth. No one made Evan proud unless they were doing exactly what he expected, and his expectations were unreasonably high for everyone but himself—most especially Ben's.

I fought back the heavy sigh growing in my chest. "Come on. Let's go eat."

Where he could play, and I could put my Google skills to work because I had a coach to check out who was arrested and in jail and was now a part of my kid's life.

3

DOMINICK

She was there. Again. I tried to fight finding her in the small crowd that had admittedly grown from just a handful of moms to now at least a dozen dads and older kids, presumably once word who the new coach was got out. Especially a week ago, after a few practices and then my first game coaching, when Gabby and Joey Taylor showed up to lend their support.

If our owner considered the mayhem that would follow once people found out there was a Viper coaching a youth team as his community service for assaulting a drunk fuck at a bar on Christmas Eve, he was definitely getting it.

But there was Ben's mom, gloved hands cupping a cup I figured was coffee or hot cocoa from the concession stand, never once dipping her attention to her phone like most of the other moms.

Nope.

Her focus was on Ben, cringing every time he fell or missed a pass, silently throwing up a fisted hand when he nailed a drill.

Her smile could light up the arena if the lights went out. She was so damn proud of every stride and skill he hit.

As for me, I couldn't figure out the tightening sensation in my own chest every time I caught sight of her.

Yeah, she was attractive. A blind man could see it from the simple and sweet way she talked. The way she laughed. Add in those dark green eyes of hers, a small dimple in her cheek, and her bright pink lips, and yeah, she was hot.

But I didn't fuck innocent women, especially single moms who were looking for their next marriage proposal and resettling down.

The women I took to bed, rarely more than once, knew the score. I came over, we both came, and I left.

I didn't have time for anything else during the season and I didn't care enough about relationships in the off-season to ever attempt something so demanding.

And in my experience, women demanded a lot. Time. Attention. Affection. Care. Effort. Commitment. Rings. Weddings. Vows.

Please.

None of that was me outside my commitment to continue being the best damn defenseman in the league.

A shot went wide and a kid two sizes bigger than Ben slammed him into the boards. Not hard. Enough to make him lose his footing.

"Ben!" He spun, grabbed on to the wall to rebalance himself. I waved him over and glanced at my roster. Our team was scrimmaging and even though it'd been two weeks since I started coaching, I still struggled to remember their names. "Stephen. Go in for Ben."

"On it, Coach." He leaped over the board like a pro and slid onto the ice and into his spot before Ben made his way across the ice to me.

"I screwed up, huh?" he asked, his eyes only meeting my chest.

Ben grew up in a part of Vegas—and I knew that because for some damn reason I looked them up—where the homes held happy marriages and the standard two point five kids, most yards with pools and probably pool maintenance men as well as lawn care companies and housekeepers on a bi-monthly basis.

He just had an asshole for a dad. Probably friends with dozens of kids who had dads who were proud of them and felt that burn every time his dad criticized him.

I knew that because I'd been one of the kids with a good, decent dad. It was easy to spot one living vicariously through their kid.

Although, it was his dad who sealed the deal on proving he was a dick at the last game. The man stood at the wall, as close to the bench as he could get, and shouted louder than any of us coaches on either team combined. None of it good. All of it critical of his kid. From the way he stood, to missed passes, and every time Ben skated to the bench for a line change, his dad was right there, drilling him before the assistant coaches or I could say anything.

"Actually, I was going to tell you that shot was good. Nice and hard, just off on your aim, but it looked good."

"Really?" Two blond brows arched and his gaze rose to my shoulder.

So the shot was soft and *way* off its mark. Who gave a shit. The kid was ten.

"Yeah, kid. You were looking good out there today. Been practicing?"

I listened to him chatter about all the hours his mom brought him in for free skate while keeping an eye on the team scrimmage, but other than Ben, most kids had been playing for years and knew what they were doing. The kid who slammed Ben into the boards, Carter, had an attitude but at least he was an equal opportunity offender when it came to defense.

"My uh… my dad says I don't skate right. Too bent over. Said it's why I keep missing everything."

Yeah. He did. Simple mechanic practice could fix that with a bit of work though.

"Here's what we're going to do," I told him without thinking for a damn second about what I was actually doing. "You're going to come here tomorrow at this same time. I'll talk to your mom. And you're going to skate with me and some of the guys before we need to get warmed up for our game later."

As I mentioned the team and our practice, his eyes turned to the size of hockey pucks. "For real?"

"Yeah." What the fuck was I doing? I couldn't take it back now. "I'll hook you up with Joey. You know him?"

"He's like… the *fastest guy in history*."

And it'd be good for his ego to hear that from a ten-year-old, too.

"Sure he is." He wasn't. Not in history, but he was by far the fastest skater on our team, neck and neck with our center Kane. "I'll call him. He'll give you tips if you want him to."

What the hell was wrong with me? I was throwing out names left and right and now I had to ask the guys on the team for a goddamn favor. I could already imagine Gabby's smile. So damn bright it was infectious, even when I didn't want anything to do with anyone.

"Holy cow."

I blew my whistle, signaling a line change, and grabbed Carter's attention as he skated toward the bench.

"You want it?"

"Yeah, I want."

"Good. Now get back on the ice, and remember, tight and quick snapshots. That'll improve speed and accuracy. Got me?"

"Yeah. Coach. I got you. And um… thanks."

He skated off the ice, wobbled a second before straightening his ankles like I'd been teaching him, and before Carter skated up to me, took the time to glance back at his mom.

Her smile was soft, a slightly worried look on her face. I gave her a nod, trying to let her know all was good before looking at the bruiser in front of me, standing with attitude and a pinched expression.

"Can I tell you something, kid?"

"Name's Carter."

I knew his name. Obviously. Hated his attitude. "Yeah, well, until you're eighteen, you're a kid and I gotta ask you something."

He didn't respond. Little shit. He was ten, for fuck's sake. When he stayed silent, I asked, "Do you know, even if this team wins a championship at the end of the season, all you get is a piece of shit plastic trophy?"

His pinched expression fell.

Fuck. Maybe that was too harsh.

"So?"

"So, you're not out there playing for scholarships and agents and getting signed to a junior league."

"I will someday." At least he had a goal.

"Until then, you're risking ruining our team's roster by chucking them all into the boards so damn hard. I'm not even sure that move is allowed in the league at your age yet, and we won't win *any* game if you're in the sin bin or ejected. So chill the hell out for a hot minute. These kids are your *teammates,* not your enemies. Work with them and not against them and they might actually give you the puck more."

He glanced at the ice. The scrimmage happening where most of the kids were playing tough but still giving each other a hard time and smiling, playing well, and having fun.

And they should. I was never happier than when I was on the ice, even if I wasn't fighting.

"You understand what I'm saying?"

After a minute, he nodded, and the anger dissipated. "Yeah. But I still want that piece of shit plastic trophy."

"Don't say shit," I reprimanded him and rolled my lips together to fight a grin.

Maybe these cocky little kids didn't completely *suck.*

"Yeah, yeah. Can I get back out there?"

I glanced at my stopwatch. "Thirty seconds. You can go in for Darren."

"You mean Derek?"

"Whatever." So I didn't know all their names.

He trudged off to the bench, grabbed his water. Right as I

dragged my gaze back to the scrimmage, Ben got the puck. He drib-
bled it cleanly until a stick got caught on his skate. He fell forward,
tripping over it, lost control of the puck but at the last second, he
flicked his arm out, hit the puck.

And it went straight between our goalie's knees before he could
stop it.

"Nice goal!" I shouted while Ben spun out on the ice, on his
belly, all four limbs straight out, making him look like a starfish.

But that grin he had while he spun in a circle?

Might have... maybe... matched my own.

Fuck.

4

———

HOLLY

ominick Masters was, in fact, a hockey god. Since that night over a week ago where Ben talked about him non-stop at dinner, I'd done some looking into him. Mostly, I wanted to know more about his arrest. Then I couldn't stop myself.

He'd been on more sports and men's health magazine covers than any human had the right to be. He had more photos of his abs shown on fitness magazines than I could count. And boy—did I try to stop myself from counting—both the blocks of abs *and* the magazine covers.

It'd been midnight before I could tuck away my phone, feeling a warm throb between my legs. It'd been *way* too long since I'd felt that lick of attraction dancing in my veins.

Did I take care of myself thinking about Dominick Masters one night? Or two?

Maybe more?

What woman wouldn't? The fact the viewing area in the stands for parents seemed to have grown since word slowly got out who our team coach was proved my point.

Yet there he was, talking to my kid. Coaching him. He wasn't raising his voice or screaming at him or scowling at him.

He was *coaching* him.

And I swear when Ben spun out and Dominick's shout of *nice goal* echoed through the arena, well—his smile might have said he was damn proud.

Which meant there wasn't only a warm throb in places there should never be at a youth hockey practice, there was also one thumping in my chest.

Get a grip, Holls. The last thing you need is a crush on a professional hockey player. Three months and the season's done, and he's back to living his life and you'll never see him again.

Despite the warning, I couldn't stop my grin from blooming with pride for my son, there was a flutter of excitement as the coach called the practice. He slapped his hand on Ben's shoulder, and skated out to the ice, removing the goals and sliding them toward one end before he skated off the ice and disappeared down the hall toward the locker room.

It was habit to meet Ben back near the home team bench after he was done in the locker room, a habit made during his first season when he still couldn't carry all of his gear without tripping over his feet, so I waited, ignoring the buzz of my phone in my purse which could only mean one thing.

Only one person texted and called repeatedly until he got what we wanted—which was ridiculous, since he had the 'all new' life he wanted. I figured he'd leave me alone, but no chance in hell of that.

I swore now that Evan and Kristi were happily together, his second greatest joy came from not letting me forget it.

My frustration bubbled as my phone continued to buzz and I decided to end the madness. I was digging in my bag when the soft scent of pine mixed with sweat and cold air, somehow, a thrillingly sexy combination wafted in my direction and I looked up, froze as Dominick strolled toward me, looking as equally comfortable walking on skates off the ice as he was on the ice.

"I got a favor I need to ask you."

"Me?" My hand found my phone in my purse as it vibrated

again and I quickly pulled my hand out, leaving the phone alone. What in the hell kind of favor could he need from me?

"Yeah." He cleared his throat, and a sliver of pink crept up his neck.

My spine turned to steel. Was he... nervous?

"Yeah, so, I kind of told your kid if he came here tomorrow, I'd have some guys on the team ready to help give him extra tips and skating time."

"You did..." My brows rose. "What?"

"Yeah. I mean, I gotta clear it with them, but we have warm-ups before a home game tomorrow anyway, so I don't think they'd mind."

"Um, wow. I'm sure Ben lost his mind when you offered that." This definitely explained why he looked so excited.

"A bit, yeah." A twitch of his lips was all he gave me. He could barely even look at me he seemed so uncomfortable. But if he hadn't wanted to do this—why did he?

"Why?"

His lips curled and then he swiped his hand over his mouth, heaving a sigh. "Can I be honest?"

"I'd prefer that, yeah." I'd had enough lies to last me a lifetime.

"Because I kind of think his dad's a dick, and I'm not sorry if that offends you or anything, but I've seen the way he talks to your kid and I don't like it. And I don't like how Ben makes a simple mistake and gets down on himself. Figured some tips from some pros would build him up *and* have the added bonus of sticking it to your husband."

"Ex." As if that clarification was the point of this conversation.

"Right. So?" He crossed his arms over his chest. Shoved his hands to his hips. That sliver of pink darkened and spread up his neck and he scratched at it.

"So you're offering extra help to my kid to shove it in his dad's face how big of a jerk he is?"

"When you put it that way, it doesn't sound good."

"Why Ben? You have fifteen on the team."

He pressed his lips together, shrugged, and I swore a muscle ticced in his jaw like he was getting pissed. "Don't know for sure. But if it's a hassle—"

"No. No, it's not. If you've already offered it to Ben, I can't say no now. Hell, this will make his year and I thought you being their coach was enough. But yeah… we can make it work. Definitely."

"Good. Good." He nodded, like we'd somehow decided something of ultra importance, spun on his heels, and took off back toward the locker rooms.

"What was that about?" A shoulder nudged me, and I grinned at Karly. Her son Tanner had become one of Ben's best friends in the last year. She was also one of the best friends I'd made in the last year. The night she heard about Evan and Kristi, she showed up at my house with a few bottles of wine and a voodoo doll, surprisingly bearing a strong resemblance to Evan. I hadn't asked how she got her hands on that so quick, but shoving tiny needles into his body while I cried and screamed and vented over wine helped make me feel better.

"The coach invited Ben in for skate time with the guys from his team."

"*Wow*… That's…"

"Weird, right? It's weird."

She winked, gave me a playful scan of my body. "Maybe he has a crush on the hot mom."

"Please." I rolled my eyes. In my ridiculous, borderline stalkerish search of him, I'd seen dozens of pictures of women he was photographed with. All candid, all on the streets of Vegas somewhere. Never a formal event but random pics of him with random women—none ever identified and not one seen more than once.

If that was his type, I was most definitely *not* hot in his eyes.

She bumped her hip into mine. "You don't see what I see. What men see when they look at you and trust me, even Blake has said we need to get you back out into the dating world."

"I've dated." Kind of. Sort of. If downloading dating apps, swiping for hours, and then deleting them two days later counted.

"The guy you met for a drink who didn't look anything like his profile doesn't count. And didn't he smell like cheese?"

He'd been hot as hell in his pictures. Then he'd shown up for our date without a hat and dressed in nice clothes. His body was still nice, so was his style, but without that hat... he was just... *no.*

"Catfished by a backward hat," I muttered.

Karly laughed. "We've all been there. So, are you bringing him? Ben?"

"Yeah."

"Think I can come too?"

She wiggled her brows playfully.

"You have a husband you can't even keep your hands off of."

"So." She shrugged. "Hockey players are top-of-the-line sex fodder for my *personal* times."

"TMI, honey, T.M.I."

"Fine. But we're doing dinner and drinks next time Ben's with Evan." A slightly psycho gleam swept across her face. "Hey... do you think if they go out, we could fuck with Kristi? Like stick ghost faces on their windows so she pisses herself when she opens her blinds? Harmless shit that'd scare her? Oh, I know! You could put one of those ghost voice makers in Ben's pocket or something so she has to hear some creepy sounds all night. That'd be hilarious."

"You scare me," I deadpanned. "Truly, I don't even... can't even handle what must go on in your mind."

She grinned. "It's like one of those funhouses at a carnival where it's all mirrors and madness and tricks and stuff."

Karly was crazy. Certifiably. God love her for it. I patted her shoulder. "Let's maybe just keep it to dinner and drinks."

"Fine," she huffed and knocked her hip into mine. "If I have to."

"Mom!" I spun at Ben's cry and jolted as he dropped his bag and threw his arms around me. "Did Coach ask you?! Did he tell you what he said I could do? Isn't it cool?! He even said he'll get Joey Taylor to help me! Dad's going to FREAK."

Dad. Right. Of course he'd be excited about his dad. Dominick's words flickered through my mind.

Yeah. I'd love to see his face too when Ben told him.

More, I'd love to see him go a round with Dominick. He obviously didn't like seeing a dad being too hard on his son. Was that because his dad was like that? Or because he was the opposite?

I shook my head. Dominick Masters was my kid's coach. And that was that. His personal history was none of my concern. Still, I couldn't forget that pink blush creeping up his neck.

"Come on. If your dad's home when we get there, you can go tell him, okay?"

"Awesome!"

I rolled my eyes behind his back, directed at Karly. She made a gagging sound and then turned to grab Tanner's bag as he followed with some of the other kids.

"Bye babe," I called out.

"Drinks and madness soon!"

Always the madness with her.

Frankly, some days I needed her level of madness.

Karly made me realize life wasn't over just because I'd learned my marriage was and my husband was a jerk. I'd love her forever for that alone.

~

OF ALL MY DARN LUCK.

"Dad's outside!"

"Close the—"

Slam.

"Door," I muttered, finishing the sentence long after Ben hopped out of the SUV and ran to his dad. Not shocking, Evan had a habit of being home from work early on hockey practice days, seemingly working in his garage or cleaning out his car, all for the excuse to be able to talk to Ben as soon as we got home.

Which wouldn't be bad, except…

His hands clasped onto Ben's shoulder and he gave him a gentle shake. "You do what I tell you to do?"

"I scored a goal," Ben said, and his excitement deflated like a helium balloon, one small breath at a time. "But—"

"Did you keep your head up?"

"I tried, but…"

"What did I tell you?"

I climbed out of my SUV, Evan's words were clear as day considering our driveways were so close and his authoritative voice always boomed. He wasn't even shouting, but it could sure sound like it sometimes.

With a sigh, keeping one eye on Ben and his reactions so I'd know when to call him back, I walked around the SUV and gathered his gear from the back.

"Bend at the knees," Ben replied, his chin now wobbling. "But something awesome happened. More awesome than the goal."

"Yeah? Like what?" Evan's brows yanked together, his tone full of sarcasm Ben didn't notice. Thankfully.

"Well, Coach told me to come back tomorrow for extra practice."

"If you did what I said, you wouldn't need extra practice."

It was illegal to kill your asshole ex-husband, right? Knifing the father of your child would probably carry a severe penalty. Still, the thoughts flickered.

This *jerk*.

"Ben—" I called. Time to end this.

He looked back at me, chin jutting out. I wanted him to stand up for himself, to work through this—but no *child* should have to stand up to his own father.

"He's getting guys from the team to help me. Just *me* before their game tomorrow."

Evan's face flashed with surprise and then he stood back, crossed his arms over his chest, and narrowed his eyes.

What a dick.

"Why would he do that for you?"

I was certain, a year or more ago, I wouldn't have noted the condescension and doubt in his voice. Now, it just made me want to scoop Ben in my arms, rush him inside and then figure out a way I could keep them apart. Forever.

I opened my mouth, but before I could speak, Evan's head spun in my direction. "You talk to the coach?"

"Of course I did. He's the one who mentioned it to me."

His gaze dropped, and I swore it dragged slowly up my body. An icy chill cascaded down my body at his inspection.

I'd ditched the winter coat, hat, and gloves in the car, but I was wearing jeans and a UNLV hoodie sweatshirt. My hair was pulled back halfway with bobby pins shoved in to prevent hat head. I barely had on makeup.

I certainly wasn't dressed to impress.

"Yeah, I bet he noticed you."

If it was supposed to be a compliment, he was far off the mark. I had no idea how it was possible to go from loving a man to despising him so quickly, but Evan sure as hell made sure I excelled at it.

I moved closer to Ben and tugged on his hand. "Let's go get dinner ready, okay kiddo?"

"Yeah." With his head dropped low, defeated because his dad couldn't be happy for him for one freaking second, probably because he was jealous his son got something he'd kill to have, I stayed quiet until Ben went inside the house.

"I'll be taking him to the practice tomorrow," Evan declared. "Make sure the coach knows what's what."

"What's... what?"

"Yeah. That you're the parent of one of his kids, not someone he can fuck around with."

"You're a dick, you know that? What, you don't want me, but no one else can have me?"

"You like that guy?"

I swore. I needed to learn Krav Maga or something. Being capable of slamming Evan's face into the cement at our feet would make. My. Day.

"What I *am*, Evan, is none of your business, and I stopped *being* your business the night I caught you and Kristi sucking face through our master bathroom window. So don't *stand* here and pretend you're doing any of this for me. And you're sure as hell not doing it for Ben. You want to do this because you're jealous he gets an opportunity for something you never had and you can't stand when the attention isn't on you."

His eyes flashed, jaw jutted in that same way Ben's had earlier that had been so cute and brave on my kid but made my hands curl into fists when Evan did it.

And then something else skated across his eyes. That flash of regret, or remorse, for hurting me and hell, even six months ago, it would have affected me. Made me think I could get him back or give me some foolish idea of having the perfect marriage and home and not having to fill out *divorce* on papers for crying out loud.

But those days were long gone. I was smarter now.

"Holls—"

"Save it." I turned, hurried back to our house, and ignored him calling out to me again.

Evan liked games. He liked winning those games.

And I was no longer playing.

Twenty minutes later, he proved me correct when my phone pinged with a text from him.

Since I couldn't get a word in earlier with your temper tantrum, I'm making this clear. I'm taking Evan to that practice tomorrow.

"Dick," I muttered, slid my phone away, grabbed a bottle of wine and filled the glass.

Then I got to cooking dinner. Spending time with my kid. Read a book.

Later—it was possible I went to bed, that sexy romance book in one hand and a toy in the other.

And somehow—that romance book's hero reminded me a lot of Dominick.

So I went to bed thinking of him—and not how big of an asshole I used to be married to.

5

DOMINICK

The night Gabby Taylor, then Dubiak, swooped into my life, I hadn't intended on going to Malley's bar. I only did because Coach Vik made me. Not that he grabbed my arm and dragged me there like a sullen child, but he might as well have.

"You only have two years left on your contract. Guys don't know you. Hard to trust a player they don't know even if we all know you're the best out there. Do this. A favor to me. You don't have to spill your guts out all over the table to have a drink and be a guy they can depend on."

So whatever. I went. Wasn't like I had anything better to do. I grabbed a drink from the bar and sat my ass in the booth. Like usual, Max and the rest of the guys were drunk as skunks so I sat back and didn't do much talking. Not that they expected me to.

Gabby sliding into my booth was a hell of a surprise. More so when Max shoved his way in next to me, threw his arm over my shoulders like we'd ever spoken off the ice and a few minutes later, Gabby was goading me into playing quarters. She started talking about the last series we played, shooting off my statistics like she spent every night memorizing them.

The coolest thing about her was she just talked. Laughed. She didn't ask questions. She somehow saw the invisible Post-it Note on my forehead warning people to *stay the fuck away* and decided it meant nothing.

She gave me shit like we'd grown up together.

For some damn reason, she slid straight through my walls and defenses like they weren't even there.

Hell if I didn't respect her for it.

Crazier than that, was when Joey and I started working out together. Then they were reunited, and the first person she invited over to dinner was me.

The fuck?

She'd caught me on a night when I didn't have shit to do anyway, not that my social calendar was ever packed, and she'd been so damn excited I couldn't bring myself to tell her no.

So I went.

And there I was again, four months later, showing up for a pre-game night dinner she always cooked and invited single guys on the team over for.

Like she was our mom or something taking care of a bunch of high school boys.

"Hey, you." She wrapped her arms around me in a hug even though I stood statue-still every time. Joey came around the kitchen behind her and smirked at me.

He knew I hated this. I think he got a sick satisfaction from watching it.

"Hey." I patted her shoulder, my signal for her to let me go and she did, stepping back. "I cannot wait for you to tell us all about your hockey team. I've been dying to text you and ask, but Joey keeps telling me to chill out."

The woman had no chill whatsoever. "You can do that?"

"Absolutely not." She smacked my shoulder as I handed her a bottle of wine, one of her favorites because she always had it stocked on the kitchen counter wine rack.

I might have checked it once.

Why?

Who the fuck knew. People were probably talking and I was bored. Not like I cared.

"How's it going?"

Joey slapped my arm and we clasped hands. "Good. Glad you could make it. Gabby cooked enough for fifty guys tonight."

"I did not." Joey arched a brow at her and she smirked back. "Fifteen, tops."

I chuckled. "Your wife is insane."

"No doubt about it. Just the way I like her."

And... I was going to let that one go.

The house smelled like garlic and carbs, and my stomach growled in response. Gabby could *cook* and it was possible I had actually started looking forward to these nights.

I certainly wasn't showing up at the last minute anymore, after everyone else was there and ready to eat, so I didn't have to make small talk.

In fact, this was the second time I was the first one there.

Odd. I scratched my temple. It didn't mean anything.

"How's the salon?" I asked Gabby while Joey grabbed me a bottled water. Gabby would be the only one drinking at the dinner since most of us tried to refrain before games. Well, they did. I rarely drank and if I did, never more than one. In fact, one of the few nights in my life when I'd actually gotten drunk was that first night with Gabby. Her fault, somehow, for making me not think about anything except the *slight* fun I was having. At least until Lucy called.

She slapped her hands on the counter and gave me an over-the-top, dramatically excited look that would have looked fake on any other woman but fit Gabby like a glove. "You will never guess what's happened."

She arched her brows, practically bursting at the seams and yet —said nothing.

Oh. She was waiting. "Tell me."

She huffed and rolled her eyes. "You and Joey. Neither of you can play along."

I glanced at him and he shrugged, drinking his own water, but the look he gave Gabby was full of damn pride.

My gut tightened. How did they do this? Hell, the two of them were practically strangers barely six months ago when they somehow woke up married after we won our last game and became champions. Then they went on some crazy road trip, living in a camper. Something happened to separate them, but when Gabby's brother Garrett and his wife had their twins, she raced back down here, moved in with Joey the next day.

They went from strangers to two sappy, crazy-in-love people.

It was insanity—even so, my chest tightened with an unknown pain whenever they were together, giving each other those *looks*.

"Okay." I took a swig of water, gestured for her to give me a second, and once I swallowed and plastered on the fakest expression I could muster, I rose my voice an octave. "OMG. What. Happened?"

Gabby's jaw dropped and she threw her head back and laughed. "Holy crap. That's hysterical. You're the best, Dominick."

I wasn't. Far from it. But even Joey was laughing at my dumb ass. Gabby wiped tears from her eyes and fanned herself to calm down.

"Are you going to tell me or not?"

"I am... just... you'd make a perfect girl. That was sooo... like, oh my God, totally California Malibu Barbie of you."

"I'm quickly losing interest in whatever you have to tell me."

"Okay. Okay." She inhaled another breath and rubbed her lips together. "So, I think word got out who I was or who I was married to or whatever a few weeks back because business started like, booming. Just, crazy busy. It's so busy I might have to add another hairstylist soon."

"That's awesome."

She'd leased a building and started her own salon around the time she returned to Vegas. I didn't know all the details, just that she loved her job and loved running a salon more than she even liked working with clients.

"Yeah. And at first, I didn't get it. I thought they were groupies or puck bunnies or something, you know? Because the women would all ask questions about Joey and Garrett. Right?"

"Sure."

I stayed the hell away from puck bunnies. Too terrified to end up with a hole in my condom or some shit so they could collect child support.

"Anyway, they're not groupies. They're *WAGS*."

"Sorry?"

"Wives and girlfriends. I've been doing hair for the center of Las Vegas's basketball team's wife *and* their shooting guard. A whole bunch of them are coming in. And the new football team. It's like... WAG central in my salon, all day, every day." She leaned in and smiled. "Want to know *why?*"

"Because you're talented and do good work and they want to go to the best?"

"That's what I said," Joey said, sliding up next to me. He still hadn't erased that look of pride on his face he kept trained in her direction across from us at the island—an island that was larger than my childhood bedroom.

The realization of how much money we had blew my mind at the most random times.

"Well obviously. But it's not that. They started coming and then told everyone about me because they knew they could be honest with their lives. Because they don't have to worry about anyone selling their stories *or worse,* not being able to talk about their lives at all. *I* give them that."

Her excited smile turned to something softer and she turned, sniffing while she went to stir the spaghetti sauce simmering on the stove. When she spoke again, her voice shook.

"It's just, really cool, I think. Because I get it. Even though Garrett was only my brother and not a boyfriend or anything, people would get close to me when I was younger and I never quite knew if they liked me, or my brother and what I could give them, you know? And these women all face the same thing. It's hard to spend like *hours* in a salon chair and not feel like you can talk to someone. That's what we do. We chat. And so yeah... business is awesome, but it's even awesomer because I give them security and freedom to be themselves."

She flashed me a soft smile, glanced at Joey, and shrugged.

A lump lodged itself in my throat, making breathing difficult. I swallowed it down with my water.

This. This was why I didn't hate Gabby or Joey.

To an extent, the extent to which I allowed, they gave *me* that too. Hell, I was certain anyone who interacted with Gabby felt that from her.

She was wild and goofy and hilarious, but mostly—she was genuine.

A rare combination in our world of professional sports.

A diamond in the rough from what I'd become accustomed to.

"I'm happy for you," I told her. And hell, I was. Making people feel good made Gabby feel good. And she was damn happy right now.

"I have a favor to ask you," I said, turning to Joey, giving Gabby the moment to get herself back together. Her eyes were still shimmering with happy tears.

"Me?" Joey asked, head jerking back.

"Yeah..."

Their front door slammed open, making Gabby jump. Max's booming voice quickly followed and then what sounded like a thump against the wall.

"Hey," Alix Halvrick called out. "We are not on the ice."

"Tough shit," Max returned. They came around the corner, Max gave Alix another shove, almost tossing him into another wall. Guess that explained the thump.

Alix pushed him back, both of them laughing.

Next to me, Joey chuckled.

That familiar sense of being out of place, a voyeur in a land where people communicated and bonded easily, took over.

"You wanted to ask me something?"

"Nah, man." I shook my head. "I'll catch you later."

"Sure?" His head tilted to the side. I understood his confusion. I didn't ask anyone for help. Or a favor.

Ever.

"We're good." I took a swig of my bottle and was suddenly jolted. I squeezed the bottle in surprise, splashing water down the front of my sweatshirt.

"What the fuck?"

"Sorry big guy," Max said and slapped my back. "Didn't expect that. How're things?"

How're things?

I glared at him, our team's self-proclaimed party animal, at six-two and two twenty, he had me beat in weight by about twenty pounds and was two inches shorter, but his size made him seem bigger.

Didn't matter when I was meaner. Max and I spent the most time together at practice since we were both first-line defenders, but I could never get past his boyish charm and looks and attitude.

Everything was one big game to him. Must have been nice to skate through life so easily.

Was I jealous?

Maybe. What I would have given to have grown up with a family like his and know no matter what happened, I didn't just have one person at my back, but a half-dozen.

I shook that off, cleared my scowl at my wet chest and Max's dopey, puppy dog expression, and shoved him. "Things were good until you showed up."

The asshole ruffled my hair. "Ah. You love me. It's okay to admit it. Didn't you know it's now *cool* for men to show and express their emotions?"

"The only emotion I currently have is wanting to punch you in the face."

His smile didn't falter.

"Is that the kind of emotion we're talking 'bout?"

Hard as I tried, when Max was around, it was difficult to stay angry. He was similar to Gabby in that way. Where Gabby's kindness was so genuine I felt like a dick being rude to her, Max's was more abandoned puppy at an animal shelter, silently begging for people to take him home with them and hug him.

"Close. You're getting closer."

Idiot.

Alix had said hello to Gabby, snagged a crouton from the salad she was putting the finishing touches on, and tipped his chin up at me. Our second line center, he had future captain written all over him. While he played as much as Max, that playfulness vanished the moment he tugged on his gear and laced up his skates.

Maybe because he'd been in the league since he was eighteen, drafted straight from his junior league team in Switzerland, that made him grow up faster than Max.

Maybe it was his blasé European attitude that did it.

Either way, I didn't hate him. Truthfully, I didn't hate any of my teammates. I just stayed away. The best way to keep my family drama firmly in the dark was to keep my mouth shut.

That was easy before Gabby slipped into my life and before I opened my mouth at Ben's practice.

"I have a favor to ask," I blurted.

The room froze. Jaws hit the floor and eyes turned to saucers. The kick of the heat turning on was the only sound as everyone gaped at me, glanced at each other, someone else, and turned back to me.

"Uh, what?" Joey asked.

Goddamn, I hated being on the spot like this. "There's a kid on my team. Dad's a dick, but he really wants to do well. I told him if he came to the skate center tomorrow before our warm-ups, I'd get some guys there to help him out."

"Ummm."

"Uhhh…"

"Huh…"

"Wow…"

Fuckers. All of them. I didn't pay attention to who made what noise, but it was Gabby's smile that sent ants sliding down my spine.

"Not a big deal if you can't make it." I drained the rest of my water bottle and fought against rolling my shoulders.

They were all. Still. Staring.

Gabby's head tilted. "Why this kid?"

How in the hell should I know? "Dad's a dick is all. Just thought it'd be good for him."

"Holy fuck," Max shouted. "You *do* have emotions."

"Fuck off." I shoved his shoulder.

"I will help you," Alix said, and I swore there was a small smile on his face. Like he knew something I didn't. It was just skating with a kid. Why would that make him so happy?

"Of course, I'll be there," Joey said.

"No way in hell am I missing this." Max laughed.

"Great. Then can we eat?"

I was starving. Then things would go back to how they should be.

Me… on the outside. Not standing in the goddamn middle of a social circle.

"Sure, Dom," Gabby said. "We can eat."

Great.

6

———

DOMINICK

My chest was burning. Maybe I was getting sick. There was a tightness there that made breathing difficult. Swallowing harder. And when I blinked, there was a slight burn in my eyes too.

I blinked harshly and then sniffed.

Yeah. I was getting sick. Had to be. And playing sick, sucked.

Shitty timing considering it wasn't just Joey, Max, and Alix taking the ice while I was already out there, slowly warming up my legs.

It was half the goddamn team. Kane. Braxton. Arlo. Garrett. Even André, the backup goalie.

"What's going on?"I asked Joey, my jaw tightening. What in the *hell* was happening.

"We're a team. You needed us."

"I didn't..." Need them. I wanted to show Ben a good time, but I didn't *need* them.

His hand slapped down on my shoulder, almost taking me to my knees. I was weak. Definitely getting sick. My muscles *hurt*.

None of what I was feeling had *anything* to do with the fact half the team was here, giving us the chance we could actually do a full scrimmage with Ben.

"Where's the kid?" Max asked.

I was still confused. I'd changed into my gear in our locker room with Joey and Max. I hadn't even seen the rest of the guys, but I hadn't been out here that long.

"Where'd you all come from?"

Garrett knocked his stick against mine. "Youth league locker rooms. Thought the surprise would be fun. Based on the look on your face, I'm not sure. Are you going to kill us?"

Was that how I looked? There was definitely *something* going on inside me that felt a little murderous. Aching. Frustrating.

"Not today," I admitted.

"Good. Good."

As he skated by me, I turned, caught the doors opening at the end.

"Shit," I muttered, loud enough Joey heard.

"That the asshole dad?"

"Yeah."

I'd expected Holly. Had *almost* found myself looking forward to seeing her today. Had planned to be knocked on my ass by her smile.

Seeing Evan walking in with Ben's gear bag banging against his entire side, with swagger like we'd planned this for him, made me grit my teeth.

"Too bad we can't get him on the ice," I said to Joey. "Wouldn't mind being able to shove him into the boards once or twice."

"No giving the parents a concussion."

"I'll try." It'd be hard though.

"Hey, Ben!" I skated to the open doorway and gave a quick thanks to the security guard who had escorted them.

"Hey." He glanced at his dad and then me, not smiling or showing a mere hint of the excitement he had yesterday.

I stepped off the ice. Much as I wanted to slam my fist into his dad's face, I extended my hand instead. "Dominick Masters. Thanks for bringing him."

"Evan Myers. Glad we could make it. This is a great experience for him." He let go of my hand and focused on Ben. "Remember what I told you, right?"

"Yes, sir."

Whatever he'd said had killed Ben's excitement. "Come on, Ben. I'll take you to our locker room to get your gear on."

"*Your* locker room?"

"Yeah."

The kids had to use the secondary locker rooms for their practices. Since we stored personal gear in ours, it was always locked for youth league times. In a swift move, I tugged his strap off his shoulder and threw it over mine.

"It's not special like the one where we play our games or anything, but it's decent."

His skates swung from his other shoulder and the handle of his stick clomped against the floor as we headed back that way.

I'd effectively dismissed his dad without a look, and I glanced back but his attention was on the ice, almost like he was judging the guys out there, who could skate circles around him in a second.

I waited until we got to the locker room, and watched his eyes bug out. "See? Nothing all that special..."

"Still. Your names are on the lockers and everything. It's cool."

The excited look was back on his face, so I took him to mine, right next to Joey's. "What did your dad say that you were supposed to remember?"

His brows puckered and he dropped his skates. "Nothing much. He just doesn't want me to embarrass him."

Dick. Absolute dick.

I should definitely slam him into the boards.

"You won't embarrass anyone. You know that, right? I wanted you here today to get extra practice and have fun with some of the guys on the team. It's all for fun."

He kicked at his skates and unzipped his bag. "I know. My dad just likes things a certain way. Ever since he left my mom and moved next door, he's... I don't know... he wants me to be perfect all the time."

Whoa. Hold the hell up. "Next door?"

"Yeah. Said he's gonna get married again. Lives in her house next door to where Mom and I live."

Holy shit. This guy wasn't a dick. He was a *dick*. My jaw tightened, and I swallowed down my thoughts on the subject.

I knew I'd had this guy figured out in a second, but what Ben was saying made him sound so much worse.

Still... none of my business.

At all.

Hell, I was still trying to figure out why I wanted to give this day to Ben.

"All right. Suit up. More guys came than I expected today, so once we warm you up and do some drills, we'll be able to get a scrimmage in. Sound like fun?"

That wonder sparked in his eyes. "Yeah. That'd be cool, all right."

"Goal!" The shout came from half the guys on the team, cheering on Ben. Dubiak who'd let the puck get through his legs, faking it out and trying not to make it obvious, did a good job of feigning annoyance while grinning.

Ben threw his hands in the air, and before he could lower his stick, two hands hit his waist and lifted him in the air.

"Way to go, Ben!" Max shouted as he rose him high in the air, skated around the ice with the kid in his arms above his head, looking like a rag doll in the big guy's paws. "You're awesome."

I shook my head at Max's antics. Yeah, the guys were giving this kid praise all day long, but truly, he caught on quick to some of the basic footwork drills and pointers the guys gave him, too.

His shots were harder and passes were more on target than I'd seen yet.

His wobbly skating was improving along with his ability to stay on his feet.

More than once, I actually found myself laughing and smiling with not only Ben but the guys on my team, too. Odd how that was happening more and more. Before the scrimmage started, I took to playing referee and coaching, coaching Ben while the guys on the team joined in.

Max finally set Ben back on his feet, and I blew the whistle while everyone skated back to their positions near center ice for another face-off.

"Hey Ben," Alix called out, sliding out of his typical position at center. "Take my spot."

Behind his cage, his eyes grew round. "Really?"

"Sure. I'll take yours." He slid into the winger position before Ben could make it into the center ice where Kane was already set up.

"Careful, kid," Kane growled. "I'm going to eat your dust."

Fear or nerves made Ben's chin wobble before he grew serious. "Big talk for such a slow skater," Ben volleyed back to a round of jeers from the guys.

Shaking my head, I tried to be serious for a half-second and blew the whistle. Kane fought for the puck half-heartedly but in the end, he didn't give it to Ben like he easily could have, but that was good.

I wanted the kid to have fun and learn, not think we were handing him *everything*.

The puck flew toward the opposite end of the ice, and Ben hustled over to it. Since we didn't have to worry about vicious penalties, I skated back toward the bench where I could see everything, but since I hadn't looked behind me, I was surprised when Evan was there.

"You're not teaching him anything by letting him always get his way out there."

This man. Fucking *dick*. At least, that was if he had one at all.

"Point of today was to have fun and get him extra practice."

He'd been yelling all practice, but as soon as he'd made his first negative comment, coaching from the bleachers, the guys had just gotten louder, talking over him so Ben couldn't hear.

"Don't know why you have a problem with that."

"Kid needs to learn nothing in life comes easy. You gotta earn it."

Said the guy who moved in *next fucking door* to his ex-wife.

"Yeah. I bet you'd think that." I'd had it with his attitude. His whole *I'm better than everyone* vibe the guy put off.

"What's that supposed to mean?"

"Not a damn thing."

"Really? Because it sounds like you have a problem." As he spoke, his chest expanded. Please. I had him by thirty pounds on an off day. And even off my skates, I'd have him by inches. Evan was nothing more than a pocket-sized man with small dick energy.

"Nah. I don't gotta problem with men like you. You're nothing but talk."

I put my back to him, felt his fury bubbling behind me, but screw him. Screw men like him in general who thought everyone owed them something but everyone else had to earn their place.

"Men like me?"

Oh he was seething. Raging. Probably had purple cheeks, a vein throbbing somewhere and his fists curled. If I gave a shit about any of it, I'd look at him. Instead, I kept my attention on the guys, on Ben dribbling the puck and passing it to Joey. Screw my social filter or keeping my mouth shut. I didn't know why this guy got to me so much, or why I wanted to do so much for Ben, but I didn't care what this guy thought of me, either.

"I know exactly the kind of man you are, and that is you aren't one. You've probably cheated on your ex-wife plenty over the years and quit caring about getting caught because you thought she'd be too weak to leave you. You also probably enjoy the fact you still live next door to her so you can keep an eye on her, ruin any chance of her happiness because you might not have wanted her, but you don't want anyone else to either and you're keeping your options open for when you get bored of this new woman."

"That bitch tell you all that?"

Oh yes... definitely seething. No matter. I didn't mind a good fight.

I glanced at him and smirked. "Nope. She didn't say a damn word. Ben told me you live next door. You told me all of the rest with your attitude and the fact you're so goddamn easy to read, I could have known exactly the kind of asshole you were before you took a seat on those bleachers today. And the last thing I'm going to tell you, I'm *glad* you cheated on Holly. I'm glad you treated her like trash. Because someday, she's going to have it good and she's going to know exactly how miserable she would have been with someone like you."

God freaking damn it. What was wrong with my mouth? And why was it this guy who pissed me off so much? I didn't know these people. Didn't give a crap about them.

"That man going to be you?"

Fuck no, it wasn't going to be me. No way did I want someone as sweet as her being mired in my filth. But to stick it to this guy? I had no problem letting him think that.

"I guess we'll see."

I blew the whistle and skated toward center ice. We needed to wrap this up and get to the arena soon for our own pre-game meals, routines, and warm-ups.

We all trudged off to the locker room, guys chatting with Ben like he was a member of the team and not a little kid, but mostly it was Max who had surprised the hell out of me.

I caught up with him. "Thanks uh… for today. You were good with him." Better than I could ever be with any kid, really.

He shook his head. No sweat at all in his long locks, which proved how easy he'd taken it out there. "Hell yeah, I was. I'm great with kids. I got two nephews who think I'm the coolest."

"You have nephews?"

He rolled his eyes. "If you'd ever listen, you know I've got four brothers and a sister. There's six of us. My oldest brother has a son and my other brother is getting married next summer to a girl who has one. Those kids love me."

I ignored the part I didn't ever listen to him. That was probably true.

"Probably because you act like a kid."

"And?" He scratched his head, like the idea of a thirty-year-old still acting like a kid wouldn't be something he'd want.

I shook my head.

"Thanks," I finally said, meeting them all in the eye.

"That's what teammates are for," he said.

We hurried out of our gear and the guys took off. I stayed back with Ben.

"That was fun, huh?" I asked.

"It was great. So awesome. Kids at school are going to lose their minds when I tell them about today. You're the best coach ever."

A compliment from a ten-year-old shouldn't have made my chest burn so much. Maybe I wasn't getting sick. Perhaps it was heartburn. Either way, I definitely needed to see the team doc.

"Good. I'm glad. You looked really great out there. Remember what I said—believe you can do it and the rest will fall in line. No doubts, right. Doesn't matter what anyone says. You believe you can do it, you will."

"No doubts." He grinned at me and stuck out his fist. I knocked it back.

Together, we headed back to the hall where Evan stood, arms

crossed over his chest. He glared at me, glanced at Ben with a dip of his chin and said, "Let's go."

And for a moment, I debated letting Ben leave with him. Men like him—if I'd just pissed him off, that might not be so good for him.

"You staying at your dad's or mom's tonight?" I asked Ben quietly.

"I'll go back to Mom's. Why?"

That was good. "No reason. See you at practice soon, okay?"

"Yeah, Coach. And thanks again. For everything."

His smile almost blinded me, and I itched to return it, but hell...

I didn't know if I'd just put an asshole in his place or made things a hell of a lot worse.

7

———

HOLLY

"You going to be okay?"

I sniffed. Stupid emotions. Stupid memories. I now owed Karly a lot more than a bottle of wine or a mom's night out.

Hell, she'd become my rock so much lately I should probably pay her the same rate I paid my old therapist.

"I'm fine now." I took a sip of my red wine and held it up toward my FaceTime screen where Karly cupped her own wineglass in her hands. "Can we move on?"

"From Evan being a jerk, throwing his affair in your face at every possible moment he gets, *and* now being a giant asshole to his own son?" She snorted. "Sure, we can move on from that. Any big weekend plans?"

"I wish." I rolled my eyes, and they caught on the television screen. I'd muted it when Karly called, somehow, telepathically knowing I needed to vent, but before she called, I'd been watching television.

Hockey.

Specifically, I watched the Las Vegas Vipers.

When Ben's practice was done today, I'd expected him to run

into the house, fling his hockey bag at the front door and kick his boots off in a rush of excitement to tell me about how *awesome* and *cool* and *totally lit* his afternoon had been.

Instead, he'd trudged inside like he'd gotten the crap beat out of him all afternoon. I'd taken one look through the front doorway, caught Evan's gaze, furrowed brows, hands planted to his hips, to know that while the practice may have been all those things, the ride home certainly wasn't.

Fucking Evan.

It'd taken a good hour to get Ben back into a good mood, and then I'd told him we could watch the game and order pizza if he wanted. We did, and slowly his mood improved, even if he never told me what his dad had said.

I didn't need to know. It was Evan. Nothing was ever good enough.

Eventually, Ben grew tired and with school tomorrow, I sent him to bed after the second period. The Vipers were already up three to one, and Ben loped off without a problem, proving how exhausted he was.

When Karly called shortly after, I didn't bother changing the channel. It was definitely not because I was watching Dominick, trying to figure him out. Why my kid? What kind of guy was he that he'd be arrested, coach youth hockey, *and* try to give my kid something most kids could only dream of?

What made him tick?

And if he was that good of a guy, what happened with the arrest?

Enough. No more thinking of Dominick.

"Mark and I told Tanner we'd take him out for dinner after their game on Saturday. Do you want to come with us?"

"Ben would love that." Tanner was one of his best friends on the team. "Where are we going?"

Karly laughed.

"Dave and Buster's," we both said at the same time.

"Of course." I laughed. "Should have known."

"Obviously. Okay, we'll see you Saturday, but if you need me, call, okay?"

"I will—" *Ding dong.* "What the hell?"

"What was that?"

"My doorbell," I muttered, already pushing off the couch. "Who in the hell could be here at..." I glanced at the clock above my fireplace. "Eleven?"

"Evan?" Karly asked.

"Probably. Shit, should I ignore him?"

"No. Answer it and I'll stay on the line. Put me on speaker so I can tell him what a grade-A asshole he is."

"He'd love that," I said, lowering my voice. "I don't think it's Evan." There was a shadow through my frosted glass front door. But it was taller. Wider than Evan. I should really invest in a Ring camera sometime soon for moments like this, but on the other hand, I didn't *get* company this late.

"Who?" she asked.

I'd reached the door, and since I couldn't peek out through the frosted window, I opened it. There was a storm door on the other side and I had Karly on the phone, so I was safe, right?

"Holy shit," I whispered.

Because it wasn't Evan.

It was Ben's coach. Dominick.

He shoved his hands in his pockets and faced the door, stepping back like he was giving me space even if there were two doors in between us.

"What are you doing here?"

"Who is it?" Karly hissed. "Do I need to call the cops?"

Dominick flinched. His gaze went to my phone. So Karly could be loud. Really loud even when she wasn't on speaker.

"No. I don't think so," I told her, my eyes staying on Dominick. At that, I swore a flash of amusement sparked before he wiped it away. "I'll call you tomorrow. I'm good."

"You sure?"

"Yep. Bye, Karly."

"And you'll tell me who's at your door in the middle of the night."

Maybe. Maybe not. Depending on the reason for him being here. And how did he know where I lived? "Of course," I told her.

I ended the call but kept the phone in my hand. Without opening the door further, and not reaching for the storm door, I asked, "What are you doing here?"

"Are you and Ben okay?"

"What?"

"You and Ben. Is he... is he okay?"

His face twisted, features angry. No... that wasn't anger. It was worry.

"Um. Yeah." Blood rushed through me. What in the hell was going on? And while I opened my mouth to ask, I swore I heard the motor of a garage door opening nearby.

Shit.

Like he understood, Dominick leaned forward. "Didn't like the way Evan talked to Ben earlier and it worried me because I was kind of a dick to him."

"Ben?"

"No. Evan." Pretty sure he looked at me like I had two heads. He speared the next door area with a heavy scowl. "And he's coming outside. Can you let me in? So I can talk? Or explain?"

"Who's there?" Evan called out, his voice thunderous.

"Shit."

I went to step outside, assure him everything was okay—damn Vegas and their postage-stamped size yards.

"Don't," Dominick said, his hand palm out toward me. "Let me in. Please?"

"So I can make my ex-husband more pissed off than he already is?"

A heavy, thick black brow quirked. "Sounds like fun though, doesn't it?"

Disarming. Dominick Masters was disarming and one look from him gave me a thousand questions—and more than a few inappropriate thoughts into my brain—in a moment.

"You're trouble," I said, but for some stupid reason, I was stepping back, bringing my door with me and gesturing for him to enter.

He pulled open the storm door and stepped inside, right as Evan called out again, "Who's there?"

"Fuck," I whispered again. My phone buzzed in my hand, but I already knew who it'd be.

"Your ex-husband might be the largest asshole I've ever met."

Dominick was in my entryway. Narrow, little area with very little room to move and maneuver so I could shut the front door behind him.

"Is he going to bug you all night now?"

"Well, a man just showed up, one he doesn't know, late at night, and so yeah... that's going to cause a problem."

"Okay, then I have about thirty seconds to make my point with this guy."

"Which is?"

"Shit. Okay. So he was being an asshole to Ben at practice, and I..." He flinched. "Might have suggested I knew what kind of guy he was based on the fact he left you and moved next door. And I might have told him I was glad he did that because that meant someday you'd have a good man in your life and you'd know exactly how shitty he was."

Holy freaking crap. "You *told* him that." Pleased? Amused? Angry? How in the hell was I supposed to feel when a stranger put him in his place? "He will not take that well."

"Which was why I was worried about you and Ben, because I didn't know exactly how he'd take that out on you, so I wanted to make sure you were okay."

Oh... this explained so much. So very much.

A fist pounded the door, a few feet from us, and made me jump. "Damn him," I rasped, my hand flew to my chest.

"That him?" Dominick scowled at the door.

"Of course."

"Want to piss him off? Like *really* piss him off?"

"No, never because I'm a better person, but yes because I'm also bitter. Why?"

"My guess? Your ex is such a dick, with a small one... that he'll be tempted to compete. He sees me with you and he's going to think I want you, which means he's going to try to come back, and I cannot wait to see the moment you crush him."

"That's... that's a lot of manipulating with zero reward for me." I didn't want him back. But would I like to see him in pain? Maybe I wasn't the better person.

Besides—Karly would think this idea was hilarious and really... after all the shit Evan pulled on me, didn't he deserve a little bit of his own medicine thrown back on him?

I grinned. "You're on."

"Good." He nudged his chin toward the door. "Then open it up and let him see me here."

"Now?" Because holy crap, I didn't mean *now* like tonight.

"Oh yeah." That rumble of his hit me in places I'd examine like *never*. But good God, the man was sexy as sin when he was coaching kids. His presence in my own home risked igniting my ovaries.

"Holly!" Evan bellowed like he couldn't see us standing so close to the door, like we couldn't see him or hadn't heard pounding on the glass.

"All right." My hands shook though, and worry made me bite my lip. This could go bad.

Evan didn't like to *lose*. I wasn't his to lose, but a guy like Dominick in a house I knew he still thought of as *his*?

Well... that could piss him off to extreme levels.

"I've got your back," Dominick said, his glare on the door like he was trying to melt the glass with his vision alone. "Open the door."

I reached out, pulled open the front door. Dominick's chest hit my back, one hand settling at my hip. I fought a shiver.

His palm was calloused, hand *huge*, something I could easily feel through the thin and ratty T-shirt I'd been wearing all night and oh my God.

It hit me then, as Evan stood in my doorway, bracing the storm door open with his back, which was all sorts of absolutely *not okay*, and there I was... dressed in a ratty T-shirt, stained sweatpants, my hair pulled back with a headband, no makeup, and shit... I probably had red wine staining my teeth.

Mortifying.

"You," Evan said, glaring at Dominick, and he hadn't even looked at me. Hadn't even really been worried about me at all, but wanted to know who was in my home.

It was his look that made me stop thinking about my stupid appearance. Pointless.

This was Dominick Masters offering to put Evan in his place, not *date* me for crying out loud.

"Get out of my home," I said and stepped toward Evan who was at my threshold.

"I'm not in your home," he returned, sassy and confident, and then I wasn't standing in between Dominick and him, I was at Dominick's side, gently being pushed behind him.

"The minute your hand hit that storm door and you opened it to her residence, you entered her property. And she just told you to leave. So now you're trespassing. Get your ass off the porch and go home."

"You have no say here and it *is* my business to know who my *wife* is bringing into our home with our son upstairs."

"*Ex-wife* and *her* home."

"You don't know what you're talking about," Evan spit back.

But seriously? Wife and our and holy crap... Evan was exhausting.

Dominick looked down at me, brows arched, hands fisted. Oh... he was M.A.D. *mad*. The heat rolling off his arm pressed to my side was *boiling*.

I bit down on my lip to keep from laughing. Because this... this was too damn funny. Almost too easy. I rolled my eyes up at him before he said anything, but I knew what was coming.

"You're divorced, right?"

"Yup. Official right before Christmas, actually."

"You got the house in the divorce, right?"

I nodded.

"So he's your ex, right?"

"Yup."

"Want me to call the cops?"

And he'd do it, too. He'd probably have fun doing it, most likely.

"Are you on a first-name basis with them yet?" Evan sneered and oh no.

Dominick's minuscule humor he'd had in his eyes as he peppered me with those questions flared into something so very, very dark.

"You think you're putting me in my place with that, but you should know I have no problems putting my hands on a man who put *theirs* on a woman who didn't ask for those hands to be on her and didn't want them there," he said, low... his voice so low it was a storm cloud, rolling thunder from miles away that told you something horrific was slowly creeping in.

A shiver danced down my spine as he focused that banked power and fury toward Evan.

"In fact, I enjoy it." He rolled back his shoulders and leaned closer to Evan. An inch. Might as well have shoved him off the porch for all the anger in that inch. "Want me to show you how much?"

Evan, for his part, clenched his jaw and didn't piss his pants in fear although I wouldn't have laughed if he had. Dominick was *scary*.

Instead, he turned to me. "Nice kind of role model you brought into Ben's life, Holly. Really nice."

He smirked, let go of the storm door, and stepped back right as it slammed shut, inches from Dominick's face, who didn't so much as blink.

OH MY GOD. What had I done? And who in the hell was Evan becoming?

I hurried away from Dominick. I needed a moment. Needed to get a grip on myself and stop the tremors from rolling through my body. I shook out my hands, paced to the kitchen, and out to the living room, back to the kitchen.

I poured myself a glass of wine, and as it shook in my hands, I was quickly—and quietly—relieved of both bottle and glass.

"Shit," I whispered, and licked my lips. I needed to slow my racing heart.

A full glass of wine was set in front of me.

"Did I push him too far?"

"He's never hurt us. Not physically. I don't think he would." But I'd never seen him like *that* either.

"Not thinking he would and knowing he wouldn't are two different things."

"Yeah, well I've never tried to push his buttons like that, either. I just ignore him and let him be."

Thank goodness Ben was sleeping and hadn't witnessed any of that scene.

Two strong, muscled hands with the veins popping out on the backs played a drumbeat on my counter. The thumping thump thump so rapid it matched my still racing heart.

"If I've made things worse for you and Ben, I didn't mean it."

It wasn't an apology. Not really. It somehow absolved him of all responsibility for any potential additional trouble that might come. But... did it matter?

Evan would continue being a thorn in my side for as long as I was unable to sell this home and even then, he'd be a pain in the ass, only farther away.

Awesome. A lifetime of putting up with him.

Sighing, I took a sip of my wine and set it down. I'd had enough tonight. Enough wine. Enough drama. Enough of Evan.

"Evan won't hurt us, not like that," I said, and exhaustion lowered my voice and slowed my words. "I appreciate you coming by and explaining, and being worried, but we'll be fine."

We always were. Somehow I made certain it was so, and I would, current drama included.

"Right." He pushed off the kitchen counter, gaze going to the fireplace, the built-ins on both sides filled with books and picture frames. I caught what he was looking at before bringing my eyes back to him.

His brows had furrowed, looking almost adorably confused. Sort of lost as he stood in my kitchen, in my *home*, this NHL behemoth of a man the press didn't have many kind words to say about and for a split second, with the look on his face, the pinch of his lips, forehead scrunched, I had the strangest urge to give him a hug.

He looked like a man who needed one and had never had one.

Which was the weirdest thought to have about a man who'd had no shame in admitting to his arrest or beating the hell out of a guy.

Although his reason...

"Did you mean it?" I asked.

It took a second, and he flinched, yanking his eyes off my living room display and on to me. "Mean what?"

"About your arrest. Why you did it."

"Any man who puts his hands on a woman should have worse happen."

Said with all the venom of a man who'd maybe witnessed it more than that one time.

"Right."

"I should go." He turned abruptly and headed to my door so quick I practically had to chase after him.

Whiplash. This man gave me the worst whiplash that I'd ever experienced.

"Did I say something wrong?" I asked. "Because as weird as I think this has been, and not so great to be honest, it really was nice of you to come by and check on us."

"Yeah. I figured you thought that since you just said it."

He didn't say it trying to be a jerk, but the effect was the same.

"Shit." He sighed, shoulders fell, and he scrubbed a hand through his hair. The move was as disarming as his earlier lost look.

Had this man ever done something nice for someone *and* been told thank you? Damn, the ways I wanted to dig into his psyche and figure him out, was startling.

Not my business. Not my circus, not my monkeys.

Still, I was curious....

He opened the front door. That was best. He should go. We could chalk up this entire night as well as flaunting *nothing* in front of Evan's face to piss him off as a lapse in judgment on both our parts.

Truly, what did any of it matter anyway?

He was my kid's coach for a few more months. That was it.

Right as he pushed the storm door open, I stepped back, hand curling around the doorknob.

"That woman," Dominick said. "The woman they said was unconscious when I put her in my car the night I got arrested?"

Had he known I looked him up or did he assume everyone knew his business? Either way, that lost look was back, dancing in his dark eyes. I leaned against the door.

"Yeah?"

"That was my sister. She needed help. I got it for her."

"Oh." A *sister*. No wonder he didn't like men touching women who didn't want it. It happened to his *sister*.

"Why Ben?" I asked.

I'd asked it before, but there had to be more to it than him not liking Evan. There were twenty-four kids on the team, and yet he'd helped Ben when he didn't need to. What did he see in my kid that had him taking these steps?

Maybe the media had him all wrong. Because standing in front of me, I saw a guy who protected and took care of those in trouble. Maybe that he did it with his fists was what people didn't like. But... it was the question I kept coming back to.

What was it about my son, his circumstance, that had this guy so ready to help out?

So he had a sister. It didn't make his sudden fascination or desire to help Ben, check on me, any clearer. Lots of kids had shit dads. I was betting, so did the man in front of me.

He shrugged, kicked at nothing on my front porch, and shoved his hands into his front pockets. "Hell if I understand it myself."

He hurried to his car, something black and shining in my driveway with an emblem that probably came from Germany or something. Nothing I knew off the top of my head.

And then he was gone, leaving me grasping my door handle for balance.

That look.

That confusion.

What in the hell had just happened?

8

———

DOMINICK

My sister. My sister. My sister.

What in the hell had I been thinking?

I wasn't. That was the damn problem. I wasn't thinking during the game the other night. I certainly wasn't thinking when I hopped in my Maserati after the game and drove like a bat out of hell to get to Holly and Ben's home. I certainly wasn't thinking when I threatened to beat the shit out of a parent who had a kid on my team. Jesus Christ—the shitshow that could become if Evan went public with that. If he'd recorded me.

I doubted he would though. My saving grace in the shitty choices I made, there was a silver lining. Evan wouldn't let anyone see him as weak, so I didn't have to deal with any fallout from the other night from him.

But my sister.

I didn't tell *anyone* about Lucy. No one.

Ever.

Holly had looked at me with those large eyes, that thankfulness and sweetness that seemed to pulse off her and choke my body's need for air. The nice house that wasn't huge but was warm and inviting and filled with so many happy, smiling faces of her and Ben it'd grabbed me by the throat and left me reeling.

Holly, asking why them. Why *her*. Why Ben. Thanking me. Somehow, asking questions with her eyes before they fell from her mouth.

My sister needed help. I got it for her.

For some damn reason, there was absolutely no way in hell I was letting that sweet, beautiful, kind woman think I was a monster.

It didn't matter I thought she was beautiful. It didn't matter I wanted to stay in that home and continue being suffocated by the warmth of it, the invitation she'd give to anyone who needed a loving and safe place to crash their head.

She wasn't for me.

I'd take her goodness and sweetness and I'd crush it, leaving her with all my ugly dredges and sharp, filthy secrets.

No, Holly didn't need a guy like me who would cause her death by a thousand paper cuts because I didn't know how to handle all that clean light.

She needed someone who would only pour more light on top of what she already gave.

But damn if I hadn't wanted to feel her. Just once. Take a hit off it and stay high on it.

Instead, I channeled all the rage and confusion into my practice the next day before we got set to do a stretch of away games that'd take us up the East Coast for the next week.

In my place, two other dads would be coaching Ben's team while I was gone.

I was head bent, responding to Carter's dad's email when Max plopped his ass down next to me in the locker room.

"Good practice today." He punched my thigh and ignored my answering scowl.

The guy wasn't affected by *anything*.

"Yeah," I grunted and turned back to my phone.

"We're headed out to Malley's tonight. You in?"

"Can't," I said, and blacked out my phone, slipping it into the pocket of my jeans as I stood.

"Busy?"

I had no plans whatsoever. "Yep."

"Really? Like what?" His brows pulled in. Adorably confused, like a puppy. His standard look, really.

For once, a lie or a brush-off didn't come as easily. My hesitation showed my lie and Max grinned. "Yeah. That's what I thought. One drink. I'll even buy."

I wanted that one drink too damn much, which was why I shouldn't go. I knew exactly what one drink could turn people into. What it turned family into.

"Why?" I asked.

Because I went to the team dinners Gabby and Joey hosted. I worked out with some more of the team now. And yeah, maybe Vik had been right last season. Hanging out with the guys more often, even begrudgingly, had had an effect on the team's play. On my playing. But I'd done enough, right?

"Um..." He scratched his temple and frowned. "Because when you don't look like you want to kill us, you're kind of fun to be around?"

Me? Fun?

Not in a million years.

I wasn't sure if it was slightly better he asked it as a question— like even Max didn't know. But...

"I..." My phone rang. A ringtone I'd assigned to one number and my blood ran cold. "Can't."

"You sure?" Max asked, but I was already shoving past him, not saying goodbye.

This was why it didn't make sense to get close to people.

My past always dragged me back.

I was in the hallway, yanking my phone out of my pocket and answering it, Max and the team and me being *fun* forgotten when reality was burning like a hot coal in my hand. "This is Dominick. What's wrong?"

"THANK YOU FOR COMING IN TODAY." I shook the doctor's outstretched hand. Dr. Miles so far had been as steady as any guy I'd ever met. This wasn't my first rodeo with Lucy and so far, he'd classified Lucy's addiction as one he firmly believed she could conquer and find victory in if she was willing to put in the work.

Which was good, since my own diminished every year.

"Lucy looked good," I admitted. And she had. For a moment, my sister's blue eyes were clear. She was showered, dressed in the soft, high-quality T-shirt and joggers all inpatients had to wear for their first thirty days, but her hair was washed. Her face clean. Her eyes not dull. Yeah, they still held the terror and fear and worry... but she'd laughed quietly.

That alone was a victory.

"Thanks for the call."

"She wanted to see you, and I thought it'd help her. She knows you love her, you know. And she's worried about disappointing you."

The only thing that disappointed me with Lucy was her constant willingness to forgive our mother—if she could even be called that.

And speak of the devil....

Dr. Miles and I were at the front reception, wrapping up our short consult after he let me have fifteen minutes of family therapy time with Lucy when the she-devil herself in the flesh stumbled outside on the concrete.

"What the fuck?"

"She's on the no-visitor list," the doctor said.

"Has she come by before?"

He shrugged. Which said it all.

"You were supposed to call me," I hissed. Outside, Gloria regained her footing.

I'd long since tried to shove off the shame and embarrassment of this woman. It never worked.

There she was—our crackhead, threw-her-daughter-into-prostitution-at-the-age-of-thirteen *mother* bobbing and weaving her way through the front doors.

Fucking hell, the hits never stopped coming.

"Security has it handled," Dr. Miles said and while he turned to speak with the receptionist, I beat him to it.

Screw the fact they knew. They'd protect Lucy, of course they would.

But when it came to Lucy, I didn't trust anyone to do a better job of it than I could—fat lot of good it'd done me though.

I'd failed her too many times and I loved her more than anyone.

I didn't trust anyone when it came to her.

As Gloria made her appearance through the front doors, I turned to the receptionist at the desk. "That woman is *never* to be allowed in. It's in my paperwork. It's in all of the notes. I've told everyone she's not to step foot into this building, much less be anywhere around Lucy."

The woman nodded. "Of course, Mr. Masters." She picked up her phone. I vaguely heard her calling for security, but it was only vague because Gloria, in all her destroyed and ruined mess, still had the power to knock the wind from my lungs. Dressed in clothes she'd probably owned since before life went to hell because she sure as hell never had money for anything other than drugs and alcohol, her face, what used to be soft and smell like peaches and well-done up was now leathered, pockmarked. She was ravaged from over a decade of drugs, alcohol, desperation, and shitty living in the hot Nevada sun. And as she sauntered in, locked eyes with me, I fought the urge to turn and vomit.

Goddamn. My mother. Dad would *hate* her for this, almost as much as he'd be disappointed in me.

"Aw. My *beautiful boy*. Our family's together again. How you doing, honey?"

Her words slurred, her makeup askew from the crooked, false eyelashes to her smeared lipstick.

She had to be fucking kidding me. It shouldn't have even surprised me.

Without Lucy around, Mom would be struggling to get drugs, but it sure as hell looked like she hadn't had a problem that day.

"You don't get to see her and security's already been called." I crossed my arms over my chest, planted my feet wide. Who knew how long it'd take for security to get there, but Gloria wouldn't go down without a fight or a scene.

My mother was fucking exhausting.

Before she reached me, I turned to the woman at the front desk and lowered my voice. "I repeat. She's never allowed in. Even strip-searched, she's not to go in."

Mom could hide a small baggie of drugs *anywhere* and that was an image no man should have of his mom seared into his brain.

"Of course, sir. I assure you all your specifications will be followed exactly."

"Good." I managed to get it out right before Gloria was breathing down my neck, ready to kick her attitude into high gear.

"How dare you," she hissed, but not quietly. "Lucy is my daughter."

Yeah, because she pushed her out of her body, but since then she'd been nothing to her. Neither of us ever were. "Don't bullshit me. Lucy is your ticket to keeping a roof over your head."

"Always too good for us. You think I won't tell someday? I can ruin you."

Fuck of it was, in this she was right.

"And ruin your income." Two grand a month and it all went to blow and smack and whatever other drugs she was doing now.

I peered closer—blown out pupils, the way she kept itching at her jawline. "Are you high now? Are you thinking to get her hooked in *here?* You're a piece of work."

"Lucy loves me."

"Because you keep her too damn high and used to know better."

Security moved closer. "Ma'am, I'm going to have to ask you to leave."

"You can't do that. She's *my* daughter."

She was a tool for food and rent. Had been since she was too damn young to know any different. It was days like this I cursed my talent, cursed Coach Vik for taking me under his wing. At the time, my father fresh in the grave when I'd gone to Vik, then my coach at Detroit College, I'd allowed him to convince me to stay in hockey. My dad would have wanted it, he said. I'd bought into his bullshit that this was my ticket to a better life, a way to save my family, to repair them after Dad's death.

Except the only thing my dad had ever told me to do was to take care of Lucy.

Fat lot of fucking good I'd done honoring my dad's only wish for me.

"I'd lock you up in here too if I thought it'd do a damn bit of good."

"I don't need help."

I couldn't exactly disagree. She was too far gone for any kind of help to do her any good.

"I find out you're here again, and I'm calling the cops and cutting you off."

I wouldn't. Damn it. For Lucy.

"You won't."

"Try me." Just because I wouldn't, didn't mean I wasn't damn close. Hell, maybe this time could be different. Foolish hope took root despite this being our sixth song and dance in rehab. But when Lucy was clean, she was the sweet, innocent girl I remembered despite the fact she was twenty-three. Hell, some days I swore she stopped maturing at thirteen—there could be such an innocent quality to her.

Part of her problem, really, because she still believed Mom loved us and could change. Her naive hope was her greatest and best quality and her downfall, every damn time.

"How many times you been inside, Ma? Hell, I bet the amount you have hidden on you now is enough to send you in."

I reached for my phone. Four lock-ups I knew of. One extended for dealing inside county jail. I could ruin her in a second.

But she'd talk.

I'd rather be hated than pitied and have my family filth spread out over every single sports headline website and blog.

She shoved off the security guards, who were now circling her, and pushed a fourth out of her way.

"Fine. I'll go. But you'll hear from me soon."

Couldn't fucking wait.

This... this was why I needed to stay far away from Holly and Ben.

I'd done my good Samaritan thing and checked in on them, but from now on—I was his coach.

And that was it.

Holly had enough crap in her life without having to take on mine.

No, that woman needed clean and easy.

Not filth and dark.

9

DOMINICK

Something strange was happening to me.

It wasn't a cold or sinus infection like I'd thought at practice last week when Ben came to skate with the team.

This was something different. Worse. More internal. It was making me lose focus on our game, currently two periods over in New York. It was distracting me from what was important—my *job*.

It was an unsettling in my gut, a cloudiness in my brain.

All because of a handful of screaming kids I couldn't stop thinking about.

One in particular.

I turned to my locker and checked my phone.

They had a game today, one of the few I'd miss. I'd asked the parents who were coaching to text me as soon as it was done. My phone was blank of any text alerts, so I unlocked it and opened the messaging app just in case it wasn't working right. But still, nothing.

"Damn," I muttered and tossed my phone to the side. We weren't supposed to have them out, but I didn't care.

Rules were always made to be broken.

"Damn what?" Kane asked and took a swig out of his Gatorade bottle.

"Nothing." Because it was nothing. So the coaches didn't text me. So I didn't know how the kids played. So I didn't know if Ben scored a goal, if his dad was there being a dick, or if Holly was sitting there looking all cute and shit.

None of it mattered.

None of it should have been what I was thinking of right then.

No... what I should have been thinking of was the rookie center for New York, who was completely kicking our ass. Sven Klemons was a demon. Played mean as hell and he'd left Kane, Max, and me chasing his damn tail all game long with no sign of slowing down in sight.

Instead, Kane was still giving me a confused look, brows arched, glancing from the phone I'd tossed in my locker and back to me.

"Everything okay?"

Kane was quieter than most guys on the team. I knew he was divorced, no kids, but outside of that, I didn't know much about him, but that was mostly because, like me, he kept quiet. I suspected it wasn't because he had drug-addicted family members he didn't want anyone to know about, but because it was his person- ality. The look he was giving me actually created a pinch in my chest.

Like I was fighting against opening up to him. Like he actually cared about *me* and wasn't asking because it was the socially accepted or expected thing to do. He wasn't making frivolous conversation, he genuinely cared.

And fuck... when did I start noticing these things about people?

"All right." He shrugged and went to grab his Gatorade bottle and for some damn reason, I found myself blurting out, "Ben had a game today and I don't know how he did yet."

That green bottle froze halfway to his mouth, already opened like he was waiting to squeeze the water into his open mouth.

He turned to me, and it must have been reflex because that bottle squeezed and water squirted right onto his cheek. The bottle dropped to the floor.

"Shit." He swiped his cheek, and I laughed.

Damn it. I fucking *laughed*.

What was happening to me?

"Sorry," I muttered and swiped gloved hands down my face. I needed to shake this off. All of it. Ben. Being worried about his mom.

The kids on the team.

"He seemed like a good kid," Kane said. "You like him."

It wasn't even a damn question.

He just *knew*.

I couldn't even argue with him. Where in the hell had all my walls gone? Or my shitty attitude that kept people away? More and more of them were slithering through defenses and lodging like bricks inside my chest.

Shit.

Maybe I needed to see the team doctor again. There was definitely something wrong with me.

"There's nothing wrong with caring," Kane said, like he wasn't witnessing me in the beginning stages of a meltdown, or a heart attack, right in front of him. "About Ben or his mom."

"I don't care about his mom," I snapped, and that heavy sensation in my gut curdled.

"No?" One arched brow. A slight tilt of his chin to the side. A shrug. "Okay."

"I don't care about anyone."

Because I didn't. Outside of Lucy anyway. He shouldn't have assumed anything about me. Care about people? I mean, it wasn't like I wanted them to be hit by Evan—I had a fucking soul, for crying out loud. That was why I'd gone to her house. It wasn't anything more.

Kane chuckled. Large shoulders beneath his pads shook with laughter like I'd told him the most hilarious joke of all time and he pressed his hands to his thighs and stood. "Keep telling yourself that, Dom. It might actually come true."

The fuck?

The asshole turned to leave. I should have let him. Should have turned back to my locker, taken a seat and gotten my head on straight. Five more minutes until we were back on the ice and I hadn't spent a second of it preparing for the demon skater we'd be facing for the final twenty minutes. We were only up by one goal. Twenty minutes could kill the game if I wasn't focused.

That's what I should have been doing.

"I don't know how to." The words blurted so fast out of my throat there was no way to prepare for them, no way to suck them back. No time to think about what I admitted. That burn in my chest spread through my body as Kane's shoulders pulled back, his body went taut and he slowly spun back to face me.

Two steps and he was right there in front of me, head tipped in my direction, leaning in like he had something vital to say, and I hung on his every breath. Every second. Jolted when his hand clamped to my shoulder and gave me a shake I didn't see coming.

"That tells me you already do and you're just too scared to fuck it up. Nothing wrong with letting the right people in, you know."

Fuck. My chest. Where was the doctor?

My lip curled. The *right* people?

"Yeah. The right people." He gestured to the locker room, the noise of the guys rushing back to my ears. Shit. I'd said that out loud. "Your team. Me. Gabby. Joey. Face it, Masters, you've been letting us all in slowly for months now even if you want to pretend it isn't happening. You might not be the nicest guy in the damn world, but you're a good man. Don't know why you try to hide it, but we're all here for you. And yeah... you care about Ben and his mom? Nothing wrong with that either as long as you don't fuck it up. Single moms are a different breed."

"Her ex-husband is a dick and I'm worried he's trying to keep fucking with her head."

Where. Were. My. God. Damn. Defenses?

"Then it sounds like with you in her corner, she has the right guy to keep her safe."

He didn't know shit. I couldn't keep anyone safe. Not even my damn sister.

Like he knew the maelstrom of emotions he was causing to churn violently in my gut, he grinned. Slapped my shoulder again and finally stepped back.

"Caring about a special woman is the best gift you can give yourself, because guaranteed—you do it right—and really all you need to do is *be* there and listen and care and show it. You do that, she'll give you that back one hundredfold. That's it."

It was a fucking youth hockey team. I just wanted to know if they won.

Not all this other shit.

"Not sure I should take advice from a man whose wife left him."

Because fuck him. Fuck him for making this tightening in my gut boil over. He didn't even flinch at my attack.

He gave me a sad smile and scooped up his Gatorade bottle he'd dropped on the floor. "Take it from someone who learned. You find a good woman who might just care back—you don't ever let that shit go."

He squirted the water into his mouth and walked off.

Like I hadn't been an asshole to him for no reason.

Like he hadn't made the floor beneath my skates rattle.

Care about her? Show up. Be there. Act like you give a shit.

Kane didn't know shit.

It couldn't be nearly as simple as all that. Because I'd done that.

I'd busted my ass to do that for the only female in my life I'd ever cared about.

And look where that got Lucy.

THE BRUTAL BELOW zero windchill whipped through all of us and sent a slash of ice through my coat and suit. Fuck this northern weather. It was the one thing I absolutely didn't miss about no longer living in the frozen tundra.

If I was ever traded to a cold climate team, I'd retire. Tonight we had our hats pulled down low over our ears, the celebration in the visiting locker room cut short due to the flight we had to catch to Toronto immediately after the game.

"Good game, yo." Max's fist punched into mine as we dragged our exhausted, but victorious asses onto the bus.

"You too."

Together with Kane, the three of us had managed to keep Klemons scoreless. New York had done the same to us though, too, leading to a frustrating twenty minutes of pure defense maneuvering.

I couldn't remember ever being so exhausted. I'd barely had time on the stationary bike after to get all that lactic acid out of my muscles so my legs didn't lock up and I couldn't wait to climb into a bed.

I shivered, shoved my hands into my coat pocket where my phone was a hot coal, burning through my gloves as I stepped onto the bus.

There were no texts.

It shouldn't matter.

I could find everything out tomorrow. Or when I returned.

"You were a beast that last period," Joey said, lifting his hand to slap mine when I passed him on the bus.

I returned the high-five and slid into a seat behind him, tossing my bag next to me.

Across the aisle from me, Kane slid into his seat. "Played like you were pissed off." He smirked.

The asshole.

Like he hadn't known everything he'd said to me would be taken out on the ice.

I ignored him.

Well, I tried. But his cocksure grin was too much.

"You think that was about you?"

He dug his noise-canceling headphones out of his bag and slid them around his neck. Cupping the earpieces, his grin widened. "I think I made you think about something you didn't want to, and yeah, you took that out on the ice. But it's all good."

The cocky motherfucker.

"What things?" Joey asked, turning around and leaning over his seat. He propped his forearms onto the back of his chair.

Across the aisle from me, Kane slid on his headphones and chuckled.

I'd punch him. My own teammate. Wouldn't be the first time I got into a fight with one—would be the first time it wasn't during a practice or scrimmage.

Would be the first time I only did it because he was right.

The asshole.

"Nothing," I growled, scowling at Kane, but he'd closed his eyes —that smirk cemented in place.

He probably didn't even have his music on. He was probably enjoying the hell out of this.

Maybe it was payback for the comment about his ex-wife.

Perhaps I'd taken it too far. Not that I'd apologize. He started it.

"Doesn't look like nothing," Joey said and held out his phone. "Need to talk to your bestie? Gabby can help."

He laughed. Swear to God, so did Kane.

I would murder them all.

"You're a little piece of shit," I muttered and opened my bag to dig for my own headphones. Screw them.

Screw them all. A few dinners and nights out didn't mean I had to tell them anything. I'd already said enough.

"Don't mind him," Kane said, and he was now grinning at Joey. "He's got his jockstrap twisted up over a kid—or maybe it's the kid's mom. I haven't quite worked that out yet."

As if I was a damn puzzle to solve. My hand curled into my fist as both of them chuckled.

"Yeah," Joey said. "That first gut-punch when a woman walks into your life you can't stop thinking about is the worst."

"You got so drunk you married her and didn't remember it." Had he forgotten? His love story with Gabby hadn't exactly started out all hearts and roses.

"Exactly. Who needs to live through the pain? I put a ring on it as fast as I fucking could."

That didn't even make any sense. It was all bullshit. He didn't know that. You couldn't know.

Not that fast. So it worked out for both of them. That didn't mean shit.

I readied myself to tell them both to fuck off and mind their damn business—with my fist, not my mouth—when my phone buzzed in my pocket.

I yanked it out, and swear to God, whatever vise had been squeezing my chest all damn day released like a valve when I saw the name on my screen.

Holly—Ben's mom.

It was how I put all the kids on my team into my phone so when parents texted to say they couldn't make a practice or game or whatever, I knew who they were immediately.

But this?

I'd expected Carter or Aidan's dads, the parents who coached in my absence.

Ben?

Holly?

What the hell was going on?

"Hello?"

10

HOLLY

O

h goodness....

In the words of *Annie*, leaping lizards!

Dominick's voice was the thickest, smoothest chocolate. Decadent.

Oh dear... the sinful ideas that went through my mind at that rumble.

I hadn't seen him since the night he came to my house. The night he left abruptly. Scowled and was kind and protective and then a jerk and it was well... *weird*.

I must have been seriously hard up for sex if I was unraveling over a hello.

"Mom. Let me talk!" Ben tugged at my arm and I laughed.

"Um... hey," I said to the phone. To Dominick. I'd only called him because apparently during the post-game talk, the coaches had said they were supposed to call Dom.

Ben had begged for us to be the ones to do it. To my utter shock, they agreed. What grown man didn't want to get to be the guy that could return to work on Monday and when asked about their weekend say, *So I called NHL Viper player Dominick Masters the other night* like it was no big deal.

"How'd the game go?" Dominick asked, and I stuck my tongue out at Ben who was about to *lose. His. Mind.*

I laughed at my son's hands clasped together, jumping up and down with his legs crossed like he was about to pee, taking me back to his potty training days. "I have someone who wants to talk to you."

"Yeah? How'd he play?"

"Mom!"

"I think I'll let him tell you."

"Okay. But when he and I are done, I want to talk to you more, alright?"

"Ummm..." Me? What did *we* have to talk about? "Okay. Sure."

"Mom! Come on! It's important."

In my ear, Dominick laughed. Or rumbled. I wasn't sure. I just knew the effects of that went straight to my toes and made them curl into my cool tile floor.

"Here he is."

"After," Dominick rumbled.

And oh... what another glorious idea that brought to mind. The idea of that voice, at my ear, rumbling *after* in relation to other things.

My cheeks burned as I considered it, handing my phone to Ben. "Talk quick, kid, he has to be busy."

Ben took the phone from me like it was a grenade and about ready to blow. Before his mouth was anywhere close to it, he shouted, "Coach! Guess what?" There had to be no time for Dominick to guess before my son shouted, "I scored a goal! And not just one... but *two* of them! And it gets even better. Want to guess?"

There was a quick, quiet rumble before Ben shouted again, "Yes! And we won five to one! Which means I scored almost *half* the goals."

My kid. He was damn cute.

And really, he'd earned this excitement. He played better in tonight's game than I'd ever seen him play. Faster. Sharper. Quick passes and smiles on his face the entire time. He barely wobbled on his skates and he hadn't tripped over his own feet. In fact, he hadn't fallen at all except for the one time a kid on the other team went after the puck and hooked him around the ankle.

If only I could hear Dominick's rumble I was certain came through the line as Ben's cheeks matched the tomatoes in my fridge. "Yes, I did that. Uh-huh. And that." His brows tugged in. "No... I didn't do that."

Another rumble. Ben's brows flipped, and his smile returned.

"Oh yeah... I definitely did that."

There were more quiet murmurs. Ben tended to pace when he was on the phone. I wanted to hear everything. Needed to hear what Dominick was saying to my kid, but forced myself to stay in the kitchen. The fridge was behind me, and I was pretty damn certain the bottle of wine inside whispered to me. *Have a glass of me so you'll chill the fuck out, crazy woman.*

It was probably smart to listen.

I grabbed the wine, filled a glass, and was taking my second sip, getting dizzy watching Ben pace a path in our tiled floor when he handed me the phone. "Here Mom! Coach wants you!"

My phone slid across the island, clattering and spinning.

Internally?

My insides did the same.

He wants me?

That... that couldn't be what was said.

That was... inappropriate, right? Because... he was my kid's coach. He couldn't *want* me.

He had to be wrong.

I mean, it was Dominick Masters, for shit's sake. *He* couldn't want me.

"Hello?"

That rumble. A muffled voice. Then my name, repeated, in that muffled voice.

I scrambled for the phone.

Right. He didn't want me. He wanted to talk to me.

Big difference. Hell, he'd even said that before.

"Uh yep?" Yep, yep, yep, I was cool as a clam. "I'm here."

Just me and my multiple personalities internally freaking out. No biggie.

"Ben said the game was good. That he played well."

Right... the game. That's what this was about.

"Yeah. He did. He had a blast."

"And Evan? How was he?"

He'd sat behind the team's bench, elbows to his knees the entire time, hands clasped together with that rigid jaw pushed forward like he was grinding his teeth.

In a miracle of all miracles, he'd stayed silent.

I sighed, made sure Ben wasn't standing right next to me so he couldn't hear me. As hard as it was, I tried my best to ensure he never heard me talk bad about his father. "Evan was, well, Evan."

"Did he say anything?"

"No, not that I know of. He just glared at the coaches the entire time. I credit that thick plexiglass that keeps him from being able to be heard most of the time. But he was good to Ben after."

"And you? There been any more problems with you?"

Surprisingly, no. "He's been quiet lately."

I took a sip of my wine. If he was calling to check in and hope he hadn't made things worse for us it was nice of him.

"I'm glad." There was a muffled sound, a bunch of deep voices in the background and Dominick cursed. "Listen, I gotta cut this short. We're getting to the airport to fly out, but... well... if you need anything. You can call. Or Ben. If he needs anything. I'm a call away, you know?"

I didn't. Hadn't even considered. But again... the offer was nice? I think?

"Where's your next game?"

"Toronto. We'll be back before Ben's next game though."

"Good. That's good, and listen, sorry to call you tonight—"

"No. I'm glad you did." More muffled voices. The sound of laughter. Pretty sure he told someone to fuck off. "It was nice to hear from Ben."

Ben. Right. Of course. This was about Ben. It'd be good for my mental health if I remembered that.

"Right. Good luck then… safe flight… and all that jazz, I guess."

Could he tell it sounded like he'd slapped me upside the head with that last statement?

"Yeah. Thanks. And so you know… it was good to hear from you too, Holly. Take care."

The call ended.

Right then.

I stared at my screen. The call ended flashing before it went back to my home screen. I blinked.

What was *that?*

MY KEYS WERE in my hand, my purse draped over my shoulder, shoes on, coffee cup in one hand. Ben, still riding high on his goals from Saturday's game and maybe talking to Dominick— which he'd now mentioned approximately two billion times yesterday and this morning— was up and ready for me to take him to school on Monday without being harassed and nagged to get moving.

Color me shocked.

"All right, I'm ready," he said, book bag slung over one shoulder, his lunch box in his hand.

I opened the front door, waited until he stepped out and down to the car, and was locking the door when he called out, "Hi Dad."

"Morning, kiddo."

I locked the door and sighed.

"You going to work?" Ben asked.

"Not today, I wanted to talk to your mom real quick."

I stepped off the porch, remote starting the car and unlocking the doors so Ben could get in.

"Go ahead and get settled. I'll be right there, okay?"

"I will." I slid a glance to Evan to ensure he heard.

More surprising than his appearance or desire to talk to me, was the light smile on his face he gave Ben. "It'll just be a minute."

"Good." Ben heaved a sigh of relief. "Because I can't be late today. I gotta tell my friends about my game and getting to call Dominick Masters."

"Did you now?" Evan's pleasant smile stretched. Fake as fake could be. I'd know because I'd witnessed that smile a lot over the years.

It took me too long to realize when he gave that smile, he was actually getting pissed. Luckily, Ben wasn't that astute yet.

"Yeah. I called him about my goals since he wasn't there. He was proud of me."

"Good." Evan cleared his throat. "That's good, kiddo. Get in the car, yeah?" He nodded his chin toward the direction of my SUV purring quietly and once Ben skipped off and slammed the door behind him, that fake smile was already gone.

"So we're calling Dominick now? First, he's at your house and now you're talking to him. Is there something I need to know?"

So much for the Monday morning good juju we had going. I ignored the question, along with the tone in his voice.

"What did you want to talk to me about?"

"I think I have a right to know who's in my son's life, Holly."

I forced my eyeballs not to roll to the heavens. "Yup. And you know Dominick's in his life because he's Ben's coach. But that's not what you wanted to talk about, so can we get to that part?"

There was a time when I would have cowered. I would have acquiesced to prevent an argument. I would have done and answered whatever Evan wanted because I loved him and thought we were a team. It'd taken almost an entire year to fight that urge.

But damn, it felt good to stand my ground in front of him.

"Right." His lip curled and he nodded toward the house. "I wanted to ask if I could borrow our ladder. Kristi's isn't high enough, and I need to change the air filters and smoke detector batteries."

Technically, it was now *my* ladder, but at least he'd asked first this time before helping himself which he'd done before.

"Sure. I'll open the garage."

"Thanks. And if you want, I can do yours, too, later this afternoon?"

Helpful wasn't a word I'd use to describe Evan these last few years. There was a time, sure, where I'd listened to women complain about their husbands' lack of involvement in the house or with the family and found myself with nothing to add. He'd been *perfect*. Doting on me, always doing stuff like this, cooked meals, had no problems grocery shopping. I wasn't sure when it all changed, when he became so self-centered.

I didn't trust his kindness now. I also couldn't remember the last time our smoke detector batteries had been changed, and there was no way I could reach them in our vaulted ceiling.

"Sure. I'm okay with that. I can come back after I drop Ben off at practice."

"No worries, I can handle it."

I was already shaking my head. "I'd prefer you weren't alone in my house. I'll be back here by four."

"It's really not a big deal."

"Okay, then tomorrow, while you and Kristi are at work, I'll just let myself into *your* home and have a look around. That all right with you?"

In truth, I had her home memorized. Shortly after Kristi moved in, we became fast friends. She'd prioritized her career and had never been married, so she was always up for a night when I needed a break or to take Ben when Evan and I wanted a date. We were *always* together. That had to be why it was such a shock to catch Evan and her together. The fact they'd been able to hide it so well. Even now, looking back, I couldn't find a single moment of guilty looks she'd give me, or Evan. Hell, when we were all together, they'd always been cordial and friendly, but never gave me a hint of suspicion.

As expected, Evan didn't like that idea. Whether it was me alone in their home or reminding him it was now *his* house, I wasn't sure.

Didn't particularly care.

"I need to get Ben to school," I reminded him. "Four?"

"Four is fine."

"I'll see you then." I turned to get into my SUV so I could open the garage for him. As I opened the door, he waved happily to Ben in the back seat and called out, "You're welcome, by the way."

I closed my door and opened the garage door. Waited for him to remove the ladder from the hooks and step back out. As soon as the ladder cleared the garage, I had my finger pressing it closed.

He could keep the ladder for all I cared.

"What'd Dad want?" Ben asked from the back seat.

I glanced at him in the mirror as I backed up. "Just to borrow the ladder for some things in his house."

"Is he mad at you?"

When wasn't he? "Of course not, baby."

"I'm ten."

"You'll always be my little baby."

"Yeah, yeah."

I reached back and squeezed his knee, making him giggle. It sucked, absolutely sucked that any interaction with Evan left Ben in a soured mood. His excitement over telling his friends about Dominick was well gone.

Some days I prayed Evan and I would be able to co-parent together more easily, for Ben's sake at the very least.

I figured getting a narcissist to begin being a decent person was most likely too much to ask.

Maybe if I started asking Santa now....

11

DOMINICK

From New York to Toronto, down to Pittsburgh and now out to Chicago, there had been two consistencies with this trip.

One, we'd won every game so far, only Chicago left to go later tonight.

Two, the pressing, unending desire to pull up Holly's number on my recent call list to see how she was doing.

Which was ridiculous. The kids had a game tomorrow I'd be back for. I'd emailed the coaches and they sent me video of last weekend's game where I was able to watch Ben's goals on the flight down to Pittsburgh. The dads had this handled. It was youth hockey, not rocket science. Hell, I didn't even not only have a kid on the team, I was assigned to do this for community service. I hadn't even volunteered.

It shouldn't have meant so much to me.

Neither should the cute and slightly sassy mom with the large green eyes and blunt-cut blonde hair and full lips with a great rack. I was just worried about her asshole husband.

It had to be it.

Somehow, Holly brought all the protective instincts I had toward Lucy and bewitched me into turning them on her.

Stupid, since I'd never been able to save Lucy.

Even more ridiculous that Holly seemed to be able to take care of everything on her own. She didn't need me.

Hadn't even asked for help.

No, like an asshole and overbearing alpha asshole, I'd forced myself into her life, her home, her presence.

Maybe I needed to make another appointment with the team doctor. My head took a pretty serious hit back in Toronto. Maybe I had a slight concussion?

Unfortunately, after I went and saw him about my heart problems and been deemed healthy as an ox—whatever the hell that meant—if I saw him again for another injury that ended up not being real, he might just pull me from the game anyway. Especially if I mentioned my head.

No. I needed to focus on the game tonight. Focus on helping my team score another win. Halfway through the regular season and we only had five losses. To say we were looking at another Stanley Cup run wasn't arrogance.

It was fact.

Since hockey was the only good thing in my life, ever, I needed my head in the game.

Not thinking about Holly's easy laugh, the teasing gleam in her eye when she joked about Ben. How fucking sexy as hell she looked when her smile lit up for him.

"Damn." I shoved my hands through my hair and scratched my beard. This was the time of year I usually started growing it out but I'd shaved earlier, my thoughts on Holly while I'd debated. Would she like the longer shaggy look? Did she even like facial hair? Evan was clean-cut, gelled hair, not a wrinkle in sight perfection.

Yeah, I definitely needed my head examined if I was thinking about her preferences when it came to my body or my hair.

"Fuck this." I grabbed my sneakers and tugged them on. We had a morning skate earlier, a light warm-up on Chicago's ice, and then had a lunch delivered, but until the bus left to take us back at five, I had hours to kill.

Most of the guys were probably napping, but I never did on game days. It left me too groggy. Today, I had energy to burn. I needed to do something to take the edge off my constant distraction.

Grabbing my key card, I snagged my AirPods. There was a gym here. I'd do a light run to get in the right mindset. A protein smoothie I could DoorDash after. Then I'd be chill and ready.

Distraction free.

The door across the hall from me opened at the same time I stepped into the hall.

Garrett Dubiak, the league's best goalie, and a guy who played here in Chicago for seven years before being traded to our team last December stepped out, eyes flashing with surprise as he saw me.

"Hey. How's it going?"

It was a blow-off question. He didn't expect me to answer. The guys had stopped trying a while ago.

Imagine the surprise in his eyes when I replied. "Good. How's it feel to be back here?"

It wasn't his first trip. We'd been here last year. From the team rumors that flew through our locker room faster than hockey pucks on ice, I'd learned that was when he'd found out his now-wife Lizzie was pregnant. They got married right before last season's final playoff run and his twin boys were born before this year's preseason started.

If my interest surprised him or seemed any more sincere than his blow-off question, he only showed it in a slight flare of his tired-looking eyes.

"It's always strange to take the ice here." He shoved his hands to his hips, rocked on his heels. "Where you going?"

"Gym."

"Want company? Ever since Archer and Gavin were born, I

travel like shit. It's either get in a quick workout or pass out from all the pacing I'm doing."

Since I had no idea what being a father entailed, I had nothing to add. "Yeah. That's cool."

"Cool."

Awkward as hell is what it was, but he'd shown up for Ben—for me—when he didn't need to and had no reason to. Especially given his current family situation.

We were silent at the elevators, Garrett hiding a yawn behind his fist.

"Tired?"

"Yeah. I don't know if I'm getting too old for this shit or if my body hates the fact I can actually sleep a full night while we're on the road."

"Twins must be hard."

"Gavin's a walk in the park. Sleeps all night. Barely cries. Archer, on the other hand... it's hard for Lizzie to do it alone so much and it's harder when I can't be there to help. Thank God Gabby is still close though. She helps out a ton when she's not at the salon."

That didn't surprise me one bit. Gabby talked about her nephews like they were her own kids.

He scrubbed at his eyes and there was such a heavy weight to his words. That he now *hated* traveling. He'd found something bigger than hockey to love in his life.

There was a black hole in my heart that tightened. Grew smaller. Because Holly—everything he said about hating traveling and being away from Lizzie.

Was that why I kept fixating on her while I was gone?

No. Stupid.

Hell, I barely knew her. So her kid wasn't an annoying little prick like other kids. He wasn't obnoxious. He didn't think he was too old to learn yet. He was a bit awkward. Kinda loud. Talked really damn fast when he was excited.

But that was it.

Like Garrett knew exactly where my train of thought was headed, he asked, "How's the hockey team thing going? That was a blast that day out there with that kid."

"Ben."

"Yeah. Ben. He's a cute kid."

"Team's okay. I'll be back for their next game tomorrow."

"You don't mind that? Coaching those kids? I imagine picking up trash would be more relaxing."

Funny how that'd been my exact same thought only a few weeks ago.

"It's... I don't hate it."

Garrett laughed softly and shook his head. "I feel like that coming from you means it's probably pretty damn awesome."

Dick. So I was grouchy and wasn't social. I wasn't an asshole. I just didn't like *talking*.

I shrugged, like what he'd said was true. And hell, maybe it was. Because I definitely didn't hate it. Was that why I'd been so obsessed with the team while I was gone? My own little baby I couldn't stop thinking of?

Hell, I hadn't even called Lucy at the facility like I usually did. I hadn't talked to her in days.

We reached the floor and headed toward the gym. Fortunately, no one was inside the room, so we'd have it to ourselves and the hotels we contracted with for traveling always had decent equipment. Not enough for a full workout, but that wasn't why I was there.

"You know, Masters," Garrett said as I pulled my AirPods out of my pocket.

I arched a brow while he paused.

"Whatever happened at Christmas time—"

I sneered on instinct. He ignored it. "You can talk to us. Or whatever. I know you keep to yourself, but this team took me in when I was new and treated me like a brother from the first day. That's all they want for you."

"Them but not you?"

"We're not the enemy and sometimes when shit gets hard, it's nice to have family and friends at your back. Trust me, with all the help Lizzie and I have needed these last few months, there might come a day when you need it, too. That's all I'm saying. We might talk a lot and fuck around, but we're here if you ever need it."

"I don't think you're my enemies," I stated.

And fuck—that burn. How in the hell did I get rid of it? Maybe I needed a better doctor.

"I'm not even surprised with all I just said, that's the part you clung to."

He shook his head and I got the slight sensation of disappointing him. A larger pang that I'd *hurt* him.

Which didn't sit right either.

Not anymore when I know for a damn fact six months ago, I wouldn't have come close to having this conversation. It's not like it totally sucked to talk to someone.

I still had my AirPods in my hands, hovering outside my ears, Garrett climbed onto the bike like he knew I wanted the treadmill. I stepped up to it. Caught his attention in the mirrored wall in front of us.

"It was my sister," I said, and at his confused look I continued before the heat spearing my entire torso set me on fire. "That girl on Christmas Eve. It wasn't some girl I was assaulting. It was my sister."

I shoved the earbuds into my ears and slapped the green button on the treadmill.

But none of that meant I didn't miss the look of utter and complete fucking shock on Garrett's face as I did it.

Fortunately for both of us, he didn't say a damn word.

"How's practice going?"

I caved. Fucking caved. I was back in my room. Post shower. I should have been getting dressed. Instead, I swore the entire time I ran, the treadmill belt had whispered Holly's name with every slap of my feet to the rubber.

Holly. Holly. Holly.

It'd been about ready to drive me mad, so after a thirty-minute light jog, I powered off the treadmill and got the hell out of the gym before Garrett and I could have any more life-altering conversations.

My sister. I'd told him about Lucy.

Not a lot. But enough that he could spew my shit to the entire team and hell, even if I'd started opening up to Joey and Gabby, they only knew I had family problems. They didn't even know I had a sister.

And I wasn't even close to Garrett. Barely talked to the guy outside practice. Since he had Lizzie, he never came to Joey and Gabby's dinner and since they'd been so busy with the babies, they'd only come to our formal event over the holidays.

We talked at practice, on the ice, and that was it.

I'd chosen *him* to tell my shit to?

Now, I must have been certifiably insane, because it was Holly's low, quiet laugh coming through the phone line that had me finally starting to feel settled after the day... fuck, the whole week, of constant madness in my head.

"I can put you on FaceTime so you can see for yourself?"

And see me looking feral? Not a damn chance.

"Maybe next time," I replied, and that laugh again.

"Ready for your game tonight?"

"You know my game is tonight?"

"Seems you've single-handedly created a monster in my house. Ben's your number one fan of all time with how much he's been following your games this week."

Damn.

I knew kids went apeshit over pro athletes. I knew they idolized them. I didn't know if it was because I was on defense and wasn't the guy who got all the glory usually or if it was because parents were too afraid to let their kids look up to someone like me, but this was the first time I'd ever heard that.

My gut twisted and my knees buckled so much I collapsed to the bed.

"Yeah? That's... well, that's cool."

"It's driving Evan absolutely insane. Between you and me, I'm kind of encouraging his fandom."

What does his mom think of me?

Not my business. Shouldn't matter. Still, the question boiled my tongue so much that I grabbed a bottled water from the fridge and cracked it open.

"Is he being a dick?"

"No. Surprisingly helpful."

"Hmm," was all I said. She would probably be the only person surprised by that. I wasn't. Not after he saw me at his house. Not if Ben was talking about me. He was probably being the nicest prick on the planet trying to remind her he was better for her, even if he didn't want her.

"Oh! Shoot."

"What is it?"

"Ben tripped. But he's back up. I don't know if it's because I'm his mom, and I always think he's awesome, but it really seems like he's finally getting this whole hockey thing."

I laughed at her use of *hockey thing* like it was merely a hobby and not something I did for a living.

"He is." In two weeks, I'd seen the difference. It wasn't my coaching. He was finally getting confidence.

"You two have plans tonight?"

"Oh. Um... yeah. Sort of." She sighed, laughed, almost like she was nervous.

My interest piqued. "What are you doing?"

"Oh, Ben's having a friend over—Tanner, from the team?"

Tall, lanky but athletic brunette kid. He was one of the two fastest kids. "I know him."

"He and his mom, Karly, are coming over tonight. To um... watch the game."

"No shit?" I laughed, and I swore it was the first time I'd done that in ages. "You're going to watch me play tonight?"

"The kids are," she stated.

Quickly. Too quickly. Yeah... she'd be watching. I suddenly wanted to know if she *and* Ben had been watching all my games. Thank God I hadn't fucked up.

A vision of Holly in that warm living room of hers, surrounded by pillows, all those happy pictures, probably curled in a blanket, maybe the fireplace on...

My dick swelled at the image and I bit back a groan.

Was it actually possible I was starting to *like* this woman?

It'd be a disaster.

Unfortunately, I rarely ran from disaster, more like straight into them, and I was starting not to care. Even if I already knew it'd blow up in my face.

"And what? You and Karly will be sipping wine in another room, totally ignoring it?"

"We might watch a little."

A pounding thump hit my door and I cursed. "Oh sorry. Shit. I need to get going. But tonight, you'll be watching?"

"Fine." She sighed. "We'll all be watching."

"Then I'll be sure to make it a good one. Tell Ben my first goal is for him. And, Holly?"

"Yeah?" Her voice was husky. Was she imagining me playing? God, stupid of me to hope so. "I like that you'll be watching."

I hung up before she could say anything, but I took a second to imagine her. Bundled in her coat and hat and gloves, feet probably bouncing on the cement floor to stay warm, thinking of me, knowing I'm glad she'll be watching.

It probably only made me feel good because no one had since Dad died.

That was the lie I told myself as I grabbed my luggage and hit the hallway as other guys from the team were leaving their room.

For the first time though that I could remember, the lie I told myself didn't sit right.

12

HOLLY

They lost four to three. From what the announcers said, they weren't surprised, considering Chicago had already beat them once. The game had started out going in Vegas's direction. Chicago racked up a bunch of penalties early in the game, giving them ample chances to score during multiple power plays.

Dominick scored a goal in the first period. Ben had *lost* his mind, especially when Dominick skated back to the face-off and made what looked like a lowercase b with his fingers at his chest.

"That's for me!" he'd shouted. "He did that for me!"

"I want a goal for me," Tanner had said, pouting only until the puck dropped and the teams were back at it.

His second goal came in the second period to take the team's lead three to one, and Ben, always trying to help others, thumped Tanner on his shoulder. "Maybe that one's for you."

"Maybe."

Their gloom quickly took over when Chicago came out for the third period, focused and fast, not seeming to lose any energy but like they'd all chugged energy drinks. They scored three unanswerable goals. By then, it was well past Ben and Tanner's bedtimes, so they grumbled up the stairs while Karly and I finished a bottle of wine and hung out for a little while longer until Blake came and got her.

"Thanks for a great night." I hugged her at the door.

"Thanks for having us. And getting me sufficiently liquored up enough to make Blake's brain scramble soon."

"TMI, sweetie. TMI."

The girl had no boundaries. Nor any sympathy for the drought I'd been under if you weren't counting self-induced.

"You should let him know Ben thinks he's awesome."

"Who? Blake?" I teased.

She'd made more than one crack about Dominick earlier. Once I told her Ben said Dominick would score a goal for him, I'd been peppered with questions. "When did you talk to him? How often? He calls you? Holy shit. He wants you."

Her stream of consciousness was never-ending.

I was definitely starting to want him. At least his body. Because... damn...

But I had a feeling, despite the friendliness of his call earlier, that Dominick spelled trouble. There was a distance to him, the things I'd read about him. He was not a guy I could easily crack open and get to know on an emotional level.

I'd spent enough of my life with a difficult man, I wasn't all that geared up for another round.

No, I needed easy. Stable. Someone who didn't travel nine months out of the year and probably had all manner of possibilities for his own enjoyment.

Despite that, I still wanted to make sure he was okay after the loss. He'd ended up in the penalty box twice himself, but that didn't seem too different than any other game.

But what was his attitude like after a loss?

That'd tell me a lot about him, wouldn't it?

"I'll think about it," I told Karly.

The game had just ended. It'd probably be forever before he

could check his phone and they had to be flying back tonight since he'd said he'd be at the game tomorrow.

Maybe it could wait.

"Text him," Karly said, the words slurring together. "While you're drunk. If you say something stupid, you can blame it on that."

I rolled my eyes. "I had three drinks all night. *You're* the drunk one."

"Yeah." She grinned lazily and stepped off my porch. Next door, Evan and Kristi's lights were on, and his car was gone. Either another business trip or a date night.

Also none of my business.

Still, as much as I wanted to claim I was over him, it stung every time I saw that house. Him.

Her.

"Good night, Karly." To Blake, climbing out of the driver's side to open the door for his wife and help her stumble to the car, I cupped my hands and called out, "Thanks for letting me steal her tonight."

"Any time you want her, you can have her."

I shook my head, laughing.

He didn't mean a damn word.

"Thanks for keeping Tanner for us, too."

"Anytime, definitely."

They, after all, had a life.

Not like I did.

I closed the door, watched as their lights disappeared before locking it, and stepped toward my kitchen.

Where my phone sat along with another bottle of wine we hadn't opened.

"What the hell. What's the worst that could happen?"

I poured myself a glass, pulled up my contacts and sent a text before I could talk myself out of it.

Ben was really excited to see you get that goal. Made his night.

Then I slid my phone away from me, grabbed the wine and remote, and changed the television to Netflix. It was late, but the boys were still upstairs, faint giggles coming from Ben's room told me they weren't yet asleep.

While I waited for them to settle, I'd watch a show. Enjoy another glass of wine.

And ignore my phone in the kitchen.

He'd be tired. Too busy for me. Probably too upset to want to talk. Maybe my text would make him grin, even if for a moment.

My phone pinged on the counter seconds after I sat down on the couch. For a moment, I froze, stared back at my phone. Debated.

Then I climbed off the couch and by the time I got to it, it'd pinged again.

Good to hear someone was excited.

That second goal was for you.

It was a wonder my jaw didn't hit the counter in shock. Even my heart rate thumped a little harder. The wineglass in my hand shook as my hand trembled. How could one simple little text affect me so much?

I pushed back my nerves, the stupid excitement I got from gaping at his words. He had to be joking.

Curling back up on the couch, I debated how to respond and then decided to ignore it.

Sorry your team lost.

His response was immediate. **It happens. Can't win them all. Will you be at the game tomorrow?**

With bells on, I texted back and cringed. Lame. That was absolutely lame.

We're leaving for the plane. Can't wait to see them.

I tapped my phone on my forehead and groaned.

Tomorrow, I texted back. **Hope you have a safe flight.**

Good night, Holly. See you tomorrow.

Three little gray dots appeared. Vanished. Re-appeared. Vanished again.

A text never popped up and my phone stayed silent.

And it made me wonder... had he been as nervous getting those texts from me as I was from him?

A thrill went through me at the thought and sent a warm pulse to my lower stomach.

Which meant that night by the time I crawled into bed, my body warm and fuzzy from the wine, I didn't hesitate.

I reached into my nightstand, grabbed my vibrator, and I felt no shame in closing my eyes, thinking of Dominick, growing wet from the vibration and thoughts of his body and all the things he could do to me.

So I had a crush on my kid's coach. And the crazy thing was, I was starting to think he might actually like me back. Would anything happen? I had no idea, but I was no longer going to keep pretending I wasn't imagining it was Dominick when I found pleasure.

"Did you hear from him? I swear he keeps looking up at you."

I sipped my hot cocoa and trained my eyes to stay on Ben where he was warming up on the ice. Karly wasn't wrong. I could feel Dominick's focus on me from across the arena where he was standing on the ice, right outside his team's bench.

Every time I glanced in his direction, I caught his gaze. More than once I saw him smirk, dip his chin in a greeting. My cheeks burned—from the memory of last night, the things I'd done to myself wishing it was him, and the silly little texts we sent.

"I heard from him. Told him it made Ben's night that he scored the goal."

Her shoulder nudged mine. "Did you ask him if he wanted to score another kind of goal? With you?"

Hot cocoa sloshed out of the small opening in the lid and I scowled at her. "No... and watch it with the bumping."

"Come on. Tell me. I need to know what's happening."

"Nothing is happening. He's Ben's coach and that's it. So he's nice to me. It's only because he feels bad that Evan's such a jerk."

She snorted. "Right. All pro athletes who are forced to do community service have such a huge heart and *all* this time on their hands to help a single mom out of the kindness of their hearts."

When she put it that way... it did sound a little crazy.

"Yes, and him getting a crush on that single mom like you're implying makes so much more sense."

She rolled her eyes at me, and settled her hand on my leg, squeezing. This time, her teasing grin was gone. "You don't give yourself enough credit. I know Evan screwed with your head and everything, but you're sweet and attractive and you're an awesome mom. You're a catch, Holly, and any man would be lucky to have you. *Especially* a grumpy hockey player who usually looks three seconds from tearing someone's head off when he's playing his own game."

He had looked like that last night. I figured it was the fact they lost. Karly told me he always looked like that.

"Quit bugging your friend," Blake said from her other side. "You're making her—" His eyes drifted up and behind me before he could finish that thought and then he glanced at me. "Fuck. Asshole incoming."

My spine straightened on instinct. Blake called very few people an asshole and since it was Ben's game, it could only mean one person.

So when a shadow fell to my other side, and the shiny black leather shoe followed by dress pants—because Evan never dressed casual—appeared on the bench next to me, and then hit the floor, my teeth ground together.

I focused on the ice, my cup of hot cocoa gripped in my hands and brought it to my mouth like a defense tool. "What are you doing here?"

"It's Ben's game," he said, sitting down. I tried to ignore him. Tried not to look. But curiosity killed me, so I slid my eyes to the right and then almost shattered my teeth from grinding them.

"Kristi."

Her lips were pressed into a thin line as she nodded. No fake smiles today. At least she looked as uncomfortable as I was feeling.

"I can't believe you," I muttered quietly and yanked my gaze back to the ice, where it landed on Dominick.

He wasn't even pretending not to stare across the ice. Dark eyes met mine and his brows rose. If I wasn't mistaken, his jaw jutted forward and his hands curled into fists.

"I'm trying to be civil," Evan said. "For Ben's sake. I figured you'd appreciate it."

Because *all* of life revolved what Evan wanted. *Please.*

"Bullshit," Karly muttered from my other side.

I knocked my knee into hers. Now was most definitely *not* the time for her shenanigans or her large mouth that had no problems expressing every opinion that popped into her head.

Who cared.

I'd had to live next door to my cheating husband and my ex-friend for a year.

I could manage an hour and a half at our kid's game.

A few minutes later, the buzzer sounded and the teams skated back to their bench before lining up for the face-off. The game started slow, the other team getting a goal.

Ben looked shaky on his skates, but to Evan's credit next to me, he kept his mouth shut, never once screaming anything that might throw Ben further off.

More than once, Dominick bent down and said something to him. Patted his shoulder in an encouraging way.

By the time the first period buzzer went off, Ben was skating steady even if he still wasn't doing as well as I know he could.

As soon as the kids skated off, Blake stood and leaned toward me. "I'm getting more drinks. Do you ladies need anything?"

I'd forgotten about my hot cocoa as soon as the game started and it was probably cooled off, so I accepted Blake's offer. If he could spike it with some vodka, though, that'd help get me through the rest of the game.

"I'll go with you," Evan said, standing. He smiled down at Kristi who looked about as uncomfortable and unhappy about being so close to me as I was to her. "Want anything, honey?"

"No," she said and pulled out her phone, ignoring Evan.

But I caught the jump in his cheek. Oh... he wouldn't like that at all.

For a brief second, I felt a flash of compassion for her. Yeah, she started an affair with my husband long before I realized there were problems with us, but she'd now been living with him for a year. Perhaps she was now starting to learn Evan wasn't always the great guy he wanted everyone to think he was.

Her problem now, though.

The guys left, Blake not at all thrilled with the company but kept his mouth shut, and once they were gone, I was turning back to Karly when Kristi twisted in my direction.

"I'm sorry if we're making you uncomfortable. I tried to tell Evan to find somewhere else to sit."

Yeah, she was not a happy girl.

Also, not my problem. Really, neither was Evan. Would I like to have a co-parenting relationship where we could get along? Perhaps forgive and move on and all become friends, one giant, mixed family where exes and new wives or girlfriends could get along, find common ground?

Sure.

That'd be nice.

But truthfully, as much as it hurt—that pain no longer affected me.

"You can do whatever you want," I told Kristi, shrugging. "I don't care."

And as I turned back to the ice, I realized it was true.

They were nothing to me anymore, as long as they treated Ben well.

13

DOMINICK

I f I could have a parent kicked out of the arena simply for showing up, I would have. I recognized the change in Ben as soon as his dad showed up and sat down next to Holly.

The guy had to be the biggest narcissist I'd ever met. It took until the end of the first period for me to pull Ben to the side in the locker room, tell him to shake it all off. His parents' deal was theirs, not his, but screw Evan for all of it.

Fortunately, he scored a goal in the third period and as he swung his stick high in the air and accepted the congratulations from his teammates, I caught his mom, standing on her feet, proud and clapping. Next to her, her friend was jumping up and down and I figured it was her friend's husband standing on her other side, taking the space between Holly and Evan.

"Way to go." I shook Ben's shoulder.

"Thanks, Coach."

If there were awards given at the end of the season, Ben would earn most improved. Once he shook off the nerves of his dad, something that took time if Evan was around, I'd noticed a drastic change in his performance since the day with the team. So much so,

I briefly wondered if we could get another scrimmage, this time with the whole youth team included.

Some of the other kids had heard about what I did for Ben and asked. I'd put them off saying, "Maybe someday," but in truth—I hadn't considered the fact they'd find out.

Was I showing favoritism to Ben?

Maybe. I hadn't intended to. I'd just wanted to stick it to Evan.

But now that some had asked—hell, I could see if the guys could do it.

I ran a hand through my hair and refocused on the game. How had I come to this?

Before I had to coach, I'd never spent time with children. Now, I was finding myself on the bus or plane, not just thinking about Ben... or wondering about Holly... but I was constantly thinking of all these kids. How I could improve their game. What they needed to work on.

It shocked the hell out of me when I was on the road last week and couldn't sleep, I found myself preparing plays to teach them this upcoming week.

For the first time in a long time, possibly forever, my thoughts weren't consumed with Lucy, how much trouble she was in, what shit my mom would be pulling now.

She'd been quiet in the last couple of weeks. Lucy was still in the rehab facility, doing well. I was under no delusions Gloria's silence would last forever.

As the clock ran down on the game, and my team won four to three, the exact score of my game last night, but this time going in my favor, it felt good.

Damn good.

For once, I didn't have a heavy weight on my shoulders. I wasn't constantly fearing the next phone call I'd get and if I'd have to run off and save Lucy or worried if I'd get a call to find her in the morgue or something.

No—for the first time in my life—good things were happening.

But could they stay? And did I have the guts to reach for them and risk them not?

"Nice coaching."

I jolted at the voice I recognized, surprised and not at the same time. When I turned, Gabby and Joey were right there, hands clasped together. Wide smile on Gabby's face and a backward Vipers hat on Joey's head, covering his dark hair.

"Hey. What are you two doing here?"

"Figured we'd come watch. You know, because there's not enough hockey in our lives at the moment." She grinned at both of us and then pointed a finger at me, wiggling it in a circle. "Looks like you're enjoying doing this. I swear I saw a smile or three on your face."

How in the hell had I become that transparent? "It's all right."

"Right," Joey said. "Ben looked good after a while. He's improving fast."

"I was just thinking the same thing. But really... what are you doing here?"

"Gabby's idea. Since we have ten days at home and no practice for a couple days, I figured it'd be fun to come out and be a kid again."

That was... nice of them. Shouldn't have surprised me. They were good people.

"I appreciate it."

"That must have taken a lot of effort for you to say without glaring at me," he teased.

He wasn't too far off the mark. Although admittedly, my assholish behavior was coming harder to lean on in the last couple of weeks. "That his dick of a dad?"

As he asked, and to my utter non-surprise, Evan was heading in our direction. Of course, Joey would recognize him since Evan had come to the practice.

"Which one's the ex?"

Because of course, he'd not only brought his new woman, but

he was hot on Holly's heels, her friend—Tanner's mom and dad, pulling up the rear.

"Holly," I whispered. "The blonde."

Close to the other woman, whose name Holly had never mentioned, they were nothing alike. Where the new chick was taller and lean with long brown hair and a pinched expression that said she was none too happy to be here, Holly's smile was still shining bright enough to power the entire arena. She had a bounce to her step and her blonde hair bounced on her shoulders. She tugged on her gray stocking hat as she got closer.

"Hey. Great game," she said.

"It was good," Evan said. He stepped up, shoved his hand out in front of me. Had he stepped two inches more to the right, he would have shoved Holly off her feet. "Good coaching."

I couldn't avoid his hand without looking like a colossal dick, so I shook it.

"Ben played well," I replied instead, and squeezed his hand until he flinched, flexed his fingers—not a *colossal* dick move—just a minor one. But he deserved it.

"This is my girlfriend Kristi." He gestured to her, and she shuffled on her feet.

"Hello."

I let go of Evan's hand and nodded toward her. "Hello. Thanks for coming."

Behind me, Gabby chuckled. She had to know how difficult it was for me to be nice. Joey slapped my back.

"Joey Taylor. Your son is a great kid. Improving quick, too."

"Yeah. Never thought the kid would take after me athletically, but he's doing well. Surprising the hell out of me, too."

Behind him, Holly's eyes narrowed. If daggers shot from her pretty blues and landed into his skull, I would neither be surprised nor sad about it.

I couldn't help myself. "Maybe he just needed the right coach to give him confidence."

Evan's lip curled. As if he hadn't just been a complete shithead about his kid. If he thought Joey or I were the kind of guys who would think that was funny, he was an idiot. Although that wasn't a surprise. "Right." He turned to Holly. "I'll see Ben tomorrow."

"Bye," she said, and barely looked at either of them.

The brush-off must have pissed Evan off because he opened his mouth to say something, but right as he did, a thunderous noise of young boys with too much energy left after a full game came barreling down the hallway.

"Mom!" Ben shouted and ran right to her. As he did, he practically threw his bag into her arms.

"Great game!" She held out her hand and he slapped his against it. "Nice goal."

"I know. I'm awesome." In a complete, mini-arrogant move, I swear he didn't learn from me, he held out his arm, pointed his two fingers at his inner elbow. "Ice in my veins." Then he turned to me and winked. "No doubts, right Coach?"

"No doubts, little man." He held out his fist and I tapped it back.

Evan stood, turning red in the cheeks and a vein appeared at his temple.

"Ben."

I winked at Ben as his smile started to fall and he turned. "Hey, Dad."

"You played great, buddy," Evan said.

Holly rolled her eyes. Kristi stood there, tried to smile but failed as she glanced to Evan and Ben, and Ben?

Well, he shuffled on his feet, almost like he was waiting for the insult to come on the heels. "Um. Thanks."

"You be good to your mom, and I'll see you tomorrow night, okay?"

"Yeah. Okay." He nodded, and Evan smiled at Ben. Then he looked to Joey before finally, looking back to Holly. "Take care. If there's anything you need, help around the house or anything, I'm happy to do my part to help."

Her jaw might as well have slammed against the cement floor. "Uh. Right."

Brows furrowed, she glanced to Kristi. "Thanks for coming to support Ben. That was nice of you."

She nodded, that smile still barely there. "Have a good weekend, Ben." She gave him a small wave and they scooted around the other parents grabbing their kids.

It took a half hour to get out of the facility. Joey and Gabby stayed close, parents and kids alike losing their minds getting to meet the great Joey Taylor in person. He was his cordial and fun natural self with all of them. Ben and Holly stayed too, even after her friends and Tanner left, but that was because Gabby had grabbed Holly's hand and tugged her off to the side. She chatted with Holly, about whatever, and it wasn't the least bit surprising when she turned to me and said, "Hey, Dom. We're thinking of having some people over tonight. Mind if Holly and Ben come too?"

"Of course I don't," I said—at the exact same time, Holly said, "Oh... we couldn't."

"Mom!? Dinner with guys from Coach's team? It'd be awesome! We have to!"

"The more the merrier," Gabby said.

"She's right," I cut in. "Gabby loves to feed people. It's her hobby."

"I'd be offended if you said no."

"Please Mom, please." Ben clasped his hands together and jumped up and down excitedly and then he turned to Gabby. "Can my friend Tanner and his parents come? They're so cool. You'd love them."

"Ben—" Holly tried to hush him.

I bit back a laugh.

"Of course they can!" Gabby said to him.

She was off her rocker. Had to be.

Holly looked no more sold on the idea but I cupped her elbow. "You should. It'll be fun."

Because seeing her again? Spending more time with her? It was the only thing I'd thought about since that first phone call on the bus when the guys were giving me shit.

That was when it hit me. Joey told Gabby about Holly and she'd had this planned since before we stepped back into town at two o'clock this morning.

She'd probably begged Joey to come to the game, for this very thing. I wasn't even surprised I'd been played.

Hell, my cheeks were starting to hurt and as I reached up to scrape my beard, I realized I was smiling.

Joey winked at me, shaking his head like he thought his wife was the most adorable woman in the world.

I couldn't even argue with him. Would I have had the guts to do it myself?

Doubtful.

An added bonus: Evan wouldn't miss the fact this invite happened after he left.

"Okay then. We can come." She glanced at me and raised her brows. "If you're sure."

"Definitely. And call Tanner's parents. Like Gabby said, the more the merrier."

It'd probably make her more comfortable.

"All right then." She turned to Gabby. "We'd love to come. What time and what can we bring?"

"Bring nothing but your smile and your friends. I'll take care of the rest."

"Food's already cooking, isn't it?" I asked.

Gabby shrugged. "Possibly."

"Enough to feed our entire team," Joey replied, completely throwing his wife under the bus.

"Of course."

Gabby rolled her eyes, that smile that had somehow drawn me in so quickly and without my knowledge as she turned back to Holly. "Hand me your phone and I'll text you our address. We have security, but I'll make sure I leave your name and if you can let me know Tanner's parents' names, that'd be great, too."

As they worked out the details, I grabbed Joey's attention. "She's been planning this since what... Thursday?"

"She told me yesterday." Which was Friday. "And you can thank me for it later."

Right.

I wasn't sure I'd ever thanked anyone for anything in my life.

But Joey was right.

This... I'd be thanking him for it later.

14

HOLLY

"Holy cow, Mom. Their house is enormous!"

Ben was not kidding. My own eyes had grown exponentially with every house we passed after we made it through security. Karly and Blake were behind us, and I imagined Karly's expression being the same as mine. We shouldn't have been surprised. Joey Taylor was one of the highest paid players in the league and he'd been in Las Vegas for years.

As soon as Gabby mentioned the fact they had security, I should have guessed. But nothing could have prepared me for a neighborhood full of homes with up to six-car garages from what I could count and the size and width of the homes, as I pulled into the curved driveway of Joey and Gabby's home. All white and gleaming with black windows and terra cotta tile roof, there was a three-car garage attached to the house, a covered portico to get to the next three-car garage at the end of the curved driveway. Through the portico, I glimpsed what was probably a pool. A pool house beyond that was a miniature version of the main house.

The *main* house.

My agenda this morning started with laundry, cleaning the kitchen, then Ben's game. Afterward I was supposed to go grocery shopping, vacuum, sweep and mop the floors and finish typical weekend decluttering and cleaning that got put to the wayside during the week. I had some work for my medical billing job I hadn't been able to finish last week.

In no way, shape, or form, had I imagined driving, much less being invited, into a neighborhood with what had to be multi-million dollar homes to have dinner with professional hockey players and potentially, more girlfriends and spouses... especially while wearing my nicest Old Navy jeans and Amazon ordered tank top bodysuit beneath an ankle-length cardigan.

Oh God. I was going to puke on their professionally landscaped bushes outside their front porch.

I slowed to a stop behind an Aston Martin, next to a neon yellow Corvette. A T-wing door styled Tesla behind that and I was pretty certain some sort of Maserati.

My palms were sweating, squeaking on the steering wheel and gear shifter as I slid it into park.

"This is so cool," Ben said, his voice so filled with awe as he looked up to the house.

"Yeah." All of it was cool outside the gut-churning embarrassment or the fact we were so much *less than* and there was no way in hell I was going to fit in with anyone.

I was twenty-eight and divorced. All the insecurities tumbled through me and made my eyes burn. *What am I doing here?* So a guy texted me. So someone asked me to hang out. That didn't mean I was ready. Prepared.

I was not at all close to being the kind of caliber of woman he'd want for something long-term. I was a single mom now. Even if, let's say the craziest cosmos came together, exploded, and Dominick was somehow attracted to me, I couldn't rely on that. I had Ben to think of. A future for him. I needed stability and loyalty and a man who would love him and build him up and be there for him.

What in the fuck was I doing?

A slap hit my window and I jumped, hand thrown to my chest.

"What the—?"

"Get out, loser." It was Karly, grinning like a maniac who'd been invited to the ball and was ready to take advantage. Of course she was. She had nothing to lose by this.

Me?

What did I have to lose?

Self-respect, mostly.

"Mom?" It was Ben's voice that had me scowling at Karly and quickly turning to the back seat.

"Yeah, kiddo?"

"Are we getting out?"

Geez. I'd parked but still hadn't turned off the car. His door was still locked. For the briefest moment, I debated. We could throw this puppy in reverse and hightail it out of here. But there was the sadness and worry wrinkling Ben's brows.

I never wanted to make him feel that. He gave that look to his dad.

Shit. Talk about a rock and a hard place. My son's excitement or my own self-preservation.

Of course he won. Every damn time he'd win.

"Yeah." I hit the button and turned off the car, grabbed my purse, and opened the driver's door so forcefully Karly laughed as she jumped out of the way.

"About time you gather your courage."

"Why are we even friends?" I mumbled.

She threw her arm around me and we headed toward the front door, Blake behind us. Fortunately, as soon as Ben climbed out of my Aviator, Tanner had him by the hand and both of them took off toward the front door.

It opened as if someone had been waiting for us, and for a moment my heart stopped.

Had Dominick witnessed my freakout?

Fortunately, it was Gabby, dressed in the same simple outfit of jeans and a cream sweater, gold necklaces draped around her neck she'd worn at the game earlier.

They weren't Old Navy and Amazon Prime deal clothes, but they didn't scream *rich* either. She smiled down at the boys. "Come on in, kids. There are other kids and most of the guys are here, so help yourself to the food."

"Sweet!" Tanner shouted.

Ben, the sweet kid he was and perhaps more slightly aware of his mom's moods, a failure on my part, for sure, stopped at the threshold. "You coming?"

"Right behind you," I assured him.

He inspected me, those eyes and those looks so much like his dad, but I hated... *hated* that at ten he felt the need to take care of me. "Cool."

He disappeared behind Tanner, behind Gabby and then we were there, stepping up to her door.

She had disarmed me almost immediately. There was something about this beautiful brunette who had already asked me what I did, told me she owned a hair salon. She was so damn friendly, I'd lost myself in conversation with her earlier.

I mean... she didn't *need* to work, and yet she'd talked about her job with such passion. Such excitement.

She loved what she did and that was obvious.

If only I could say the same about mine. I was envious of her instantly and yet not turned off in the way some people could make you jealous of what they had.

No, Gabby had the gift of gab for sure... like her naming had been prophetic.

"You made it. Come in, come in. There's food, drinks. Moms, babies... oh dear sweet Jesus, there are babies galore in here, so many your ovaries will pinch with need."

"Yes." Karly fist pumped next to me and her husband rolled his eyes. "Don't even think about it. My balls were iced and closed years ago."

"There are options." Karly waved him off, laughing, and that glimmer in Gabby's eyes brightened.

"I like you already," she said to Karly.

"And Holly told me you own that new salon in the new gentrified area of Vegas. Which means you're my new stylist because your hair is…" She threw out a chef's kiss. "Divine."

"Salem did it for me. I'll get you her contact info. She's amazing."

"Please do." As if it wasn't offensive to touch a woman's hair, much less a stranger, Karly flipped Gabby's long brunette, and gorgeous shiny locks, over her shoulder. "I can't wait to have my hair done by someone who knows what they're doing. Good stylists are hard to come by."

She sauntered into their house like she owned the place and I couldn't stop myself from turning and teasing Blake. "What did you see in her?"

"An adventure I'd never get tired of."

Damn. I knew their love was deep. Sincere. Fun. All the things I'd always wanted. Like usual when I was around them, my heart pinched with the green-eyed jealousy monster and a hint of happiness. Some grief for what I had and lost.

"You, lady." Gabby grabbed my wrist lightly and pulled me toward her. "I have women for you to meet and Dominick, even if he won't say it, is anxious for you to arrive." She turned to Blake. "I'm Gabby, Joey's wife. The guys are spread out—movie room, workout room, kitchen. Help yourself. Our house is yours and everyone is always welcome."

"Thank you." He dipped his chin. "I'm Blake, the crazy woman's husband. Thanks for having us."

"Always. Like I said. Cooking is my therapy and entertaining my drug."

He laughed. She still had her hand on my wrist, and Blake gave me a look. "You good?"

I wasn't. Not at all. My knees were knocking together and I was pretty sure I was still ready to vomit. How was I supposed to speak?

"Yup," I managed. "I'm good."

"We won't scare her off too much. I promise," Gabby assured him and gave me a good squeeze to assure me as well. Odd how she could be terrifying and welcoming in equal measure.

Blake sauntered off, equally comfortable as Karly had been.

Maybe this was my own issue I had to get over. After all, Dominick asked me to come. Gabby had invited me. I was welcome here.

How freaking bizarre.

By the time Gabby dragged me into the kitchen, Karly was already sipping a glass of champagne, or something equally fizzy, eating what looked like a stuffed mushroom in her fingers of her other hand. Next to her were two other women. A blonde, with an older infant sitting on the edge of the counter in front of her, munching on a Goldfish. Based on the crumbs around the edges of her mouth, it wasn't her first.

"Help yourself to anything you can find to eat," Gabby said. "We have lasagna because the guys love when I make it, but there's also some vegetarian options, chicken, and seafood."

Wow. "You really do love to cook," I said, my gaze trailing along the massive kitchen island. It was fully covered with all manners of dishes and bowls, piled high with more food than I'd seen at some buffet-style restaurants.

I'd barely stepped toward the food when a brunette, her hair piled messily but cutely on top of her head, black-framed glasses perched on her nose, and panic in her eyes, stepped in front of me.

"I don't know you, but if I don't pee in three seconds I'm going to make a mess all over Gabby's floor, so here." A weight was thrust at my chest and I grabbed it, and then... she was gone.

"Uh…" The weight at my chest squirmed in my arms. "She just handed me a baby."

It was a cute baby. New. Really new based on the tiny wrinkles on his face, a baby that was so new he hadn't quite filled out and the only thing that gave it away that the baby in my arms was a *he*, was the blue and white blanket with matching outfit bundled up inside.

"That's Willow. Lance's wife. And this little guy," Gabby cooed and brushed her finger over his teeny little hat on his head with the words *MILK JUNKIE* stamped on it, "is Lucas. He was born on New Year's Eve. Adorable, isn't he?"

I was still stunned stupid that a stranger had shoved a baby into my arms. It took me a minute, but the more I looked, I felt that craving deep in my uterus.

Babies were the best. "Yeah. He's cute. So little."

"Almost three weeks. She said he's so mild-mannered and I swear, if Joey and I were married longer, I'd be begging him for one, too. It's like it's in the water around here right now. My brother and Lizzie and their twins, Sophie over there with Ilsa, who's almost ten months old." She pointed at the pudgy little cutie munching on another Goldfish. "This little guy is our newest addition."

Her voice turned to that quiet, soft tone all women instinctively used when near a sleeping baby.

As for Lucas, his little lips pursed and sucked, and I imagined him dreaming of his next feeding.

"Hey… what…" Dominick's eyes widened as he finally found me, glanced at the baby in my arms. Back to my face. The baby.

"He's not mine. It's Lucas."

"Lance and Willow's boy," Gabby said.

Dominick rolled his eyes. "I know who Lucas belongs to." Still, I swore his face lost some color as soon as he saw the baby. "Ben and Tanner found me as soon as they ran inside. I had to beat them in a quick game of air hockey."

Well that explained where he was.

"We've only been here five minutes."

"I'm that good at hockey in all forms."

"Humble too," Gabby teased.

He smirked at her but didn't move closer. Was it me he was avoiding? Or the baby? I wasn't certain until he tilted his head in the direction of all the food. "While you're holding him, can I get you a drink?"

I'd learned how to do things one-handed right around the time Ben was this size—although, he was ten pounds as a newborn, this baby had to still be under eight. He was like snuggling a pillow.

It'd also been a long time since someone had taken care of me. "White wine please, that'd be great."

"Good." He glanced at Lucas again and took off, jaw jutting forward.

"So I take it babies make him nervous." Gabby chuckled.

"Oh my goodness, thank you. Thank you so much for holding him." The woman, Willow, who'd thrust her baby into my arms returned, eyes a little less panicked, hair still askew in all manner of directions. "I'm so sorry for just shoving him at you, but for real, it was an emergency."

"It's no problem. He's sweet."

"Yeah." Her googly eyes went to that new mom lovey-dovey look.

"I can hold him for a minute if you need a break." Now that I'd gotten used to him, I wasn't quite so sure I was ready to let him go. It'd been so long since I'd snuggled someone this tiny and helpless. And oh, the smell... baby powder and bath soap. Ugh. Babies were so damn sweet.

"Oh thank you for that, but even thirty seconds away from him drives me bonkers." She smiled up at me. "I'm Willow, by the way. And again, thank you."

"Holly." I handed back her son to her. "A friend of Gabby's."

"And Dominick's," Gabby said. "He coaches her boy's team."

"Right. How's the team doing?"

"Ben's loving it." So was I, really, even though up until this season I'd never enjoyed hockey. I told myself it was because Ben was finally improving, but really, I was also learning it was mostly because of Dominick. The way he was with Ben. And just who he was. Was there any point in continuing to lie to myself?

"That's great. Lance always talks about how he learned to skate before he could walk, practically. This hockey drug infects them at such young ages."

That was definitely how it was like for Evan, but I wasn't about to bring him up.

"I don't know if Ben feels that way yet, but for now he likes it."

"Of course." She brought Lucas's head up to her lips and kissed him, snuggled him closer. "Where is Dominick? He here?"

"I was getting Holly a drink," he said, stepping up behind her.

"Oh. It's been a while since I've seen you. How are you?"

He glanced at the baby and I was pretty sure he gave her more space than necessary to scoot around her to get to me. So he didn't like babies...

No surprise, really figured most guys probably didn't until they had their own.

"Good. Congratulations," he murmured, almost like it pained him.

Weird.

"Here you go." He handed me my drink and stepped back. If I wanted to talk with him, I needed to put space between Gabby and Willow, but they turned to each other, talked about Lucas's sleeping and eating, and I suspected that was Gabby, making it seem more natural than it felt. "I'm glad you came."

He looked uncomfortable. Eyes scanning the room around me.

"Really? Because you don't seem like even you want to be here."

"Yeah," he huffed. "I'm not... well, I wasn't, didn't used to be, really close to the team."

From my search of him online after Ben telling me about his arrest, I'd learned he was a brawler. That definitely wasn't the first time he ended up in the papers. With me, he'd seemed protective, but was I missing something? I sipped my wine to take the edge off my nerves. "Is there a reason?"

"Mostly because all of this..." —he gestured to the room with a quick sweep— "makes me uncomfortable. I'm not great with the family... or friend stuff."

I thought about diving in further to that, but he truly seemed tense. He wasn't joking. It wasn't just babies he didn't like being around, I was beginning to think it was most people.

So why me? Because he hadn't yet acted like that around me.

"Oh. I miss my family. All the time."

"Where are they?"

"Wisconsin. Right in the middle of the state in a small town called Wausau."

"No shit?" He chuckled and crossed his arms over his chest. "How'd you end up here?"

"Evan's job. He got a job in pharmaceutical sales that brought him here after graduation. Ben was barely walking." I must have still had babies on the brain. Crazy how he was already ten and I remembered his first steps like it was yesterday.

"You got pregnant with Ben young then."

"During my sophomore year of college. We got married. As soon as Evan graduated, he got a job here, so we moved."

"Do you regret it?"

"What? Ben? No, absolutely not."

"No." He smiled softly, like he hadn't even considered Ben being a regret. "Marrying Evan."

Wasn't that a million-dollar question? I sipped my drink, tried to find a way to explain it. Even with all that pain he put me through, it wasn't always all bad. Sure, now I knew he was a lying jerk and hid who he really was for a long time. Or maybe he'd become so obsessed with his career he changed. Either way... "No. I don't regret it. We had some good early years, and for a long time, he took really good care of us. But some days, I wish he would have tried to get a job closer to home. I miss my parents like crazy."

"You see them often?"

"I fly out there at Christmas. They usually come here a few times a year. Ben and I always go back for the summer for a trip to their lake home and to escape the heat here."

"What about Evan's family?"

"They're still there. Which makes it weird now, but his mom is great with Ben, too. Loves him like crazy so I make it work."

"That's... mature of you."

It was. That was me. Always doing the right thing. Although he looked like he wanted to vomit.

I took a sip of my wine and tilted my head. "You don't like talking about families, do you?"

15

DOMINICK

Shit. She was right. I hated it which was why I always minded my own damn business. Asking questions always led to being forced to answer them and this was not the place. I was making this awkward, but I liked her.

I wanted to know more about her. Everything, maybe. I wouldn't get that if I didn't *try*.

I cleared my throat and gave her as much honesty as I could. "Let's just say I didn't have the best."

Her head tilted to the side, and she chewed her bottom lip. "You mentioned your sister... that night."

"Lucy."

It was all I said. But how did I describe my sister who stopped being full of life the first time I came home from college after Dad died and found my mom barricading her door in our house, her cries echoing through it. And below those cries there were grunts. Masculine grunts.

I was twenty-one. Enraged. How in the hell could I fight my mom? How in the hell had she turned into this so quickly after his death? She kicked me out until she received her drugs from the guy she'd given my sister to.

I couldn't tell Holly any of this. Shit like this, I imagined, happened to her only in movies and even then I doubted she liked dark.

And still, somehow, I knew by not saying more, I'd fucked up.

"Right," she said and for the first time since I met her, the light dimmed in her green eyes.

I'd done that. When I wanted to do the opposite.

She took a drink of her wine and I reached into a nearby bucket filled with ice, water bottles, and beer. I was desperate for the alcohol, but I grabbed the water.

Fuck, I had to salvage this. Already the awkwardness between us, my fault, was growing. Thickening. I shoved a hand through my hair, cringing as it flopped back over my ears and to the collar of my light gray dress shirt.

The crap I'd gotten when I not only showed up for a *family* event, but actually dressed like I cared was something I wasn't sure Joey would let me live down anytime soon.

"I don't like talking about them." I hadn't had anything good to share since Dad died. "It's a long story."

Gently, like she knew I was one more question away from losing my shit, she asked, "How'd you find hockey?"

You'd think it'd be an easier question, but it was still all wrapped in my mess. "Made my dad put me in it when I was eight."

"Eight?"

"Yeah, I was ancient. My sister was a year old and I think I was jealous of the attention she got, so I asked to play hockey."

"That's... kind of cute."

I wasn't cute. Never had been. Even as a kid, I was serious, especially when it came to Lucy. Didn't mean I couldn't be a prick though, either.

"Let me guess, you were an immediate star."

"Something like that." But only because I then made my dad build an outdoor hockey rink in the winter so I could skate all day long. Once he became my coach, I wanted to get all his attention, spend all my time with him.

"I think that's impressive," she said, all soft and sweet with that cherry blossom scent of hers and the light in her eyes making me feel invincible.

"Thanks." It came out garbled. When was the last time I'd thanked anyone and meant it. I couldn't think of a time.

"Oh my gosh," Karly, Tanner's mom, mumbled, coming right up to Holly's side. "This food is amazing. If Gabby couldn't recite all the recipes off the top of her head, I'd say she was full of shit and had this stuff catered."

There was no shame on her face. I think I liked this woman. She was who she was and she didn't care who liked her.

Holly's cheeks turned rosy pink at her friend's announcement while she popped another stuffed mushroom into her mouth and hummed around it. "God. So good."

"Quiet down. No one needs to hear you making those sounds."

Karly winked playfully. "Blake likes them."

And that was enough for me. That statement alone gave me other ideas. Like what noises Holly could make if I....

Nope. Nope nope. I struggled to shake off the errant train of thought while Karly kept talking about the food, Holly smiling at her.

"You should eat," I said. "I can go check on Ben or grab the guys for food."

"Oh. Well sure. If you're okay with that."

"Yup." I needed a minute to douse the heat sizzling in my blood. If I sprouted a hard-on now, I'd never live it down.

I turned and left, found Ben and Tanner now going at another air hockey game this time with Max and Garrett. The guys towered over the kids, Max and Garrett both much wider than me and the kids so damn small and gangly. So much kid left in them. Such an easy, joyfulness to them.

I waited until the game was done, Max and Tanner beating Garrett and Ben. "Hey boys. Your moms want you to get some food."

"Aw man," Tanner pouted. He was the opposite of Ben. Quieter definitely, more athletic for sure. Dark brown hair instead of Ben's blond like his mom's, but both of them wore it shaggy, almost like mine. Hockey boys for sure. "We got one more game to go."

"It's all right," Max said. "Listen to your moms. We'll be here when you're done."

"Fine," Tanner mumbled. The boys took off toward the kitchen and once they were gone, both Max and Garrett flashed me strange looks.

"So the mom is here, huh?"

"Gabby invited them. Couldn't stop her even if I tried."

"Ben's a good kid," Max said, and the expression on his face was more serious than it usually was. "You know my brother's dating a single mom. Engaged to her, actually."

I knew that. He talked about the boys a lot recently, although in his defense, it could have been for years and I'd never paid attention.

"And?"

"And so you don't mess with single moms."

Anger spiked so fast and furious, Garrett took a step forward. Probably to stop me if I punched Max. I wouldn't, I got what he was saying, but he could fuck right off.

"I'm not messing with anyone."

"No? So you like her? Because Ben said you've been calling and texting her. Sounds to me like you're making an effort and I'm just sayin—"

"I know what the fuck you're saying."

"You have a trail of women left in your wake all over the damn city and half the ones we visit," Max said. He was the playful guy on the team. He and Alix Halvrick were the playboys. They acted like nothing ever bothered them. Nothing could bring them down.

If I wasn't getting so fucking pissed at what he was saying, I might get it.

"Are you calling me a whore? Sex shaming isn't cool."

"No. I'm saying from what Ben said, she's recently single. She's probably been through a lot of shit. She doesn't need someone playing with her and fucking her kid over."

"He's got a point," Garrett rumbled.

I knew all that. Was why I'd tried to stay away. But when I was with Holly, even texting her briefly, I didn't feel that dark heaviness clinging to my skin.

Garrett continued as if I wasn't one more comment away from beating the shit out of both of them. "All we're trying to say is take care. Her kid is cool. We just don't want you fucking it up."

So close to the message Kane gave. *You got a good woman. You take care of her.*

I could do that, though. Or I could at least try. Hadn't I been trying? What did they want from me?

My phone rang in my pocket and ice picks slammed into my spine. Shit. I knew that ring tone.

I yanked it out of my pocket, dread pooling in my gut.

"This is Dominick."

"Mr. Masters, this is Dr. Miles—"

"What happened?"

Vaguely, I caught Max and Garrett flashing each other worried looks. Could they hear through the phone?

"It's Lucy. I think... well, you need to get here. One of our assistants allowed her a visitor earlier and she's in trouble. If you can get here, that is..."

Blood boiled. Red edged my vision. A visitor? He had to be kidding. No one was on the list allowed but me.

"Be there in twenty minutes."

"Everything okay?" Garrett asked. His thick brows were furrowed and now his arms were crossed over his chest. Concerned.

Genuinely worried and asking.

"Same shit different day," I muttered.

If they needed me...

Fuck. Gloria got to her. It had to be.

I rushed out of the house, tunnel vision with my need to see Lucy.

It wasn't until I pulled into the parking lot there I remembered I took off on Holly and Ben. Didn't even say goodbye. Hadn't even considered her.

Fuck. Maybe Garrett and Max were right.

Maybe I had no business messing with her life.

Because this? This would always be a part of mine.

16

DOMINICK

"This is one of the most fucked up things I've ever heard. In all the times I've had to put Lucy somewhere, and *this* is what you allow?"

"Mr. Masters."

Fuck Mr. Masters. And Dr. Kline. And the stupid fucking assistant therapist who thought it'd be a *great* idea to allow Lucy's "friend" Anna to visit.

I'd already destroyed the small office room where I was brought after showing up, readying to set this entire building ablaze.

Lucy was high. Fucking stoned out of her mind earlier.

All because *Anna* showed up on family day.

While I was out, having a life, not bothering to keep my sister safe and get her healthy like I promised.

Sure, he apologized.

Everyone fucking apologizes when they mess up. But this?

"Anna is another of Crank's girls," I grunted. "She's not Lucy's friend, she's the only girl around her age who's been forced to deal with the same shit she has, so she's all she knows. But if you don't think for a single damn second that Gloria didn't have anything to do with this, you are all dumber than I expected. Jesus Christ." I scraped my hands through my hair. My anger was at boiling points. Nothing good happened then.

The fist I'd already slammed through the walls and drywall dust speckling the floor beneath clear proof.

Crank. If this was payback for his broken jaw and nose, I'd kill him. Slice him open from throat to dick and then I'd chop that off. The world would be a better place.

"I can't believe this."

"I understand, and like I've said, we are so incredibly sorry. Since Anna wasn't banned on the visitor list and Lucy has mentioned her in therapy, the assistant assumed it'd be okay. They weren't unsupervised. We have no idea how Lucy got the drugs. If they even came from Anna."

"What do you mean, you don't know if they came from Anna?"

"It's a drug rehabilitation facility, Mr. Masters. Inmates in federal correctional facilities with some of the strictest security can smuggle in drugs. Do you think it's one hundred percent possible our guests can't figure out a way occasionally?"

Red flared at the edges of my vision and drifted inward. This idiot had to be kidding me. "I am paying you a shit ton of fucking money to ensure that does not happen."

We could go round and round in circles all day for this. Of course he was fallible. Lucy had snuck in drugs before. Logically, obviously it happened. I wasn't a total moron.

What I was, was a brother who'd been out trying—poorly, most likely—to get to know a woman I was attracted to. And I did it by skipping a family visit. An afternoon where I could have been here, ensuring Lucy was safe and happy, and most of all, fucking *clean,* but instead, I was thinking of bright smiles and sweet laughs and innocent happy smiles.

Fucking hell.

I'd never needed a sledgehammer to double down on a point before, but this entire evening, from the phone call and way I left Holly earlier, and now learning that Lucy was on IVs getting the drugs she'd taken flushed out of her system, sure as hell felt like one.

"We truly are sorry, Mr. Masters, and will endeavor to ensure this doesn't happen again. According to Lucy's therapist, she was doing so well, she believed it would benefit her to see someone from her life."

"Her life is shit and so is everyone in it." I couldn't even say I was an exception today. "Lucy will always believe the absolute best in people, even if there isn't anything good in them. For some, that's a good thing. I'm not going to begrudge anyone a positive outlook in life, but for Lucy." I sighed, shook my head. They *knew* all this, but still the words kept coming. "Lucy's hope is her downfall. Every time. I don't know if it's been her way of coping. I don't know where she escapes when those men did those things to her, when Crank and Gloria make her still do them, but I imagine it's a place of fairy tales. It *has* to be. Otherwise, how can she not be completely broken?"

At least not in spirit. And yet, wasn't being so goddamn trusting being broken? When it came with no questions? No doubts?

Lucy went so far to believe in the goodness of our mother, she truly believed we could all be a happy family again.

That ship sailed the day I came home after college graduation, because of course Gloria didn't remember or bother to come. She was high as a goddamn kite and Lucy was passed out next to her, now seventeen. I'd never wanted to play professional hockey. I'd wanted to follow in my dad's footsteps and help him grow his garage. Vik had told me there were scouts. I'd had calls from agents. I had never returned a call because I'd always planned on returning home. Then I did. Saw my mom, saw Lucy. Our house was run-down and such a fucking mess there was nothing worth saving in it. Dad's garage had been sold and bought years ago. I had nothing to go home to except helping Lucy. So I did. The day after I was drafted to the Vipers, I did.

I found her, stoned, passed out, with hair that hadn't been

washed in who knew how long, covered in who knew what kind of fluids, in our childhood home after Gloria went out.

Two days later, Lucy was showered, cleaned up, becoming more clear-eyed and she and I were on a plane to Las Vegas.

I got her into a treatment center.

I started my job.

For six glorious months, Lucy was clean. Forty-five days in the center, the rest with me.

And then Gloria found us. Somehow managed to save up the funds to drive her ass all the way to Las Vegas.

I hadn't had a single break since then.

Today reminded me why I could never take one.

There was always a demon lurking. Always a storm brewing. There was always another battle to fight. For Lucy and I, if I lost the puck—she was the one who paid the price.

"Shit. Can I see her again? Even if she's sleeping? Just for a few minutes, but I need..."

My throat closed up. I needed to know my sister was still somehow fighting.

"Of course."

LUCY HAD ALWAYS BEEN a fun-sized version of myself. Born seven years after me, I loved the hell out of her. I used to have friends that would complain about their siblings. Call them annoying and irritating and hated being around them. Lucy was never that for me. From the moment she was born, I loved her. The day she was born and my dad had come to pick me up from a friend's house to take me to the hospital, I sat with her on a small chair in my mom's hospital room, cradled my sister in my arms with my dad's help propping up her head. He'd squatted in front of me, the intense expression he always wore when he had something important to say. I'd sat up taller to make sure I could listen.

"She'll be yours to watch over and keep safe, you know, Nicky? You're her big brother and someday she's going to need you. She'll need you to be strong and brave and protect her. Help her out. Love her."

I'd stared down at the tiny bundle in my arms and knew. Dad needed me. I was important. I would absolutely, always take care of Lucy.

My throat burned as I headed down the hallway to her room, shaking off that memory that now haunted me.

If Dad was still alive, if he was watching over us, how disappointed would he be with the job I'd done so far? The one thing he expected from me and I'd let him down at every fucking turn.

I opened the door to her room slowly, the creak of the hinges squeaking quietly, and stepped inside.

She was smaller than normal, thin, somehow she'd started filling out in the last couple of weeks but with her small, five-foot-two frame covered in blankets and an IV in her arm, her skin was pale, and she looked so tiny.

Sleeping. She appeared peaceful, but that was something we only saw in her sleep.

As the door closed behind me, her eyes flickered, slowly opened. They were glassy, from sleep and drugs and meds, I didn't know, but as she blinked and recognized me, that ball of guilt in my gut spread through my veins.

"Are you mad at me?" she asked, her voice scratchy and dry broke.

I rushed to her side and fumbled through the thickness of blankets to try to grab her hand. "Never. I'm never mad at you."

And I wasn't. I hated Gloria for continuing to do this to her. I despised the woman our mother became because she was never strong enough to get her shit together after Dad. But mad at Lucy? Never.

I grabbed a chair, and she flinched from the screech of metal chair legs on linoleum floors until I could sit. Brushing back her black hair stuck to her cheeks, I bent over and kissed her forehead.

"You should be mad at me," she whispered. "I always let you down."

"You could never let me down as long as you keep fighting, Luce."

"It's so hard some days, Nicky. It hurts. I'm so sorry."

I'd been around long enough to know about addiction. I knew it was a disease. She couldn't control it. She'd been too young back when Mom first got her started, all for the sake of having someone with her. She'd never had a chance at surviving being forced into this.

"You have nothing to be sorry for." I bit back the scathing words about Gloria I wanted to say. Lucy would defend her. It didn't matter this was her fault, it didn't matter that her own *mother* was the person who kept screwing her up all because she was too damn scared to be alone, that she couldn't handle her own shit so she forced it on her daughter. Lucy was too fucked up in the head from all the shit Gloria made her do to understand it.

"Sometimes, when I sleep, I see Dad." She closed her eyes, her voice heavy with sleep. "I'd like to see him again."

"Dad would want you to get better."

Dad would probably kick my ass for falling down on the job. When I closed my eyes and saw Dad's face, his was always disappointed.

"Dad would want you to be happy again."

"I don't know if I remember what that's like." She opened her eyes, half-slits of cerulean blue. "What's it like to be happy?"

Hell if I knew. It wasn't like I could remember the last time I'd ever felt it.

I squeezed her hand and cupped her cheek with my other. "Keep fighting and we can find out together, okay? Maybe when you get out of here, we can go to the beach? Lay in the sun?"

"Mountains," she murmured, playing the game we always did. The places we'd see someday when we were young and we'd dream of being able to see the world. "I like the mountains. And the snow. It never snows here and it's so pretty…"

She trailed off, falling back asleep.

I brushed my lips across her forehead. "Dream of mountains and snow and happy times and I swear to you, I will take you there. To the grandest mountain home you've ever seen. The top of a peak with mountain views and snow for miles."

"I'd like that," she murmured, barely awake, probably too messed up from the meds she was on to remember any of this.

"Then fight this for me, okay? Just keep trying, Luce."

"Okay, Nicky. You're the best brother a girl could ever have."

She fell asleep, and I let her believe the lie. I sat by her bed, the quiet of her room, suffocating.

Happy.

There had been a glimpse of it lately. A lightness I hadn't experienced in a long time.

All wrapped up in a pretty little blonde I probably pissed the hell off tonight. And I didn't know if it was worth it to fight for that… or if it was best to let her go so she could have someone better.

17

HOLLY

For the first week since Christmas, I was not looking forward to Ben's hockey practice. Last week was his week with Evan. Continuing with his strange theme of trying to be helpful, for the first time ever, he'd offered to take Ben to practice.

Ben's mood soured the day Dominick disappeared from Gabby and Joey's house.

The same man who hadn't responded to a text I'd sent asking if everything was okay.

As soon as I realized he'd left, I'd tried to keep a good attitude. I'd actually been having fun although it was impossible not to with Gabby, Paige, and a woman I met later, Sophie, who'd had the Gold-fish-eating baby on the counter when I arrived.

It'd felt like Dominick was opening up to me. I had a feeling some of the things he told me were things he never talked about.

So what had happened? Because as soon as it felt a little bit like he *might* have liked me, he literally vanished. I hadn't even seen him leave that day. Hadn't expected anything, but a *goodbye, gotta go* would have been nice. It wasn't like he owed me anything. That night, I'd sent him a quick text, just asking if everything was okay.

Two days later, worried, but knowing enough not push, I sent another simple text.

How did practice go? Ben still doing okay?

He was home all week on a stretch of home games. He was probably busy. But the sudden silence from him was unsettling. More unsettling was how much it bothered me.

After that second message with only radio silence, message received.

I'd officially been ghosted.

I wasn't sure what went wrong, but whatever. Maybe I read too much into something that wasn't there. I was a big girl. I'd get over it. Really, there wasn't anything to get over. We had a few conversations. A dinner with his teammates. It wasn't like anything happened. At least that's what I told myself.

Didn't mean I was looking forward to the next time I ran into him, which was silly of me, really. It wasn't like I had to interact with him at practice at all, but I'd been forced to watch more Viper's games, thanks to Ben insisting on it, and I didn't know if I could handle seeing Dominick skating around with the kids at practice, too.

So there I was, like a fool, waiting in my car for Ben's practice to get out instead of watching him from the stands like usual.

The doors to the arena opened. Kids streamed out with their parents helping them with their gear. I climbed out of my SUV and stood at the front of it, waiting for Ben to help him and said hello to some of the other parents as they passed.

The trickle slowed as kids climbed into cars, chatting happily. Engines started, cars pulled out, and still, there was no Ben. I pushed off my car, ready to head inside when he appeared, Dominick with him, carrying his bag. His head was bent toward my son, Ben smiling happily up at him, a larger smile than I'd seen in recent days, and I froze.

Why did he have to be such a jerk and so damn good looking at the same time? My stomach knotted and I tried to ignore the flutter seeing Dominick grinning down at my kid sent through me.

"Best practice yet," Ben declared, almost jumping on his feet. "I didn't fall even one time *and* came in third in our speed drills."

"That's awesome, kiddo." I ruffled his hair as he reached me.

"You should have watched me."

He was right. I should have. I definitely shouldn't have let a man I barely knew keep me from it. How stupid of me.

"Next time," I promised him and looked to Dominick. "I can take the bag."

His dark eyes were on me, tiny lines at the corners of his eyes like he wasn't thrilled to see me, either. "I'll get it." His chin tilted up. "Pop the trunk."

I gritted my teeth against his demand. Still, my body obeyed and my hand went to my key fob. The trunk beeped, opening it, and he and Ben moved around me to get to the back. Fine. If he wanted to help, I'd let him, but I stood by my door, opening it while Ben hopped into the back seat and said goodbye to Dominick.

"Thanks," I said, as he came back toward me.

"No problem. I got your texts."

I glanced at Ben, buckling up in the back seat and back to Dominick. "Okay."

He scrubbed a hand over his mouth. "I didn't mean to ignore them, it's just been a hard week."

He looked it. Worn down, exhausted. He was still the most attractive man I might have ever seen close up in my life.

"You don't owe me any explanations."

"Don't I? Because... well, I thought..." As he trailed off, he shoved his hands into his pockets. Pulled them out and crossed his arms over his chest. An uncomfortable tension pulsed between us, letting me know exactly what he'd thought.

That flutter of excitement at the sight of him grew stronger. As he peered at me, there was something in his eyes. A glimmer. I couldn't tell exactly what it meant, but my skin flushed at the heat in it. Still, I couldn't do this.

Not now. And probably, not with him.

"I need to get Ben home."

"Right." He stepped back, whatever expression had been in his eyes closed down. "I'd like to explain, when you have time, at least. I *am* sorry I just took off that day. My family—"

He stopped. Jaw jutted forward. His gaze shot to Ben and back to me.

I waited for him to finish, but he didn't.

And I… didn't have time for a guy who couldn't talk to me.

"I appreciate the apology." I slid into my seat and he opened his mouth like he was going to say something, maybe stop me. But then he stepped back and out of my way.

"I'll see you Saturday at the game then." To Ben, he flashed a smile and lifted his hand. "Good practice, today."

"I was *awesome*," Ben said.

He grinned, startling me with the size of his smile, the joy that sparked for the briefest moments. "You were, kid. You're doing great. Take care, Holly."

"You too."

I shut the door and as I started the SUV, a pinch hit my chest. Like I'd just shut more than my door and might have made a mistake.

Dominick stepped back, hands at his hips, and his eyes stayed on us until we were out of the parking lot, and I knew that, because my eyes had stayed on him in the rearview mirror.

"Hey, Mom?" Ben asked.

"Yeah, kiddo."

Please, please tell me he didn't feel all the tension.

"I think I want to be like Mr. Masters when I grow up."

Great. Just what I needed.

"But I don't think he's all that happy," he said. "Except he smiles when he's around you and I like that. You should be his friend."

Yeah. Friends wasn't exactly what I thought when I saw Dominick. Although, my body definitely wanted to get friendly with him.

"Okay, Ben," I said, only to move the subject along. But questions sparked and lingered—much longer than they should have. How did Ben become so perceptive? Why *was* Dominick so unhappy? And... could I be his friend?

If his disappearing act this last week hurt me that much, how much more could he hurt me if I tried to grow close to him and he pushed me away again?

Two days later, I decided I really needed to find a way to move. Maybe Ben wouldn't mind if we had to downsize into a townhome, the only thing I could afford in this market and in his current school district. Seeing Evan almost every morning was beyond old.

I was over it, even when he'd dropped the *if there's anything you need help with* comments and had moved straight into extra helpful and super-fake-kindness mode of whatever game he was playing.

Currently, he lifted Ben's bag off his shoulder, an oddity in itself because he always insisted Ben was big enough to handle his gear himself and tossed it in the back of my Aviator.

He didn't even scowl at the car. Or frown once.

Yeah, Evan was being weird. Some might say he was growing up. I knew better, and I didn't trust him for a second.

"I'll see you there, okay sport?"

"Sure, Dad." They shared a fist bump.

"We need to get going," I reminded Ben, and moved around the front of my SUV.

"Kristi's gone for the weekend, girls' weekend with her co-workers at the hospital." Where she was a nurse, a job I'd always wanted, but Evan kept talking me out of going back to school for. Ironic.

"Okay." I shrugged and opened my door. Like I cared what she was doing or where she was.

"So it'll just be me at the game today."

If he was searching for a reaction, he wasn't getting one. We'd had to attend dozens of games together since he left me. We'd never had to discuss his attendance before.

"All right." Because whatever.

I opened my door and went to slide in when Evan called me again.

"What, Evan?"

If he heard the strain in my voice, he didn't react. That alone was odd enough.

"You look nice today."

A shiver, prickly and uncomfortable, danced up my spine. "Right."

I climbed into my car, started it, and as we backed out of the driveway, Evan was still in my front yard, hand lifted in the air in a wave and a smile on his face.

"Dad's being weird," Ben muttered, even while he smiled back at him.

"It's good he's being so helpful, though." The words soured my tongue, but I had to say them. He was, after all, Ben's dad.

"Yeah. Which is weird."

Yeah, Ben was becoming way too perceptive for his own mind.

By the time we reached the arena and Ben hustled to the locker rooms, and I grabbed the cheap coffee and a hot pretzel to munch on, I'd all but kicked Evan out of my brain.

"Hey beautiful," Karly called as she turned down the row and headed my way.

I scooted down to make room for her and Blake. "I'm glad Tanner's feeling better." He'd been out of practice this week.

"Fortunately, it just ended up being an ear infection, but yeah, he's back to normal. How was your week?"

"Normal." A week of work, errands, laundry, cleaning, and

running Ben around. Sometimes I loved the normalcy and basic-ness of my life. Other times, I missed the company. It didn't help that the last couple of weeks, I'd had Dominick to talk to.

More than once since Wednesday's practice, I'd wanted to pick up the phone and ask him to explain. He'd offered, after all, and yeah... I was curious.

Plus—that look he gave me when I told him he didn't owe me anything. How many times did I wonder how that sentence would have been finished? Countless.

"Really? Because, well, I thought...."

On the other hand, he hadn't attempted again either, so what-ever. He could go back to being Ben's coach for the last month of the season and I'd go back to watching my son practice and doing what he loves. Someday, Ben would look back at this season as his best ever because he was coached by a professional athlete.

Worse things could happen in a life.

It was just too bad I had started thinking something *great* could happen to me.

"Is Ben ready for the party tonight?"

"Yeah." I laughed softly. "Except I hate it when he's gone from me for more nights."

"I can only imagine. But the kids will have fun with Jordan."

It was Jordan's birthday and the entire team was invited to go roller skating and then a sleepover. For another Saturday night, I would be home. Alone.

"Need company?" Karly asked as if she sensed the direction of my thoughts.

I brought my hot cocoa to my mouth. "No, but that's sweet of you to offer. I bet you and Blake need a night alone."

"Eh." She shrugged. "You had the boys a couple weeks ago. If you need me tonight...."

"I'm good. Really. I'll probably catch a movie and take a bubble bath, nothing exciting." Maybe DoorDash in some dinner. Curl up with a book and a glass of wine. It might not have been an exciting life, but it wasn't a bad one.

"If you change your mind…"

"Stop worrying about me."

Karly grinned at the boys taking the ice for warm-ups and quieted. The kids all lumbered out to the ice, sticks in hands and fully padded. I found Ben immediately, number twenty-one in black on his jersey, and clapped with the rest of the parents. And then my gaze snagged on the coaches.

The two dads who helped and had coached when Dominick was at his away game were there, but no Dominick.

"Kids seem to be skating slower," Karly noted, and I realized I was still watching the tunnel. Waiting for Dominick to appear.

"It's just warm-ups."

"Yeah…."

She was right though. They didn't seem nearly as pumped as in recent games. And as they continued skating and warming up, they didn't get much more excited.

That was odd enough, but then Evan entered the stands and headed toward us. He carried two drinks, lifting one to me.

"He's lost his mind if he thinks I'm going to let him sit here again," Karly muttered.

"You and me both," I replied right before he reached us, one of the cups extended toward me.

"I got you an extra," he said. When I didn't make a move to touch it, he set it down near me on the bleachers.

"Uh. Thanks?"

"No problem, least I could do with all the work you do for Ben when I can't. Enjoy the game." He turned and took a spot with some dads several rows away.

Karly flashed me wide eyes that had to match mine. "What was that about?"

"I don't know." I didn't touch the cup of coffee he'd set down near me on the bleachers. "He's been nice these last couple of weeks. Helpful. And just... kind."

"That's weird," she muttered.

"Tell me about it."

I brushed off Evan. Whatever he was doing didn't matter to me. Not anymore. I tried to refocus on the kids and the upcoming game, but Dominick still wasn't here. Ben had freaked out in the parking lot when we pulled in and saw his Maserati—Italian car, not a German one I'd originally guessed at—so he was here somewhere.

It was none of my business, but for some damn reason, I was standing, setting my hand on Karly's shoulder for balance. "I'll be back in a couple minutes."

"Where are you going?"

"Make sure Dominick's all right."

"Oh... okay." Her brows furrowed. I hadn't told her about the run-in on Wednesday, but she'd asked why he left last weekend. Hadn't been all that happy to hear he'd ditched me without a reason, either.

"Be back," I said before she could grill me on *why* I was going to find him.

It was for Ben. The team. They needed him out there. It had nothing to do with my own curiosity or the sadness and his exhaustion I couldn't wipe away from the last time we spoke.

18

———

DOMINICK

I paced another lap back and forth in the hallway, my phone at my ear. I had two minutes to get out to the ice to salvage the damage I did in the locker room earlier.

"Lucy, it's okay," I said, as my sister cried into the phone.

As soon as I saw the number earlier from the center, my blood had turned cold. I talked to her yesterday and she was fine, but as soon as I answered, her cries pierced my ears.

"She hates me," Lucy cried, and I could imagine her frail shoulders shaking.

I hated her—not Lucy. Gloria. Because she was doing what she always did.

"Mom doesn't hate you. She hates herself." I was losing patience. Quickly. My week had been a series of errors and poor focus.

Lucy sniffed. "She just misses Daddy. And she's so sad. But she yelled at me today and it hurts so much."

I was quickly losing all confidence in the center. First Gloria gets through the front door, then they let Anna in. And somehow, Mom was able to get a call through to her today. How in the hell that happened, I was going to find out. Soon. But if I had to ship

Lucy somewhere else, I'd do it in a second. Too bad there weren't other facilities close by because if I needed to move her, it might have to be out to California.

Although maybe farther away was better. Somewhere Gloria couldn't travel to. But then I couldn't keep an eye on her either, couldn't make sure Gloria was nowhere near.

I shoved down my bubbling anger. The constant frustration. "We all miss Dad." I gritted my teeth. He'd been gone ten years. At some point, Gloria had to stop using that as her excuse. "And it's not okay for her to be mean to you, and I'm really sorry she hurt your feelings, honey, but she doesn't hate you."

"I just don't like it when she's mad."

"I know." I blew out a breath, checked the clock. Shit. I *seriously* needed to talk to the team. "I know, Luce, and it's okay. Today is just a bad day for everyone, but there's always tomorrow."

"I know," she whined and sniffed again. "I hate this place. It's so boring."

The rehab center looked more like a five-star hotel than a hospital, and when she didn't have group therapy, she had full days planned with other therapies including yoga and art and equine. There was no way she was bored if she didn't want to be.

"That place is getting you better though, right? Being nice to you?"

"Yeah." She was twenty-three, and I could never get over how much of a child she sounded like sometimes. "They're all nice. And the food is good."

"Good. That's good. A lot of cookies?"

She laughed. "And brownies."

Lucy had a huge sweet tooth. The sugar helped with some of the cravings. I figured they were keeping her plied with sweets since last week's incident to help get her back on track.

"Okay. That's good. I can come see you tomorrow, okay? First thing, as soon as I can get there."

"Not today?"

"No, Luce. Remember, I'm coaching kids? And besides, don't you have yoga today? You like that."

"I know. And then group class."

"So we're okay, right? And I'll see you tomorrow. If you want, I can come to one of your individual meetings and see if we can talk more about Mom."

I cringed, sometimes once I got her off topic she was okay. Other times, bringing Gloria back up could set her off again. But she needed to work through this to truly heal.

"Can I think about it and let you know tomorrow?"

"Of course. I love you lots. You know that, right?"

"Love you too, Nicky. Good luck."

I hung up the phone and turned, and almost ran smack into Holly.

Damn. I hadn't been able to stop thinking about her. Not since I ignored her texts. Should I have texted back? Yes. Did I want to bring her into my business and my mess?

Absolutely not.

"I'm sorry. I didn't mean to eavesdrop or anything."

"I was talking to my sister."

"Your... oh. Right. How is she?" Her head was slightly tilted, blonde hair tucked mostly beneath that cap she always wore and tucked behind her ears. There was a slight flip to the ends as she moved. It'd be soft, probably smelled like flowers and my fingers itched to reach out and run my hands through it. Cup the back of her head, tug her toward me and feel how soft her lips would be.

Instead, I'd screwed that up and my one attempt to fix it didn't help. In my defense, I didn't have a lot of practice apologizing to people.

"She's a mess." I glanced behind her. It didn't even matter right now how much she heard. I'd told her more than anyone knew. She could probably put a few of the pieces together. "What are you doing here?"

"I was worried about you when you didn't take the ice. And the kids looked, I don't know really, but it felt like something wasn't right out there."

"I need to talk to them." I slid my phone into my pocket. "I got a call and I wasn't... well, I was kind of a jerk."

"Oh." Dark green eyes widened in surprise. How she could be surprised I'd lose my shit every once in a while was anyone's guess. "Okay. Then, I guess I'll get back to my seat. I just wanted to make sure you were okay. You know... with everything."

"It's as good as it can be." Which wasn't great to begin with, but at least Lucy wasn't crying anymore.

How did normal people do this? The whole *I'm interested let's hang out, and oh yeah, I still need to apologize and explain.* I *wanted* to be with this woman. I just had no idea how to make it happen.

"Okay." She started to turn, and before I could stop myself, I reached out, taking her hand. Her fingers were small, even tucked inside thick gloves, and they curled around mine. "What?"

"Shit. Sorry. I didn't mean to grab you—"

Her smile shook.

"Tonight. Ben has Jordan's party." It was all the kids talked about this morning before I stole the wind from their sails.

"Yeah. He's excited."

"Would you... well.. could I come over? Maybe bring dinner?"

She shuffled on her feet. Pink bloomed on her cheeks. Nibbling her bottom lip like she was having to debate it, maybe actually say no. A ball of nerves lodged in my chest. "I'd like to explain more—about last week. Maybe... maybe tell you about Lucy?"

Because hell.

What was my problem?

So I had a sister who was addicted to drugs and a mom who sucked. Hadn't I just told Lucy we all needed to move on past Dad?

Maybe it was damn time I tried it for myself.

"Sure." Another wobbly smile. This time not so scared. Happier. "Sure, okay. I'd like that."

"I'll be there at seven."

"Seven. Okay."

"Good." God, I felt like I was twelve, getting my first crush. "I need to go get the kids."

"Then I'll see you later. Good luck today."

She turned to leave and seemed to think better of it. With a quick step back to me, she wrapped her arms around me. Hugging me. Before I could respond, stunned so hugely by the sweet move, she was stepping away, already letting me go. "See you later, Dominick."

She was hurrying away before I could reach out and grab her back.

A fierce, stealth hug.

Also, I was right. She *did* smell like flowers.

"ALL RIGHT. ALL RIGHT!" I clapped my hands together. We were on the verge of getting *slaughtered* out there. I hadn't made it in time to talk to the team, apologize for the jerk I was earlier, and it affected them. Even while the kids were on the bench, I tried to apologize, tried to tell them to shake it off and move on and put on their game faces, but they were ten.

I'd snapped at them, impatient, worried, upset about my own game last night where we won, but I played like crap, and it was affecting them now. It was over nothing. They were riled up in the locker room, chatting, laughing—being kids for fuck's sake, and I'd just needed a second of silence.

I cupped my hands around my mouth and shouted, "Listen up!"

At once, glum little voices stopped and all the boys looked to me.

As their coach. A role model. Seriously—what in the hell had Coach Vik been thinking, putting me on the spot like this?

It'd been almost a full month since I was arrested, and I didn't hate I was here. Not like I thought I would. The coaching was enjoyable. The way their faces lit up with that innocent joy I wished I could go back and have was something that felt damn good when they did it after I helped them.

There was a new responsibility on my shoulders now, because apparently, for some reason, these kids *did* look up to me. The words of my father came back to me, ones I'd been torturing myself with for years now.

You're the protector. You need to take care of your sister. Always be the kind of man who stands up for what is right and good and just in the world. That's what will make you a man. It's not muscles or money, but the way you treat others. You understand?

I hadn't then. Not when I was seven. Or ten. Or twelve or twenty right before he died.

Now, I scanned the locker room, caught twenty pouty faces waiting for me, looking up at me. Gone was that first day when I'd walked into the locker room, told them who I was and I was their new coach and they'd tripped over themselves, their skates and gear, and tongues with excitement.

Now I was just the coach who'd been a dick.

"Carter." I called him out, that punk with the attitude who hadn't slammed kids around unnecessarily since that practice where I told him to chill.

He had two penalties in the first period, back to being brutal.

"You still want that trophy at the end of this season?"

"Yeah," he grunted. "Course I do."

I scanned the rest of the team again. "You guys all want to win that trophy at the end of the season? The big one that says Champion on it?"

There were mumbled *yeahs* around the room.

"Okay then. Because the first thing champions do is own their mistakes, right? We *always* learn from what we've done wrong, how we can fix it, and today, this morning, I let you all down. I wasn't nice and I was a bit grumpy."

"A bit?" That came from Aidan's dad and I shoved him playfully.

"I'm trying to keep it PG, Shawn."

"Right. Carry on."

A few of the kids chuckled and then stopped when I settled my hands at my hips. "I messed up. I've had a bad week. My back is killing me from that hit I took last night—anyone see it?"

"Brutal," Carter mumbled. "Thought you were knocked out for a second."

He wasn't wrong. We played Calgary and it was always an ugly, tough game. They were right behind us in the rankings and closing in and last night, they tried to lay us out. I'd been slammed into the boards, got in two fights and during one of them, got knocked off my feet straight to the ice.

"I'm tougher than that, but my point is, I took that out on you today, and it was wrong. None of you deserved it. So, I'm sorry." The word burned my throat. I'd said more apologies in the last week than I had in my entire life. "I'm really sorry, and I'll do better, because champions learn, always, right?"

"Right," someone said, a little more pep to their tone than earlier.

"All right then." I clapped my hands. "So, what do we do to win this game?"

"No doubts?" Ben asked, his voice slightly higher than normal, wavering.

"Right. No doubts, because champions know they're the best and can do it, right?"

There were some nods. Some boys who were feeling beaten, trying to be tough and put it behind them. I waited as they pushed their uncertainty to the side and mustered up some bravery.

"Are you saying we're the best?" Tanner asked.

"I'm saying right now we're in first place, and we can stay there. So let's get out there and show that other team who they're messing with, right?"

The other two dads started clapping, cheering on the team. Slowly, those nervous looks and sad faces became smiles. Jordan, the birthday boy, stood up and held his stick in the air. "Give me a great birthday present and let's win this!"

"Yes!" I shouted, as all the kids cheered. "Let's win it for Jordan."

"Because we're champions!" Carter screamed, his face red he yelled so loud.

They chanted the word over and over again, banged their sticks on the floor, and as we made our way out to the ice, I followed right behind them.

"That was pretty good," Shawn, Carter's dad, said. "And Carter was right, you know, that hit last night looked pretty bad."

"Got the bruise on my ass to prove it, too."

He shook his head. "I know you know I'm a fan of your team. To be truthful, I always thought you're probably a dick, but you're all right, Masters. You're all right." He slapped my shoulder and passed by me, headed toward the bench.

Far as compliments went, it wasn't the greatest I ever had.

But it was sincere. Honest. And maybe... maybe he wasn't all that wrong, either.

I'd had a great dad who taught me a lot growing up. Maybe I'd spent so long feeling like I was failing him, I'd forgotten all the good he left me with.

Huh. Perhaps, like I'd been trying to tell Lucy, I was ready to finally start doing a little healing myself.

19

HOLLY

I had a date. Was it a date? I mean, we weren't going out or anything. But it was dinner. Adult company. My house. Alone.

I was going crazy and Dominick hadn't even shown up yet.

When those kids came out to the ice after the first period of the first game, they were completely different. They played with a fierceness that surprised some of us parents. Dominick had a smile on his face for most of the game, something I'd *never* seen.

In fact, both games went completely different than normal. There was high-fiving constantly, clapping and cheering. This team of kids rallied together and truly became a team of one unit instead of twenty kids trying to learn to play.

Through all of it, though, I'd thought of Dominick. The conversation with his sister I overheard.

We all miss Dad.

So many questions formed on the spot. I should have left, but I was riveted, and I'd ducked back around a corner so he didn't see me. He spoke to his sister with a soft rumble to his voice like he was trying to hug her with his words. The gentle way he encouraged her.

I couldn't see him then, but I could feel the warmth and love in everything he said.

We all miss Dad. My mom wasn't much of a mom. My sister... the girl I saved, was my sister.

He'd had it tough, and yet he'd chosen to open up to me when he said he never talked about his family. So maybe... maybe I could cut him a little bit of slack. Listen to him.

At the absolute very least, I could be the friend Ben wanted me to be to him. That was what had me hugging him so quickly.

He looked like he needed it. I doubted he had many.

I scanned my living room. I had candles out, unlit. Lighting them would probably set a romantic mood he wasn't going for.

"Oh. My. God. Holly. Get it together."

Music. I pulled up the music app on my television and clicked on a top one hundred playlist and tossed the remote back to the coffee table. I'd showered after the games, partly to warm up, mostly to make sure I looked decent for him. Gone were my jeans and oversized sweatshirts he normally saw me in. I'd thrown on black leggings, because I didn't want to be too formal. On top, I had a pink, silky camisole with lace edging at the collar and a chunky gray sweater. I'd taken a bit of extra time on my makeup, even curled my short hair into loose waves, such as they were with the length.

I debated opening a bottle of wine. A few sips to take the edge off, when I caught a flash of lights through my front door, car lights turning into my driveway.

Oh God. No time for wine now. He was here. I tripped over my feet on the way to the door, and by the time I was there, Dominick was out of his car and bending into the back seat. The doors closed, and he turned, caught sight of me on the other side of the storm door. My hands were balled into fists inside my cardigan sleeves, and I fidgeted on my feet.

Damn, he was *divinely* gorgeous, more fallen angel than innocent sure, but there was no doubt he was cut from some form of Godly masterpiece.

He strolled up to the front porch and I opened the door for him, catching the large paper bags in his hands.

Cleaver. One of my favorite steakhouses, the kind of place Evan and I went for anniversaries or birthdays.

"I haven't had a decent steak in forever." I sighed happily.

Dominick glanced at the bag in his hand, back to me, pulling open the door so I had to step back and let him enter. "You sound happy about the meal. I debated texting, and probably should have so I knew what you'd like…"

"As long as there's a big chunk of meat in there, I'm a happy girl."

My jaw fell. Did I just say *that*? "I'm… I'm so… oh my God, I can't believe I just said that."

Dominick chuckled, eyes now gleaming, and shook his head. "Then it's a good thing I brought some."

"Come in. Come in."

I stepped out of the way so he could fully enter. My cheeks had to be the color of tomatoes but as Dominick's gaze fell down the length of my body, I didn't think it was my cheeks he was noticing.

"You look great," he murmured, one corner of his lips quirked into an appreciative smirk.

"You too." Dressed in a short-sleeve tee, skin tight and tucked into jeans with a thick, leather brown belt, all the clothes looked to be vacuum-sealed to his frame, showing off ridges of abs and curls of pecs beneath cotton, built thighs, and as he stepped past me, an ass that almost had me melted into a puddle in my own entryway.

He raised the bags. "Where should I set this?"

"Kitchen. Please." I followed him and he began pulling out the containers.

My home quickly smelled better than any candle I could have lit. Steak. Potatoes. Salads. There were more containers of chicken and possibly lobster tails in other containers. With every package he slid out, including a bottle of red wine in the second one, my eyes grew.

"It's just us, right?"

He grinned. "Like I said, I should have texted to see what you liked. I requested the steak medium."

"Perfect. And this is, wow… a lot… but smells so good."

I gathered plates from the cupboard and silverware while Dominick asked for my bottle opener. After I handed it to him, I grabbed two wineglasses.

"Just water for me."

"You don't like wine?"

He was removing lids from the food and sliding them off to the side. "Don't drink much."

"Is that an in-season thing?" Not that it mattered, but there was something about his tone. I figured athletes needed to watch what they consumed, food and beverage included.

"No, it's an after my dad died, my mom became an alcoholic and drug addict to cope kind of thing and I've lived with the damage of what that can do."

My hands were raised to the cupboards toward my water glasses and I froze. Slowly I turned to him. "I don't feel like *I'm sorry* is the right thing to say here."

His eyes held me captive, frozen in place. "Figured I came over to explain and I should get the shitty part out of the way. Are you going to move any time soon?" He nodded at my hands still frozen in the air.

"Right." I jerked them back, grabbed a water glass, and went to the fridge to pour it from my filtered water pitcher.

"I am sorry you went through that, though. Losing a parent can't be easy."

"I was twenty, sophomore year of college in Detroit. Lucy was thirteen."

My parents were the most supportive people in my life, always had been. Even now, I called my mom more than once a week to talk and laugh at whatever silly things Ben did. They were at their lake home this weekend, my dad ice-fishing and my mom probably quilting and they didn't have good cell phone access. Had they been in town, she would have FaceTimed us immediately after Ben's games to talk to him.

Losing my dad? At the age of thirteen? "Poor Lucy," I whispered, my throat catching.

There was so much my dad taught me after that age. So much I learned from him. And to lose it.

"Yeah. Poor Lucy."

"I'm sorry, I'm didn't mean to not include you in that."

He gave me a look. Soft. His jaw was tight and I knew he didn't talk about this. "I know what you meant, Holly. Come on." He handed me one of the plates I'd set down. "You go first."

I hesitated for only a moment and soon my plate was piled high with a New York strip, lobster tail, side of potatoes, and I grabbed two bowls for a salad and dressings from the fridge.

Once we were seated at my kitchen table, Dominick taking the seat across from me, we tucked in and to more than his dinner. "My mom, she was never a really strong woman, you know? And I don't mean muscles, just in fortitude. She leaned on my dad a lot. He did everything. Worked, came home, cooked dinner. He carted us around to practices, always helped around the house. Mom always tired easily or I don't know... she was great. Back then, when I was little. Played with us for hours, was always at the craft store helping us make things for school, but life... when I got older, it somehow seemed like she never really grew up.

"Then Dad got killed in an accident at work. He ran a garage, was a good mechanic. Awesome one, really. Something went wrong and a car fell on him. Totally fucking freak thing. No warning. He just went to work and didn't come home."

Tears burned my eyes. "I'm sorry."

"Me too. I was off at college, playing hockey. Never wanted to go pro and hadn't even really planned on playing in college. I'd always planned on going to work for my dad, but when I started getting scholarships he told me to take it, said I never knew what opportunities I could have with a college degree. After... well after, Mom fell apart. I didn't realize it was so bad since I was still playing, not able to come home much. By the time I did that next summer, I came home to Mom drunk and passed out, and Lucy was next to her... high as a goddamn kite, right along with her."

His jaw shoved forward and he looked beyond me. He might have been feet away but he was in another world. A different state. Reliving that memory.

I gave him silence, at a loss for words myself.

"Mom got Lucy hooked on drugs because she couldn't handle being alone and wanted someone with her. Lucy, she was like Mom, so damn sweet and naive, and I'm not saying she didn't know what she was doing, but the first time I got her cleaned up, she told me she thought Mom would snap out of it someday and then they'd both be fine."

A mom who forced her kid to get high with her. I couldn't begin to comprehend how that would happen. No wonder why he was so angry.

"I can't imagine how painful that must have been for you."

He held his knife and fork in his hands, gripped tightly his knuckles were white. His forearms rested on my table and veins popped and slithered down his arms like a beautiful, twisted map. "The day my sister was born, my dad placed her in my lap and told me it'd be my job to protect her." He cleared his throat, sliced through his steak like he had a personal vendetta against it.

Oh. I felt the weight of that implication like a bomb in my lap. The guilt he must carry... "You were just a kid, then, Dominick. You're what, six? Eight years older than her?"

"Seven, but that doesn't matter. He made sure I knew it, all growing up. Fucks with me daily to know how bad I've failed him. And her."

Shit. If this was any other person, I'd yank them into my arms with a fierce hug and hold them. My hands burned to cradle the back of his neck and wrap my arms around him, but that wasn't what we were.

"Anyway, I get Lucy cleaned up. She stays clean for a while. As soon as I hit the pros after college and got drafted here, I brought Lucy with me. She was clean for almost a year. I thought we'd be good. Then Mom somehow saved the money or stole it, probably, to get here, and it's been one mess after another. That night, Christmas when I was arrested?"

"Yeah?" I nodded and sipped my wine. The dryness of it closed my throat, but that was mostly from emotions I was fighting to let fall. This was his story, and I suspected he'd needed to get this out for a while. If he wanted to throw it in my lap, I needed to be strong for him.

"The guy I beat the shit out of, that was her pimp. Soon as she hit sixteen, Mom started selling her to pay for their drugs."

"Oh God." My hand went to my chest. Tears fell before I could fight them. "Your sister."

"So much for fucking protecting her, right? Even when she was here, and I was keeping an eye on her, Gloria can fuck her up worse than anyone. And she still fucking thinks Gloria loves her. She called me that night because that jackass wanted her to do shit she didn't want to do and she knew I'd help. So I beat the shit out of him. I put her in a rehab center and that's where she is now. Some shit happened last weekend there, Gloria got to her and I still don't fucking know how it happened, but that was why I left."

He paused, finally, chest heaving like his heart was racing. Something flared in his eyes and he ducked his head, stabbed his food like it was Lucy's pimp. Or maybe his mom. Gloria. He didn't even use her name. That was how much he hated her.

"I've never told anyone any of that. Coach knows. Back when I was in high school, he was the coach at Detroit, where I went to college. He recruited me. Became an assistant coach out here, that's most likely why I was drafted. He was the only one in my life who knew my story."

"Your friends don't know?"

His thick black brows furrowed. "I don't..." he huffed. "To be honest, I don't think I've ever had a friend, not since everything fell to crap. I never wanted to bring anyone into this shit."

His team didn't know any of this. No wonder the media called him the lone wolf. He wasn't just as fierce as one, he was a wolf without a pack.

"Ben said sometimes you looked sad, and he thinks we should be friends."

A glimmer hit his eyes. "Your kid is smart."

"I know. Takes after me."

"No." Dominick shook his head and slowly set down his fork. He leaned forward incrementally, but he might as well have been touching me with the heat in his eyes, the intensity in his expression. "If I said he was fucking beautiful, that'd be taking after you. Not that you're not smart, but you're gorgeous, definitely."

My lips parted, body warmed. We stared at each other until Dominick cleared his throat and broke the spell. "After that shit last week, I figured it'd be best to stay away from you. No one needs this shit in their life and it's not a problem that fixes itself. It'll follow me for fucking ever. You don't need that. Ben certainly doesn't."

I didn't care. I liked this man. Knowing how much he went through, how much he survived, the guilt he carried only made me like him more. I told him that and his eyes widened in surprise, then narrowed as I said, "I really want to hug you again."

His silverware clattered to the table and he pushed back from it, spreading out his arms. "Then get your ass over here and do it."

He arched a brow in challenge, and holy shit. I was doing this. My legs were unsteady, a baby deer came to mind as I scooted around the small table and when I got close to him, his hands hit my waist, yanking me down to his lap.

"You're too sweet, too good for me. I already know that."

"I don't care." And then I did what I'd imagined doing before. I slid my hands to the back of his neck, one up into his thick, shaggy black hair, and I wrapped my arms around him, resting my head on his shoulder. I hugged him tighter than I'd ever hugged anyone before, my chest pressed to his. My nipples hardened beneath my bra and flimsy tank as the heat of his body soaked into me. He hesitated for a moment, and then his arms were around me, his head burrowing into my neck. "I can't tell you the last time someone hugged me, not like this."

My heart squeezed, and so did the rest of me. In all the ways I'd imagined touching Dominick over the last few weeks, it never crossed my mind I'd be draped over his lap, comforting him.

But I did, and I held on to him until his heart slowed, a low rumble slipped from his throat and his hands slowly drifted up and down my back. His head turned as his palms splayed across my back and my body arched into him on instinct.

His lips, followed by the scruff of his beard scraped over my sensitive skin, and a whimper escaped me.

"We need to finish our meals," he said, lips brushing my heated and pebbled skin as he spoke. "Before I throw you on this table."

My thighs clenched and he must have felt it because he huffed a laugh and slid his hands to my hips, pulling back.

"You'd like that," he stated, and his dark eyes roamed my face.

"The idea has some merit."

We were inches apart, the heat between us nuclear and I didn't move as he leaned in, gently tilted his head and pressed his lips to mine. I inhaled his scent and seared the touch of him to me. Hot, full lips. A slight scrape of his beard around the edges of his top lip. He did nothing else but tease my lips, no tongue, and still, I was spiraling with heat and need.

"Dinner. Come on."

I pulled back reluctantly, slowly dragging my hands from his hair, and sighed. "Fine."

He pushed me off his lap, and I went back to my spot. After a sip of wine and a fresh glass of water to simmer down my parched throat, I tucked into my lobster tail that had cooled but was no less delicious. I had just taken my first bite when Dominick spoke again.

"Hey." A small smile curled his lips. "Thank you. I needed that."

He'd given me a lot and I had no doubt he'd needed to unburden himself for a long time. Still, I didn't want to go back to the heavy stuff. "The kiss?"

"No." He winked. "I've been wanting to do that and thinking of it since the first day I talked to you at practice. But in this case, I was talking about the hug and letting me dump that shit on you. I've never wanted to tell anyone before, so thank you for making it easy."

"Anytime."

"The kisses too?"

I returned his wink. "We'll see."

"Movie?" I tossed Dominick the remote after he sat back on the couch, arms spread like a king, knees spread giving me an idea that had nothing to do with movies—unless you counted the Triple-X kind.

We'd eaten. Talked about Ben a lot. My family back in Wisconsin. I told him more about my job, my life, only slightly hesitating the parts that included Evan when necessary. We'd cleaned up dinner, and both of us had refreshed our drinks. Me with a fresh glass of wine, him with another water and now we were curling up on the couch.

It wasn't even nine, and while I usually went to bed early, but with a belly full of great food, my fridge filled to the brim with leftovers that would last Ben and me for days, a couple of glasses of wine in and the taste of Dominick still on my lips, I could have run a marathon.

Dominick caught the remote and immediately flipped it to my other couch. I glanced at it, and then hands were at my hips.

"Hey!" I squealed as he yanked me forward, until I was on his lap, knees falling to outside his thighs.

"I don't want to watch a movie."

"No?" My hands found his shoulders and hung on. He rolled his hips and tugged me down against him. I could feel him growing hard, and my thighs clenched in response.

"No. I don't want any background noise for what I'm about to do to you. I only want to hear the sounds you're about to make."

He lunged, palmed the back of my head, and fused our mouths together. I immediately inhaled in surprise mixed with desire. This was a far cry from the soft and teasing kiss at dinner.

This time, Dominick kissed me to devour me, to memorize the feel of my lips and the twist of my tongue against his. I sank against him and moaned as my center rubbed against his hardness behind his zipper.

"Oh God," I gasped, as his hands tangled in my hair.

"Your hair is so damn soft. I've wanted to get my hands on you for what feels like a lifetime."

There were no words that could express how good that felt.

That this hadn't been one-sided. That he'd been attracted to me this entire time. That the night he left, looking so confused after checking on Ben and I now made sense.

He wasn't the asshole people accused him of being.

He was the best kind of protective man that existed.

My hands went to the hem of his shirt and sizzled as soon as fingertips met hot, taut, and muscled skin. He sat forward, yanked his mouth off mine long enough to grip the back of his collar and tear off his shirt.

"Oh sweet heavens," I murmured. My pulse beat so hard it was thunder in my ears and as I took in his body, his top-half bared to me and the wild gleam in his eye, my entire body rolled with a delightful shiver.

I placed my hand on his chest. Felt it jump beneath me. "You are the most gorgeous man I've ever seen."

"And I haven't seen nearly enough of you." His hands settled at my shoulders, shoved down my cardigan. One strap of my tank top fell down as I helped him wiggle the sweater off my arms.

And then we were kissing again. Mouths clashing, tongues tangled, my hips rocked with abandon against him as his hands explored my arms, my back. He slid it down beneath my tank top and his thumb dipped beneath the waistband of my leggings.

I whimpered into his mouth and his hand palmed my ass, pressing and rolling me against him. The friction sent shocks of electricity, enough to power a city, through me, and my core pulsed with desperation.

This man was a god. Knew exactly how to touch me, and in a second, the briefest of moments, I remembered the pictures of him with all those women.

Thought of me. My experience with Evan...

"I've only been with Evan," I rasped, pulling my mouth off his throat. "I don't..."

Dominick removed his hand from my waistband and cupped my cheeks. Brows knitted together. "Do you want to stop?"

"No. It's just, I don't have a lot of experience."

Another smirk, feral with wicked intent. "I'll teach you everything I like."

And then he was moving, adjusting us, laying me down beneath him and propping my calf at the back of the couch, the other shoved to the floor.

With his body above me, he lowered himself, settled his groin at my center and my eyes rolled back to the heavens.

"You good?" he murmured, peppering my chest, my collarbone with soft kisses, little swipes of his tongue that drove me mad.

"Never better." I gripped his hips and held him against me. Truer words had never been spoken.

"We can stop at any time. Just say the word."

"I don't want that."

He slid his mouth into mine again, slowly, sucking my bottom lip, little teasing nips with a firm grip of my hair at the back of my head, he twisted and tugged, tiny shocks of pain mixed with mind-boggling pleasure before he shoved up my shirt, exposed my stomach and scooted down.

Ding-dong.

Both of us froze.

Dom tore his mouth off my belly and glared at the door like he wanted to set it on fire. "You have got to be fucking kidding me."

In a moment, I was hauled to my feet. Daggers shot from his eyes and I imagined that night he saved his sister. How he must have looked. He barely knew me and he was ready to rage.

"Stop." I pressed a hand to his chest. "I'll handle this."

"It's Evan."

"Has to be," I agreed. "But if you tear his head from his neck, Ben might not forgive you."

The doorbell rang again, followed by a knock that sent an icy blast, dousing the heat from moments ago.

"You get to handle it until he's a dick. And then he's mine."

That, I could handle.

"Deal."

20

DOMINICK

I left my shirt off, flung who knows fucking where, and followed Holly to the door. I could have been decent and tugged it on, but screw this asshole.

They were divorced, for fuck's sake. This shit had to stop.

Hell, I'd buy her out of this house myself just to get her away from this asshole who thought he could infringe on her personal time with no warning whatsoever.

Screw him for ruining her night, on a weekend, when I was betting damn well he knew where Ben was. Almost like he figured she'd be alone, would want to come over and chat.

"I need to move," Holly mumbled, echoing my earlier thought. She straightened her tank top and combed through her hair, but there was no hiding what we were doing—or getting ready to do. Hell, my dick was still rock hard, aching to be set from the confines of my jeans.

She reached the door, and I stood several steps back, arms crossed over my bare chest with an ankle kicked over the other. I'd give her space to handle this, and step in when needed. "Remember," I said quietly. "You get him until he's a dick."

She shot me a smile. "Then this shouldn't take long at all."

Turning, she opened the door. Evan, at least learning about not entering her home, was on the other side of the storm door. From my view, I caught the appreciation in his gaze as soon as he saw her, trailed his gaze straight to her perky, full tits I'd barely managed to get my hands on before the interruption, and then finally met her face.

Since he was so caught on her, her body, he didn't notice me several feet back until I faked a cough.

"Oh, you're not alone," he said.

Like he hadn't seen my car sitting in her driveway.

"Hello to you too. What do you need?" Holly asked. Her hand was at the door, holding it open enough for him to see how messed she was, how half-naked I was, but not inviting entrance.

He gestured toward the storm door. "Can I? Please? I'd like to talk to you for a moment. Alone, if it's possible."

"Can this wait until tomorrow?"

"Please, Holly. A few minutes."

Had to give the guy credit, his eyes were focused entirely on her, not once did he glance at me. Had to give him more credit, because he was a good-looking guy with a smooth voice. My bet, he was a hot shit in high school, possibly a big man in college. He could most likely sell a tree farm to a school of fish he was smooth enough. Probably why he was able to cheat on Holly and not have her figure it out, but from what she said, she no longer bought what he was selling.

"I can give you a minute," I offered, dropping my arms so he could be reminded exactly what he interrupted. As she glanced at me, I caught his sneer tossed in my direction and ignored it. "If you want."

Might as well give him what he wanted so he could leave.

Her lips pressed to the side and she sighed. "Fine. Two minutes, Evan. Come in."

She stepped back enough to give room to enter. I pushed off the wall slowly, letting him see my body. He sneered at me again and rolled his lips over the front of his teeth. I'd pissed him off. Good. Hopefully he was feeling a bit insecure or challenged, but let him.

I never lost. Besides, Holly wasn't a game. She was a woman I cared about, and I'd always fight for that.

"Thank you," he finally said, returning his attention to her.

I strolled to the living room and grabbed my shirt from the floor. Whatever mood we'd had was killed now anyway. After I was redressed, I topped up Holly's wineglass and filled my water. Although screw it. A glass of wine wouldn't kill me tonight. Pouring a half glass for me, I kept one ear toward the entryway, thankful she hadn't fully invited him into the house.

"I've been doing a lot of thinking lately."

"And?" Holly asked. She sounded bored, and I grinned.

"I guess... I've been thinking lately. Since Christmas really and when I was out of town, that I don't know... I don't know if it was for the best we got divorced."

There was a heavy beat of silence and then Holly's quiet, "I think it is."

"You can't mean that, Holls."

I cringed, took a sip of my wine, and set it down. This guy...

"We can do better. I know we can. I've missed you. I've missed our family."

I knew it. Called it the first time she told me he started acting nice.

"You have Kristi," she stated, and there was now a tired tone to her voice. Thank goodness.

"She's not you."

That was it. I'd heard enough. The balls on this guy to do this while another man was here was bad enough, but if he thought I'd stand back while he attempted to manipulate Holly, Evan was dead wrong.

I started moving through the kitchen, headed their way to break things up when Holly's voice rang loud and clear.

"Then you should have thought about *me* and our family before you started an affair with my friend..." She paused, and then, "You know what? This is ridiculous. You had time to attempt reconciliation and you didn't bother. And when I filed for divorced, you signed your name like you were writing a check to get me out of your life for good. I have no idea what you've been thinking lately, but I can tell you I'm over it. So go home, Evan."

"This is still my home."

Like hell it was. *Dick.*

I turned the corner, near the stairs where I'd been before, but Evan had his back angled where he couldn't see me. Holly saw me though, glanced at me, and back to him. If he caught it, he didn't see it. But she knew I was there.

She leaned in, and a spark of anger I didn't know the sweet woman was capable of possessing flared. "Kristi would disagree. And it stopped being our home the night I saw you two making out during her birthday party."

Damn. I hadn't known that part.

"It was a mistake. All of it."

"No." She stepped back and gripped the door. "It was a choice and if you now regret that, it's not my consequence or problem, it's yours. But on behalf of women everywhere, and hell, even for Kristi, if you're tired of her, then figure out what you want before you do more damage. But what you will *not* be getting is me, in any capacity other than being your child's mother."

He stepped back, crossed his arms, spread his feet. Oh dear God. If I had to throw this guy out, it'd make my night. "I want my family back."

"That option's not available for you. Besides, you don't want me back, you just don't want Dom to have me."

She nodded in my direction and at that, he glared at me over his shoulder before turning back to her. "Ben will never forgive you for ruining your family."

"Don't you dare."

I moved then. As if Holly assumed I'd go straight for his throat, she turned, forcing him toward the door and put her back between us. I was behind her in three strides, my hand at her hip. I squeezed, letting her know I was there, but I was pretty sure she felt the volcanic heat blasting from me.

Fortunately, because I was still learning exactly how much Holly kicked ass, she didn't need my help at all.

Holly shoved a finger in his face and leaned in, her tone still quiet, but so harsh it could cut glass. "*You* fucked up this family with how you treated me. I fucked up by allowing it for so long. *You* cheated. *You* left. *You* wanted a different woman and *you* chose the time and effort you put into your relationship with your son. None of that is on me, and Ben knows exactly the choices you have made since you moved in right next fucking door and you throw Kristi in our faces every single damn chance you can. So don't you dare, stand here, on *my* property and tell me I ruined shit or even *think* to use Ben against me or I'll be contacting my attorney and revisiting the child custody agreement we have."

"And do you honestly think a judge would look at you, a woman who can barely afford to take care of her kid on her own, and shacks up with a guy with an arrest record, and think you're the best role model for our son?"

"Don't you fucking—"

Her entire body was vibrating. Strike three.

"Time for you to get the hell out," I said.

Evan turned his glare toward me. "Now you step up. Some kind of man you really are."

"You're goddamn right, for the first time since you showed up. I *am* the kind of man who will let a woman stand up for herself when needed, and then I'll have her back when she's put up with enough. But since she's now asked you to go, and you haven't listened, I'm happy to put you out."

"You think you're tough, don't you."

"A tough man knows when to let a woman fight their own fights, and knows when to protect them. Perhaps you haven't learned that because you cause the fights and you throw your women straight into the battle because you're too damn afraid of showing them how weak you really are."

His chest puffed and his hands balled into fists.

Oh... let's go. I'd happily spend another night in jail for this.

I must have broadcasted that thought loud enough because Holly set her hand on my chest.

"Jesus Christ, Evan. Just *go*. You knew he was here before you showed up tonight. This is all just a game to you. I don't know if you and Kristi are having problems, or what, but if you came over here truly believing I'd take you back, especially after all that bullshit you just shoveled my way, you might need to get a mental health evaluation. I'm *happy*. And most of that is because I don't have to walk on eggshells around you anymore."

He glared at me. Then Holly.

"You'll regret this. I'll make sure of it."

"Whatever." Holly waved him off. My hand at her hip, I pulled her back.

He sent another pointless glare at us and I was pretty certain Holly rolled her eyes.

Then he was gone. The front door slammed so hard, nearby pictures on the wall rattled. Holly stared at the door for several beats, her breath deep and ragged before she exhaled and her head fell.

"Are you okay?"

"I'm thinking he's starting to be a serious pain in my ass, and I need to consider moving even if it means losing a shit ton of money."

Yeah, she was okay.

Hell, I'd make sure of it. I'd even offer to help her move, but I figured she wouldn't accept it.

"Come on." I slid my hand off her hip to take her hand in mine. "Let's get you a drink."

IT WAS LATE, and I should get going.

After Evan left, and I'd handed Holly her wine, we settled back on the couch. As I suspected, the mood from earlier was destroyed. Instead, I had Holly's legs draped over my lap. My hand at her thighs. She rested against the arm of the couch while I sat in the center, and I listened while she ranted.

About Evan. Their marriage, how she remembered when he'd been so good to her and how she could now recall that slowly changed. How he'd encouraged her to quit college, promising her she could go back someday, but then when Evan went to school, he continually suggested she'd enjoy life better if she wasn't focusing on school and missing time with Ben after school. Then she told me about the night she caught him.

"It was Kristi's twenty-eighth birthday party," she started and went on to explain the rest. They and other neighbors were all at her house to celebrate. Holly had spilled some red wine on her blouse and she'd come back to their house to change. While she was changing, she'd walked past their bedroom window, opened and facing the loft in Kristi's. Blinds were open. And she saw them. They weren't *kissing*. Evan had Kristi propped against a wall, her legs wrapped around his waist.

"That's enough visual for me," I murmured, and ran my hand up and down her thigh.

Holly's head fell back and she closed her eyes. "It was so humiliating. I just stood there. Watching. Like I couldn't believe what I was seeing, and they didn't even care." She lifted her head and opened her eyes. "You know I never even asked how long it was going on?"

"Did it matter?"

"No. That's what I thought at the time. There was no coming back after that. It wasn't a stumble. It wasn't a first kiss because we were drunk or anything. There was passion there, the kind that only came through time and practice, but sometimes I wonder—how long was I a fool? How was I stupid for so long?"

"You weren't stupid. Evan's a manipulator and he knew you so well, he knew exactly how to play you. That's all on him, and him twisting and ruining your trust. None of it's on you."

"Ugh.... You're right. I know." She paused and shook her head, like trying to shake the last hour off her and grinned. "What a night. I'm so sorry I ruined it by all of this."

"You didn't ruin it. Evan did, and I suspect that was his intention."

"Fucking Evan," she muttered and drained the rest of her wine.

Couldn't argue with that. "Need more?"

"No. I need a shovel, some chloroform, and someone to be able to dig a six-foot-deep hole so I can bury him alive. You in?"

"It's definitely an idea." I laughed. If she could turn this into a joke, she was doing okay. "But I think I have a better one. One that won't get us sent to the slammer."

"Must be one hell of an idea."

It was risky, but screw this. There was no way I was leaving her tonight. I had no doubt once my car was out of her driveway, Evan would be back. And hell if I wouldn't really love to have him stewing in his own damn home, right next door, wondering what was going on in his old bedroom, with his ex-wife.

I slid her legs off my lap and stood, reaching down to take her hand and pull her to her feet.

"If you're not opposed, I think we should go to bed."

"Bed?" Her brows rose and lips pressed together.

"To sleep. I'm not comfortable leaving you with him next door."

"Um... I haven't slept with anyone—"

"I know." I cupped her cheek and brushed my lips softly over hers. "I already know, Holly. And by sleep, I mean sleep. You're tired, it's late. As much as I loved what we were doing earlier, I think it's safe to say that mood has been killed tonight."

"Oh."

If I wasn't mistaken, disappointment tugged at her brows. I ran my thumb over them to smooth them out and she smiled sleepily, and adorably, up at me. "Trust me, I want that, whenever you're ready, but the first time I have you isn't going to be after that. We'll wait, okay?"

"When you put it that way, that makes sense."

"Besides." I guided her around the living room table and winked at her. "I want Evan to see my car in the drive all fucking night long just to really piss him off."

"Not as good as a grave, but I suppose I'll take what I can get."

"Gracious of you."

21

HOLLY

I woke surrounded by Dominick. For a moment, I considered the fact I was still dreaming. The way he'd taken care of me last night after Evan left came back to me. Dominick took me upstairs, gave me privacy as I got ready for bed, and went back downstairs and locked everything up, before returning. I'd slid into a casual, cotton, and absolutely unsexy tank top and short set and was already in bed with the covers practically tucked up to my chin when he returned.

He took one look at me and chuckled, shaking his head before asking if he could use my restroom or should he use the one in the hall.

The very consideration he gave me in asking, had me pushing down the covers and relaxing.

He cared. Truly cared about me. There was no reason to be nervous.

"Mine," I'd told him, and then pointed out the extra toothbrush I'd left out on my counter.

Once that was done, he flipped off my bedroom light before stripping out of his clothes and dressed in only his boxer briefs, which I couldn't even see clearly in the dark, he slid into bed.

"Come here," he'd said, and pulled me into his arms.

That was exactly how I woke up, the room still dark from the early hour and room-darkening curtains. At some point, we curled onto our sides, but Dom's arms were still around me, one of his hands at my hip, the other arm slid beneath my neck. His breath was shallow and warm at the nape of my neck and his chest was a warm, solid shield at my back.

Exactly how he'd been last night.

Even our legs were tangled together, twisted beneath the sheets, and I inhaled a deep breath, settling back into him.

"Mornin'," he muttered. His voice was gravelly from sleep and thick, and while I couldn't see him, I imagined his dark eyes blinking away the haze of sleep quickly. Dominick didn't strike me as a man who didn't wake up and become alert in a moment. "How'd you sleep?"

"Heavy." I'd expected to toss and turn, my dreams tortured by Evan's mind games and threats.

You'll regret this. I'll make sure of it.

Like he was some sort of Mafia boss who had armed men at his beck and call. He might not have been that, but I had no doubt he could make my life hell and enjoy the sick thrill of trying to bend me to his will.

"You snore," Dominick muttered and his lips brushed over my shoulder.

My skin awakened beneath that gentle touch and I elbowed him in the gut playfully. "I do not."

"Okay, so it's not a snore, but you make these cute little noises. Tiny little sounds. Drove me crazy all night long. And then you'd press against me."

He groaned and shot a heatwave racing through my veins. Teasing him, I said, "If sleeping with me is so miserable, I'll make sure you never have to do it again."

"Fuck that," he said and in a second I was tugged to my back,

Dominick looming over me. "That was the best damn night of my life."

He smirked, and I wanted to kiss that look off his face, but morning breath and nerves held me back.

"You have a plane to catch today, don't you?"

"Not until noon." He glanced at the nightstand behind me. "It's only seven. What time does Ben get home?"

"I need to pick him up at eleven."

"Perfect. Then we have time." He leaned down and kissed me and then was gone, jumping off the bed before I could reach for him, pull him back to me.

"For what?"

I shoved to sitting, letting the covers fall to my waist. My hair had to be a mess, and a burst of cool air, along with the sight of Dominick tugging on his jeans, tightened my nipples.

His gaze dropped right to them, making them peak further.

"Not for what you're thinking," he teased, spinning his finger in a circle at my face. "I know that look, and that's not what I meant."

"What *are* you talking about then?"

"Breakfast. I want to take you out, and I need to eat."

At eat, my cheeks burned and Dominick swore. "None of that. I made you a promise last night and intend to keep it."

"But—"

"No buts. *I* need to know I'm doing right by you. And Ben."

My heart fluttered. He *meant* it. Every word. Truthfully, he was doing more *right* for me in the last twelve hours than Evan had done for me in twelve years. With everything he said last night, his guilt about letting down his dad and Lucy, I understood.

"I get it." I waited until he dressed, biting down a whimper as all those muscles disappeared beneath his shirt. "But I want Denny's or Bob Evan's or something. Nothing fancy."

His hands settled at his hips. "Demanding in the morning for such a small creature, aren't you?"

"Vertically challenged," I argued. "And I guess you won't know exactly how demanding I can be in the morning."

I stuck out my tongue, flung off the covers, and hurried to the bathroom.

"Evil!" he shouted through the door and I laughed.

This was more flirtatious than I'd ever been in my life. More sassy too. I had no idea where it came from. Just opened my mouth and it spit itself out. Maybe I'd been spending too much time with Karly. Maybe the exact right amount because I kinda liked being a little sassy.

I liked being with a man who could handle my attitude, as rare as it was.

In fact, based on that gleam in Dominick's eyes, he couldn't just handle the attitude that came as a surprise even to me, he rather liked it.

"Not that I'm complaining, because this bacon is incredible, but you don't have to keep feeding me."

Although this bacon... applewood and drizzled with honey, I could eat a pound of it with no regrets.

"I'll keep that in mind."

I'd stuck with bacon, eggs, and toast. I didn't usually eat a lot for breakfast unless you counted a venti coffee—okay, two—as breakfast, but I was thankful the waitress sat us at a booth for four instead of a small table for two.

Dominick's meal more than took care of the remaining room.

Cinna-biscuits. Four eggs. Bacon and sausage. Waffles. Toast. Hashbrowns. The man was probably consuming more at breakfast than I ate in two days.

He'd dove into his food like a man possessed and shockingly, we were finishing near the same time.

"I can't even fathom how you can eat that much."

"Fast metabolism. Need the energy for tonight."

"Where's the game?"

"Dallas. We'll be there by three. We'll do a warm-up skate, eat, play, hit the bus, then get on the plane and head to Arizona. Back on Wednesday."

Every time I flew, I was exhausted. It didn't matter if the flight was an hour or four, the entire process of packing, unpacking, security, wore me out. "How do you manage all of that for an entire season?"

"Mostly because we're used to it and you adjust to things like sleeping in hotels and being on planes. It becomes second nature. Hell, I have a suitcase I take that always has ninety percent of what I need in it. I just need to add an outfit, change out a suit, and I'm pretty much ready to go whenever."

"It takes me a week to pack for a weekend trip."

He shook his head, gave me a look like he found me adorable while he drank his coffee. "I bet if you did it twice a week, you'd be a pro, too. Besides," his expression warmed and his tone deepend, "when it came to the traveling, up until very recently I didn't have anything to miss at home, so it didn't matter where I was."

He meant *me*. "Oh."

"Yeah." He winked. "Oh."

Damn those eyes. That wink and that crooked little lift in his grin. "For someone who the media claims is the bad boy, you sure say the sweetest things."

"I'm honest."

He was also turning me on. My body was warming and I shifted in the vinyl booth. Dominick's eyes heated, and his hands flexed and fisted.

"Any chance you have time to come in when we get back to my house?"

He dropped his head. "You're killing me. And no," he said once he lifted it. There was regret and no small amount of desire on his face. "But I'll be able to give you one helluva goodbye kiss."

"Deal."

∼

I LEARNED DOMINICK DROVE A MASERATI, which meant I'd been wrong on the German assumption, and for someone who knew squat about cars, the fact it was Italian didn't tell me anything. All I knew was the purr of his engine at a stoplight vibrated in his seats in the most distracting way. All the way home, I'd clutched the door handle, and it had nothing to do with the way he took off from stoplights or swerved in and out of traffic like a professional. It had everything to do with the tight space, the warmth of his hand at my mid-thigh, and the look he flashed me that said he knew exactly what he was doing to me.

By the time we returned to my house and I unlocked my front door, I was three point six seconds—the time he said it'd take his car to reach sixty-five miles per hour—from dropping to my knees and begging him to let me make him feel good.

A thought I'd *never* once experienced.

"Thank you," I told him, trying to fight through the insane lust pouring through me. It'd been so long since I felt desired. Hell, it'd been a long time since I felt respected—which I considered the bare minimum to a relationship—that this whip of passion I felt by merely looking at Dominick kept throwing me for a loop.

Since he'd said he didn't have time to come in, and we both had places to be, I expected him to hold open the storm door, give me that kiss he promised and take off.

"Thank you for last night. And everything, and well, for being you and so good to me," I told him.

He blinked, eyes darkened. I inhaled a sharp breath as his gaze dropped to my mouth and lingered.

"I lied to you," he said and his hand was at my stomach, pressing me firmly, but gently into my house. The doors slammed behind us and the wall was at my back.

My purse hit the floor.

"About what?" I rasped. That was not at all what I thought he'd say to me.

Dominick's body pressed against me and then his hands were at my jaw, thumbs brushing along my cheek bones. "I want to give you more than just a goodbye kiss."

His lips pressed against mine, and my hips rolled at the sudden contact of his tongue, slipping against mine. His grip on me tightened, and his hardness, well and truly erect, pressed against my stomach.

I moaned into his mouth, a truly wanton sound, and gripped his shirt into my fists as he devoured my mouth with a kiss. He made my knees wobble and the room spin all in a matter of moments.

Dear sweet heavens. This was what true lust felt like. This kiss. The scrape of his beard against my cheeks. The savage way he pinned me between the wall and him and the firm move of his hand, drifting down my side until he grabbed my thigh and settled my leg at his hip.

He rolled against me and my head hit the wall as he tore his mouth off mine and trailed the column of my throat.

"Oh God," I whimpered. "Please."

I didn't even know what I was begging for. For more. Everything. He kissed my collarbone, back to my neck, my ear, and I writhed against him until the friction at my center demanded clothes were removed, and we could be skin to skin.

"Can't fuck you," he murmured. And I swore I hadn't spoken my pleas out loud. "But I'm not leaving here without hearing you shatter."

Oh, but I was already so close.

He tore at the button on my jeans, flung down the zipper. He only paused in kissing me enough to shove down my jeans. I began kicking them off, but as I got one off an ankle, he dropped to his knees in front of me and yanked down my underwear.

Oh God. Embarrassment and nerves hit me for a moment and I

tensed, too terrified to look down at him. There were stretch marks from Ben. Hair in places I would have normally taken better care of, but I hadn't expected this. Hadn't done a full self-care routine before he came over last night.

"You are so fucking sexy, so pure," he murmured, and if he noticed any of my insecurities, he didn't act like he gave a shit as his lips pressed right to a stretch mark at my stomach, and then trailed lower.

His hands ran up my inner thighs, draping one leg over his shoulder. Oh God.

Never. Never had I ever thought to have sex standing up. Beds. Maybe a couch. But the wall in my entryway? I'd never be able to enter or leave my home without blushing again. Without remembering the heat of his mouth at my inner thigh, the crease where skin met hip.

"You okay?" he asked, and he glanced up at me with desperation burning in his dark eyes, his hair a mess. "Because if you're not..."

"I'm good. Great." Losing my damn mind over this man.

"Then hold on, honey." He actually took my hand where it was plastered on the wall, curled it around his head. My fingers dug into his hair on instinct, right as he leaned forward and then dug into *me*.

"Oh shit." My hips bucked and I clawed at the wall, gripped his hair. If I hurt him from the slight tug, he moaned against my sex, sending a wild vibration through my clit as he pressed a finger into me, ate me like he hadn't consumed a meal in weeks.

I was going to lose it. Pass out. Fall to my knees and possibly injure the man before his game if he kept at it, but as he continued, my sounds grew louder. Nails scraped over his scalp when he hit that perfect spot and added a finger.

"Oh shit." I chanted sounds. Animalistic. I bit down on my tongue to quiet them until they could no longer be contained and as he worked with expert precision, I came, hips bucking wildly on his face. He spread my knee wider, held it out like he couldn't get enough until the stretch in my thigh and the pleasure zipping through me was almost too much, but oh so perfect.

"Shit," I rasped, a sweaty mess in need of a shower. I was hot everywhere. My teeth tingled and my entire body felt like I'd been dipped in lava as my orgasm continued rolling through me, Dominick not stopping until I loosened my grip on his hair.

Slowly, he settled my foot on the floor, gently tugged back on my underwear and I laughed stupidly as he pulled up my jeans and re-did them up.

I was a boneless mess, only held in my place by the wall and his hand at my hip.

"I could eat you every day. Those sounds you made were incredible." He leaned in, face glistening from me, and I didn't care one bit as I tasted myself on him as he kissed me like we suddenly had all the time to explore.

"Later tonight," he murmured, pulling back so there were inches separating us. "When I get in the shower at the hotel, I'm going to be thinking of this, the taste of you and the feel of you, and I guarantee, I'm going to come so hard the hotel might kick me out for a noise disturbance."

My sex throbbed at his words. How was I already turned on, especially by that image?

But God, I wanted to *hear* that sound.

I pressed my lips together to keep from begging for him to do just that. Mostly because I hadn't yet reformed the ability to speak. Also, I'd never had phone sex, didn't particularly want to start. But how would he sound, thinking of me?

I reached for him, hand at his jeans. "There's something I can do for you now."

His hand covered mine over his hard, thick length. Oh *wow*. That was... there was a lot in there. Dominick shook his head and smirked, like my thoughts were broadcasted for him and he was pleased. "Trust me. The frustration I'm feeling right now will only help my game. You good?"

"I think once my brain starts working again, I'll be great."

His chuckle was a vibration against my cheek as he kissed me there. "Probably the best compliment I could get. I really do need to get going though, but I'll call you when I can."

"Okay. And well, you know, thank you."

"Trust me. That was all my pleasure."

Not sure how when he was walking away with an erection the size of Manhattan, but considering I was the winner in this scenario, I wouldn't bicker the point.

22

———

DOMINICK

The Arizona arena was absolutely insane. Given we were less than five hours from Las Vegas, the crowd was an equal mix of Vipers and Bobcat fans. It was quite possible there were more Vipers fans than home team fans, but the deafening noise was making the arena tremble.

Our team was electrified by the energy, as much as we were frustrated.

There was less than a minute to go and we were up by one. We should have killed them, but Arizona took to the ice tonight like they wanted our blood. Even though they were near last place in their division, we'd had to fight for every inch of ice and second of puck time. It was only a lucky goal by Alix to put us in the lead.

Arlo, our left winger, was in the sin bin for thirty more seconds. Arizona had the power play, and we were facing off on our side of the goal. Forty-five seconds to go and they were taking out their goalie to give them an even greater advantage over players on the ice.

"No doubts," Max said, hitting his stick with mine as I skated to the face-off.

"No doubts."

"And drinks once we get home. You're coming."

It was an hour flight. We'd be home by eleven. Too late to call Holly. Or show up, even though I wanted to.

Damn, the number of times I'd jerked off to her in the last few days was embarrassing. I wanted her.

"Fine," I grunted and stopped at the marks on the ice, spraying ice all over Arizona's center's skates. Brock Myers. Big guy. We'd faced off against each other in college when he went to Minnesota.

"Always such a dick, Masters, aren't you?"

I tapped my stick against the ice. "It's big. Thick. All the girls like it. Makes them choke so good. I understand being jealous."

"I'm not jealous of your dick."

I cocked my head. "Then why'd you bring it up?"

His glare at me was perfection. Eyes on me, I'd thrown him off. Yeah, I was a dick. I was the asshole. I was also really good at distraction, so as the ref blew the whistle, and I knew I had two seconds before he dropped it, I said, "Your mama likes it—"

Slap. Puck drop, puck mine. I whipped it over to Taylor and he skated around the goal. He was thrown into the boards and tangled with two of Arizona's guys, and I came at them both from behind. Right as I reached the puck, digging it out with the tangle of skates and sticks, Max came into view. I whipped it to him. He dodged a player, then another, and with two seconds left and one of their defenders racing back to their empty goal, Max let that fucker fly.

"No!" he screamed right as the buzzer went and the puck flew right by the net by an inch. "How did I miss that?"

"We still won," Kane cried and threw his arm over Max's shoulders, bending him so his face was at his knee. Max shoved him off and turned around as the other guys came over. There were hits with sticks, gloved fist bumps, and we all skated past Garrett, tapping his helmet for being the best kick-ass goalie and saving our ass tonight multiple times.

"Drinks on the plane and at home after!" Max was in a celebration mood.

And for the first since ever, I was smiling, not *hating* the idea of a couple drinks with my teammates.

Odd, that.

By the time we were changed and on the bus, I'd already received the text I'd was quickly coming to expect from Holly.

Awesome win tonight. You looked great.

It'd been two days since I'd lost my mind with the need to have her. We'd talked every night I was on the road and after both games, she texted me the same thing. I almost wanted to know what she'd say if we lost, but not enough to throw a game. Every time my phone lit up with a message or a voice mail, I was no longer hesitating, assuming it was bad news. Instead, I found myself checking my phone like an asshole, desperate for it to ping.

I couldn't wait to see her.

Ever since I met Holly, I felt myself changing.

The kids weren't the little shits I'd thought they be. Hell, I missed them even now and I'd see them tomorrow at practice.

My teammates weren't nearly as obnoxious anymore, and since I'd told Holly how I'd grown up, I realized *not* talking about my dad, the man who'd taught me so much, wasn't doing anyone any favors. Ever since Saturday night, I'd thought of him. Not the guilt-ridden memories of the things I'd failed at, but his laugh. Boisterous. Loud enough to gain the attention of everyone in a room. The way he taught me to tie my skates and stabilize my ankles—the same way I'd taught Ben. He'd been a good friend. Honest to his customers. He taught me how to take care of women and he taught me how to stand up for myself.

Nothing good had come for the last thirteen years of ignoring all the good he gave me. Perhaps it was time to try something different.

And Lucy was currently getting the help she needed and if the center screwed up, knew I'd have my lawyers on their asses in a heartbeat.

Gloria was still out there, and I had no idea when she'd rear her ugly-hate-filled and desperate head again, but for the first time in my life, I wasn't watching my back for her to pop out of a dark alley, demanding more money. Evan, I had no doubt, would fulfill his threat of making Holly regret not taking him back, but I couldn't give two shits about him.

Things were good. For the first time in a long time, even with all that ugly shit in the background, I could see good things coming.

And I wouldn't be the man my dad had wanted me to be if I didn't take a moment and be thankful for them.

Glad you watched. Get some sleep and I'll see you tomorrow.

Her response was a kissing emoji, which meant I was smiling again, when I pulled up my music and settled into the bus.

MOST OF THE guys who came out were pretty lit by the time we arrived at Malley's. Joey wasn't with us, even though he owned the bar. The team had been coming here for years when the previous owner became too sick to keep running it. He thought he'd have to sell it, have the run-down little joint turned into part of a nearby strip mall, and was pretty unhappy about it. Joey took over the bar, including being the main sponsor of a disadvantaged youth summer baseball league. Now, it was where the team always hung out. It was far enough off the Strip and tourist areas where we could chill when we wanted privacy.

Tonight was perfect for it. We were energized by the road wins, an excitement that was only slightly dimmed to the long day, plane ride, and late hour, but that wasn't stopping Max and Alix from blaring the speaker music to the amusement of the two bartenders still working and dancing with their pool cues like they were grinding with women.

"Kids," I said to no one in particular as I watched both of them.

Although Kane, sitting next to me must have thought I was talking to him. "Harmless fun. They're good guys."

"It wasn't a criticism."

I'd never felt that freedom though. I didn't begrudge them for it. If it was a night I considered being more introspective, I'd probably realize I was jealous of them. They worked just as hard as the rest of us, and yet, they never seemed like life had ever tossed a lemon at them.

"How are you and the mom?" he asked, taking a sip of his drink. Conversation with Kane never came easy. He was about as stoic as a two-by-four, probably not much different than me, but without the angry little chip on his shoulder.

"Holly," I corrected and he smirked.

"My bad. How are you and Holly?"

My fingers tapped the side of my glass. My first and only drink for the night and I already had water for when I was done with it.

"Good. I think."

"That's it?"

"I don't know what else you want me to say."

Things were good. Great really. I liked her. A lot. She liked me. She tasted incredible and after only a brief hesitation where I imagined she cataloged every one of her imperfections, she went wild for me.

Yeah. Things were good.

Across from me, Kane brought his drink to his mouth, chuckling. "You kind of suck at this conversation stuff, you know that?"

"Fuck off." He was right. And I felt myself grin. "I'm not used to it, all right? But to answer your question, fine. I like her. I've never had a relationship and I don't know what the fuck I'm doing, okay? But she's..." I fought for the right word. She was *Holly*. Sweet, a little sassy. Definitely funny. She was sexy. *Vertically challenged.* "She's sweet." I settled on it, because really, it described everything about her in a wide variety of ways.

"I'm happy for you." He set down his drink, sucking down his last sip through his teeth.

"What happened with your woman? Your ex?"

Surprise sparked in his eyes. I figured because I was actively engaging him in conversation. "Like I said, I messed it up. Didn't appreciate what I had while I had it and she got tired of having to put up with it."

"But how?" Because I didn't want to fuck this up. Not so soon anyway, but other than memories from when I was a teen, I didn't have a decent barometer for relationships. And I found myself with the sudden desperate need to know. The good and the bad of them.

Kane sighed. "Honestly? I think I just took her for granted. Figured we were married and she'd always be there. We started dating in college, got married as soon as I was drafted, and for the first couple of years, it was awesome. But I got traded here, she came and didn't know anyone. She got busy with studying for her master's degree, I was always on the road… I stopped calling and texting all the time. Stopped asking about her. And when we were together, we started feeling like strangers. Want my advice from a guy who screwed up?"

"Yeah."

"Pay attention. Always. That's what Ava said was my problem. I stopped making the effort I used to. Didn't call as much and when I did, she said I acted like I wasn't listening. I came home and slept and worked out and we stopped going out. I think, at the core, women want to feel appreciated and important. They want a man to ask about their day and give a shit enough to listen. Ava said she started feeling like I treated her like she didn't matter. I wasn't *mean* to her, just, like I said, took for granted she'd always be there. And one day I came home to an empty house and she wasn't there."

"That's harsh."

"When I called, she reminded me how many times she tried to talk to me. I always said I'd do better. Then a week or two and things went back to normal. She got tired of asking me to treat her like she mattered. So, she found someone who did." He grabbed his glass, drained it, and signaled for another. Since there were hardly any of us left, the bartender noticed and nodded back to him right away.

"She cheated?"

Because none of this was sounding like rocket science. Or how you could fuck it up. Ask questions. Listen. Take them out. I could do all that, easy. I *liked* listening to Holly.

"No. Never. She's too good for that. Last I heard she's getting remarried soon."

"Hey grandpas." Max shoved me across the booth as he slid into it, throwing his arm over my shoulders.

What was it with this guy always thinking we were best friends? "Grandpas?"

"Yeah. You two are like, almost the oldest guys on the team. How does it feel to be so old?"

He snickered, chugged his beer.

"You're two years younger than us," I reminded him.

"And I'm still young enough to kick your ass, especially since you can barely walk straight," Kane said.

"Aw. Come on. I'm kidding and besides, you love me."

"Do we?" Kane asked.

I arched a brow at him.

"Yeah." He nodded and jostled me around until I flung his arm off my shoulder. He was always so sure of himself. "You do, you might not know it yet, but I'm your favorite. Screw Joey and Gabby. It's you and me, bro."

"How do you figure?" I asked him.

"Don't know. Just got a sixth sense about this kind of shit. You and I bonded over quarters that night. You'll never forget me." I still couldn't figure out how any of that had happened, although I didn't regret it as much as I used to.

"And you assume that's a good thing."

Max threw his head back and laughed. "Hell yeah, it is."

Whatever. The guy was one big party animal. His phone pinged and he pulled it out. Opening a text his smile stretched across his face. "Holy shit. Check this out."

Before I could act like I cared—which I didn't—he shoved his phone into my face. A blurry picture of what looked like a beach appeared and I shoved his hand back to get a better look.

"What is that?"

"My brother and his girlfriend are getting married this summer. I can't fucking wait. Our whole family. Hers and a couple of friends on a private resort island. Us Mikolajczyks are going to destroy that place."

"Get ready for the community service that follows," I joked. After all, been there done that.

"How's that going, you liking it?"

I wasn't hating it. I never actually had. The amount of time I spent thinking about those kids—and not just Ben—when I wasn't at practice or when I was on the road was reaching disturbing levels.

"Yeah. It's actually pretty fun. Remember when we skated way back then and it was all for fun?"

"Fun my ass. I wanted to *win*."

"Yeah, obviously, but I don't know. There's an innocence to that. Now it's all trying not to get killed or traded or end up with freshly broken teeth."

As I said it, Max popped out his crown and I shoved my hand in his face. Across the table, Kane barked a laugh. "I don't need to see it, you dipshit."

"I'm kidding, and I get you. Kids are awesome. I love my nephew and my soon-to-be nephew once my brother ties the knot. I don't think there's anything better than the life I had, all those kids, always someone to play with or beat up and hell, we could play three-on-three hockey easily all winter long. Mom hated it. Dad loved it."

"What was that like?"

"What?" His stupid brows pulled in. Sometimes he was dumb. "Playing hockey?"

"No."

Kane laughed. "He meant your family. All those kids. What was it like?" Kane arched a brow, and I nodded. That was exactly what I'd been asking about.

"You'd have to ask my mom, I guess. For me, it was life. I had two older brothers, two younger brothers, a sister. It was sweet. Lots of bloody noses and split lips."

I couldn't resist. "Your sister kicked all your asses, huh?"

"No, dick. But she probably could have. Probably still could. You try growing up the youngest and have five brothers. She probably hates our fucking guts. We didn't let her do shit. Still don't."

"Isn't she an adult now?"

"So?" He glared at me. Got it. I'd definitely feel the same way about Lucy.

And somehow, I didn't have the thought to filter or stew over that. "I get it. My sister's twenty-three. I feel the same way about her."

Both of them froze. Glasses in the air, heads swiveled in my direction, and I was pretty sure eyeballs were at risk of popping out of skulls and bouncing into my beer. I pulled it back just in case.

"You have a sister?" Kane asked.

"Lucy." And damn... what was happening to me? "She's in rehab right now. That night I got arrested? She needed help."

"Holy shit," Kane muttered and leaned forward, twisting even more to face me. "That girl in the car... that was why the charges were dropped."

"Yeah." I grabbed the water I'd also been drinking from. "She was in pretty bad shape that night."

"I mean, wow, not that I ever thought you'd assault some girl, and I figured with you beating the shit out of that other guy, you were helping her..."

"Really?" Because I'd tried not to care. Told myself I didn't. But a piece of me had wondered if my teammates suspected I could do something like the press made it sound like.

They jerked back and scowled. A round of *What? No fucking way. Fuck no. And don't be a dumbass* ensued.

"Shit. This makes so much sense," Kane said, but the look on his face quickly turned and he tilted his head to the side. "You don't want to talk about her problems, do you?"

"Never." I nodded. Yet right then, it wasn't so bad.

Max jostled my shoulders again. What was up with him constantly touching me? "So she's getting help. You're a good big brother, and we now actually know you are a human instead of a cyborg. But you've forgotten the most important part."

"What's that?"

"Is she hot?"

I punched him in the shoulder.

23

HOLLY

"Hey, hotshot." I slapped Ben's hand and took his bag from his shoulder. "Nice goal."

"It was just a scrimmage."

My kid was cute when he was trying to be modest. Too bad his smile gave him away.

"Still awesome." To my surprise, Ben was actually getting better. In the last two weeks, I hadn't once seen him sprawl out on the ice like he had a month ago. I wasn't sure if the skills suddenly clicked, or if it was because he was enjoying the game more. Or, if it had anything to do with Dominick's coaching. Regardless, he hadn't been bummed after a practice or game in a while, nor had I seen him worried about his dad's approval.

Not that I spent a lot of time thinking about Evan. Since he showed at my house last weekend, I hadn't heard a peep out of him. I had, however, seen Kristi in their driveway earlier when I left to come here to pick up Ben.

She'd stopped. Slowly lifted a hand. Her face looked thunderous, and I nodded and hightailed it out of there before she could say anything to me. Based on how unhappy she'd seemed at the game a couple weeks ago, and Evan's sudden appearance last Saturday, things didn't seem to be going so well over at casa cheaters, and frankly, karma was a bitch and it seemed Kristi was learning it the hard way.

"Ready to head home?" I asked Ben. Dominick was busy talking to Carter's parents around the corner, and Karly was still wrangling with Tanner's gear, chatting with him.

"Hey, Holly!" Dominick's voice rang out like thunder through the emptying arena and I turned as he jogged toward us. There was a smile on his face, and a lightness to him that took me by surprise.

I thought back to last week, the burden he shared with me. Had him opening up had anything to do with that?

As he met me, Karly stood and grinned at both of us. "Look at you kids. So cute." She waggled her finger between us.

Dominick chuckled and shoved a hand through his floppy mess of hair.

"What are you doing tomorrow?"

It was Friday. And I had no plans. Pretty standard for me. I'd hoped to see him, but it was also my weekend with Ben and I wasn't sure I was ready to throw all three of us together in a setting that wasn't hockey-related.

"Nothing. Why?"

"You and Ben want to come to the game? My game?"

"A hockey game?" Ben's mouth almost hit the floor. "*Your* game?"

"Yeah, Ben. I get two tickets." He grinned back at me, shuffled on his feet almost like he was nervous. "Thought maybe you and your mom could come watch me."

He glanced up at me. "Maybe I should have asked you privately."

"We'd love to come." If we were alone, I'd kiss him.

"Yeah?"

"Yes!" Ben shouted and threw his arms around Dominick's waist. His eyes widened and he looked down, hands frozen in the air like he didn't know what to do with a kid hugging him before he curled his hands around Ben's shoulders and held him tight. "Thanks, Coach. You're the best!"

I felt tears burn my eyes and blinked them back. Dominick was slowly melting into Ben's hug and I was done for. Absolutely gone for this man.

"So, the game, tomorrow then, huh?"

"Yes," Ben said. "I gotta go tell Tanner."

He ran off, and Dominick took a step toward me. "I should have asked you first. I'm sorry."

"It doesn't matter. I want to see you play."

"Yeah?"

I shrugged. There were still parents around. I wasn't sure what Dominick and I were doing, if we *were* anything, but I knew the fastest way to hit the gossip wheel was to do something with the other moms around. "I like you in all that gear."

"And what about out of it?"

Oh goodness. I could melt to the floor. His dark eyes scanned my body and quickly returned to my face. "Um. I haven't seen all of it yet, so I can't make an informed decision."

Someone shut me up. My cheeks burned, and the heat slid down my throat.

Dominick chuckled. "Next time Ben's with his dad, we can rectify that. If you want."

Oh. I wanted. "Okay."

He grinned that cocksure grin. "I can still taste you. It's been a week and I can't stop thinking about what I did to you."

Perhaps I should have flung myself on the ice to cool down. As it was, I was sweating in my coat and boots.

"Do you still think about it?"

We'd spoken plenty while he was gone. Several texts at least, a few short calls when we could manage it, but none had gone like this. Setting me on fire with no outlet.

"All the time," I admitted, and my throat was suddenly bone dry like the desert.

"Good." He slid his hand into his pockets and pulled out a paper. "Tickets for tomorrow's game and a VIP parking pass. And, because I figured you wouldn't say no, I put your names on the list with security if you want to come see the team after."

The arrogant little... "You figured I wouldn't say no?"

"What can I say?" He shrugged shamelessly, that damn smirk of his. "I was assuming you kind of liked me."

"Maybe a little. Sort of."

"Well, I maybe, sort of, kind of like you, too." His arrogance was gone, replaced with a vulnerability I figured very few had seen in his life. At once, my heart squeezed and my stomach flipped.

This man was going to be a lot of trouble. And a lot of fun. The question was... could there be anything serious between us?

My lips twitched, fighting a grin, which of course Dominick saw because he burst into a wide one of his own. "I hope you know if we were alone right now, I'd be kissing you."

"Who says it wouldn't be me kissing you?"

He threw his head back and laughed. The area around us silenced as the remaining parents left turned and gaped at him. Questioning looks shot between us and if he noticed or cared, he didn't show it.

"I love your sass, Holly. Mostly because I think most of it's only for me."

It was. I wasn't going to feed his ego and let him know.

"And maybe if you're lucky, you'll be able to see it sometime soon."

"I'll be lucky all right. Anytime I'm with you, I am."

Damn. This freaking guy.

"Come on. You need to get Ben home, and I still have a workout to get in." He scooped down and grabbed Ben's gear and called his name. He hurried back to us and Dominick said goodbye to the rest of the parents and if anyone thought it strange he walked us to our car, no one said a thing.

At least not to our faces, but there were looks that said there'd be plenty of talk behind my back.

After Evan left, I'd despised those looks.

This time, I figured the talk would be a lot more fun, so who cared. *I* didn't even know what was happening between Dominick and myself... but I figured the stories they created this time would be entertaining.

"OH MY GOSH, Mom. This is lit."

I nudged Ben's elbow. "Lit means cool, right?"

He rolled his eyes even as he didn't remove them from the game below us. "No one says cool anymore." He almost jumped out of his seat as Dominick skated by us, hustling his ass off after a Boston player. "Look at him go!"

I'd already lost Dominick in a sea of green jerseys who fought for the puck behind the goal. At least, that's where I assumed the puck was based on the pile-up.

The seats Dominick gave us were great. We were ten rows up across from the home team bench. Close enough to see all the action, close enough we could practically see sweat dripping off the players' chins as they flew by.

And holy cow. Hockey in real life moved so much faster than it did on television. I was almost getting whiplash with how fast that puck flew across the ice and lost it more than I'd admit.

How in the hell did the players track it?

And the speed they skated. The crunch of bone and pads into boards. The crack of sticks being broken, even the swish of ice flying in the air. Heck, even the arena's noise from the stands and buzzers was louder than anything I could have predicted.

I really needed to turn up my volume at home to get a better feel for the game. Maybe play it in fast forward motion. Then it'd be more realistic.

"Oh crap," Ben said, and I'd been focused on the group of men behind the goal I hadn't seen Dominick burst free. Number seventy-two stamped across his back, but then he was tugged around, jersey gripped in the fist of a Boston player right as that guy's glove slammed into Dominick's cage.

That was the last punch he got off though before Dominick hit him once. Twice. He hit him a third time before throwing off his helmet and sweeping the Boston player off his skates.

"That's Selkin," Ben said, and I had to lean forward. "Everyone *hates* him."

I hated him too, although I was more worried about Dominick as the refs circled them before finally wading in when blood—from Selkin—I hoped, landed on the ice and they managed to pull Dominick off him. Other Vegas players surrounded him, shoving back more Boston players. There were more scrums. More punches thrown. As the fight grew, the buzzer blared and more refs and players from the bench hopped the boards to separate the massive brawl going on.

I didn't know whether to be disgusted or turned on, as Dominick shoved off a ref and grabbed his helmet. He shook out his hair like an animal and I swore he glanced in our direction and smiled.

"Does he see us?" Ben asked, bouncing on the balls of his feet. Men and women around us were on their feet, cheering and booing in equal measure. Considering we were surrounded by Viper fans, I assumed the booing was against the Boston player for starting the fight, but it was Dominick being hauled to the penalty box ten rows below us.

"You suck, ref!" was shouted from a number of men with Coors Light tallboys in their hands. "Come on!"

Dominick tossed his helmet to the floor of the sin bin and threw his gloves. His face etched with something feral.

"He's mad." Ben's face had paled as he saw it play out on the mega screen above center ice, too short to see over the men still on their feet in front of us.

He was most definitely mad. His expression was also a very vivid reminder of why everyone thought Dominick was an asshole. Why he'd earned the nickname the bad boy of hockey.

Yet he'd been so *good* to me. Protective, sure. Walls up, definitely, at least until he ripped them down last week. But this?

This was slightly worrisome. Who was he who could be set off so quickly like this? And why was he in the penalty box and not the guy who started it? I'd watched enough hockey over the years to understand basic rules like icing and hooking and tripping and offsides. But his made no sense.

"Even Dad doesn't like Selkin, and he likes the fights," Ben said. How my ten-year-old knew I needed a teacher was beyond me.

"Yeah?"

"Yeah. And Boston is who the Vipers beat last year for the championship. Dad says these two teams *hate* each other. Told me when I told him we were coming to the game. Said he wished he could be here."

At the mention of Evan, my spine tingled. I hadn't heard from him in a week. He'd most likely be at Ben's game this weekend, but as long as he stayed away, I didn't care. When we got home from practice yesterday though, Ben had run next door to tell his dad about us going to the game.

A part of me was proud of Evan for what he said—if Ben was telling me the whole story. It was certainly better than how he treated me. And knowing what he saw of Dominick last week, and what I'd told him, I hadn't been sure of how his next visit with Ben would go.

But at least he didn't spoil Ben's appreciation of Dominick.

"Dad doesn't like Dominick anymore either," he said and grabbed his drink, popped his straw into his mouth.

So much for thinking something good about the guy.

"Some people change their mind about who they like. That's okay."

"Maybe. I still think Dominick is cool, though."

"Good. It's okay to like people your dad doesn't. You know that, right?"

"Yeah." His nose scrunched and the guys returned to the ice after a time-out. As they faced off, I caught sight of Dominick below us in the penalty box. His eyes had been up at the Megatron, but he turned his head. I could see his profile, the quirk of his lips. He was... smiling?

For a man who just got kicked out of the game for two minutes to a team they were down by one to, I wouldn't have expected the smile.

This man. He was a constant source of confusion for me. Would I ever figure him out?

Would he be worth the risk if I tried?

24

DOMINICK

There wasn't a player in the NHL who liked Selkin. Hell, I doubted his own team liked him, and yeah, I knew the hypocrisy of that judgment given who it was coming from. Worse than Selkin, we lost the game. I had no doubt the odds were high we'd be seeing them again in the playoff finals in a few months and if tonight's ugly game filled with fights and penalties on both sides was any indication, some of us would be happy if we all survived the games without concussions or serious physical injuries.

That was how hard they played. Brutally vicious, worse than any other team. I couldn't stand them and their ugly playing, and worse, how they always seemed to get away with it.

Not that I gave a shit about my own penalty. I'd take Selkin down for the hell of it any chance I got, but that didn't mean losing to them felt good.

Coach Vik ranted as half of us took a slow cool down on stationary bikes and the other half of the team stripped out of the gear to do the same. I'd been sure to get on the bike first so I didn't have to make Holly and Ben wait long if they chose to come down to the player and wives area. The bikes were detrimental after a game, especially when we had back-to-back ones like this week. They helped get rid of the lactic acid from our intense game and kept our muscles loose for the next one. Usually, I rode the bike like I was in second place at the Tour de France, the winner right in front of me, and the victory banner a half mile ahead.

Tonight, I barely paid attention to either my speed or Coach's rants. We all knew we let them get in our heads. We all knew we fell to their level, and we *always* lost when we let that happen. We'd all go home tonight, watch film that would already be emailed to us or we'd wake up early and do it tomorrow. Fortunately, Boston was hitting the road and San Francisco was headed down.

A less brutal team, but fast, they'd be just as difficult to beat but would require an entirely different game plan.

Which probably meant I shouldn't have let Selkin's comment about fucking my sister make my blood boil. Hell, he didn't even know I had a sister, but for a moment I'd wondered—had the guys on the team said anything to him? Gossiped? Spread the word about the drug addict who couldn't take care of herself?

Two punches in I realized that was all bullshit I made up in my own head, my low ability to trust people, but by then, my adrenaline took over.

My bad.

I would have felt shitty for overreacting had I been punching anyone other than Selkin.

A hand slapped the power button on the bike and I scowled as my feet almost slipped off the pedals.

"Get off," Kane said.

"The hell?"

"Word is your woman's out there and you've been riding this so hard you're going to do more damage than good."

"Shit." I looked at the speed ticking down at the screen. The max speed I'd hit. "Got lost in my head."

"Maybe go get lost in Holly instead, yeah?"

He was teasing. So I told him I liked her. Didn't mean we were fucking. Not tonight, anyway. Not with Ben around.

Although my frustration might have had something to do with Selkin's face being rearranged by my fists tonight.

I climbed off the bike and found Joey, almost done getting dressed. "Hey, Taylor."

"Yeah?" He threw on his shirt and faced me.

"Gabby out there?"

"Of course."

"I think Holly and Ben are there. Can you tell them I'll be out in ten?"

Look at me...asking for more help from my teammates. I hadn't even hesitated. Damn. I was *changing*. A weird taste hit the back of my throat.

Joey smirked. "No problem. See you outside."

I'D NEVER PAID attention to the girlfriends or wives, children, sometimes parents or siblings who waited outside our locker room. No one was ever there for me, and since up until a few months ago I wouldn't have considered any of the guys on my team friends, I'd never even looked at the small crowd gathering and chatting in the hallway. I'd always gone to the locker room, listened to Coach, done my post-game cooldown, or spent time getting a massage, showered, grabbed my bag, and gotten the hell out of there and back to my quiet condo.

I had no clue what I'd been missing until I stepped out of that locker room door, bag thrown over my shoulder to immediately see Holly, smiling and talking with Gabby and Joey, her seeing me, turning, and that smile so damn bright it could power the electricity in the arena.

Holy shit... my chest almost exploded from the heated look on her face.

And then there was Ben. He was standing next to Holly, gazing up at Joey with that hero-worship smile until she squeezed his shoulder and he too, turned and caught sight of me.

"Coach!" he cried out, tugged out of Holly's soft hold of him, and ran straight to me, arms out. He slammed into my stomach, arms thrown around me. His hug was so strong, his hit so fierce, I went back a step and had to wrap my free arm around his back to keep us both from toppling over. "Thank you. Thank you so much for giving us those tickets. I had so much fun."

Something burned my eyes and forced me to blink while I dropped the bag in my hand and patted his head. "Glad you could make it."

The words came out, scraped over gravel in my throat. *Damn. This kid.* He had no shame in his excitement, no fear in his emotion.

I had to clear my throat before I could speak again, and as I did, found myself crouching down to his level a bit. Soon, he'd be tall enough I wouldn't have to, but then, Ben was still a bit short for his age. "I was really glad you were there."

"Me too. I had to teach Mom everything."

"Yeah?" I glanced up at her. Her gorgeous, large green eyes flickered to Ben, that bright smile softening as she took us in, before meeting mine. "Everything?"

"Not everything." She rolled her eyes. "But he did explain the bad blood between you guys and Boston."

I stood. Right. Because she'd totally seen me lose my shit. Not that I didn't fight, but I usually had more restraint. "Long history there," I said. "And we hate losing to them."

"Yeah." Her lips quirked at the corner. Lips I'd kiss if Ben wasn't right there. "I got that from the blood on the ice."

"It's part of the game." Granted, not to *that* extent.

"The crowd around us seemed to love it."

"Most drunk guys usually do."

She chuckled and shook her head. I waited to see if it worried her, either my ability to lose my temper or if I'd been hurt. Not that it mattered. My body was usually covered in a few bruises, sore muscles, and scraped knuckles.

The teammates and their families around us started to disperse and as they did, we followed them down the hall. "Did you park with the pass I gave you?" I asked, to make sure.

"Yes, Ben noticed your car, so we're right there."

"Good."

"Can I ride in that car with you sometime, Coach?" he asked.

I glanced at Holly for approval first. I'd learned with the tickets. She might not like me springing a surprise on her, but she was his mom. At her nod, I told Ben yes.

"Sweet."

"And Ben?"

"Yeah?"

"How about when we're not at practice, you call me Dominick."

His eyes turned to saucers and he grinned cheek-to-cheek. Glancing at his mom for approval, getting her nod, he nodded his okay. "Okay, Dominick."

Said my name like he was testing it out. And yet my name coming from his mouth with those eyes that matched Holly's and hair so similar, a different kind of heat spread through my body. As if Holly somehow understood what that meant to me, a kid not just looking up to me, but *liking me*, she reached out, brushed her fingers over the back of my hand.

Which sent a totally different shock to my system.

Damn it. One innocent touch from her, and a rush of desires raced through my mind. The things I'd do for a touch like that.

Anything. Everything. I would do *anything* for Holly if her approval came with that gentle caress.

We reached her car, and she beeped the locks to unlock it. Ben stared at my car in awe as he walked to his. Yeah, someday soon I'd get this kid in my ride. Possibly with both of them in it, flying through an open stretch of road in the desert where we could ease the top down and see how fast I could get her going before they screamed with excitement. No doubt both of them would. The image of Holly's blonde hair flying in the wind, laughing heartily with her shining eyes on me was too much.

As Ben went around to his side of the car and opened the door, I lowered my voice so he couldn't hear.

"Have you told Ben anything about us yet?"

"No..." She glanced at him and fidgeted with her keys. "I... wasn't sure what to say. If there was an us."

"Oh." Well, shit. I figured she knew my interest from the other day. Or at least when I spent the night at her place, insisted on taking her out for breakfast.

"I didn't want to presume anything," she rushed to say. "And we don't have to define anything. For him, we can be friends. If that's what you want."

Which would be okay, I guessed. But she was right. I hadn't been clear enough. Yeah, I told her I liked her, but that could mean anything.

I smirked at her. "I think you're his mom and you know how to handle it best, but trust me, friends don't kiss the way I want to be able to kiss you, even if he's around. So there's no doubt moving forward, I like you. I want to date you and when you're ready, that includes spending time with both Ben and you."

And funny how after knowing her for a month, spending time with the sweet and pure single mom didn't seem like such a terrifying thing anymore.

She rolled her lips, and an adorable pink hit the apple of her cheeks and the tip of her nose. Yeah. I wanted to kiss her. Whenever the hell I felt like it.

She grinned. "I'll talk to him tomorrow."

"Good choice." I reached around and opened her door for her. "Drive safe. Text me when you get home, and tomorrow, be prepared for kissing. A lot of it. I don't care if Ben *is* around. It's been too damn long since I've touched you."

"Yes, sir," she teased.

Oh, the ideas that submission could spring to my mind and other places. I bit down a groan and nodded toward her door.

"Get in the car." Knocking my fist against the back seat window, I bent down and smiled through the window even though I could barely see him on the other side. "Glad you could see me play, Ben."

"I'll come anytime you want me to. It was a blast."

Sounded like the best idea to me.

No one had come to watch me play since Dad died. Knowing Ben and Holly were there?

Pretty damn awesome.

Hopefully it was the first of many.

I STOOD in front of half the kids on the bench, the other still on the ice. We were losing. We weren't just losing. We were getting our asses kicked. An experience these kids hadn't face yet this season.

They were *not* taking it well.

"It's a game," I told them. "And you're never going to win them all, but that does not mean we fall apart and stop trying."

"They're so big," Tanner said, and if I wasn't mistaken, there was fear in his voice. He was right. If I could, I'd force the other team's coach to show me the kids' birth certificates. The kids were monsters. They were also skilled. Fast. And physical. Our kids had spent more time being knocked to the ice than on their skates for the first two periods and now we were halfway through the third and had yet to score.

"They are," Carter's dad, Mike, agreed. "And they're fast. And maybe we will lose, but that does not mean we give up. Aidan, you keep skating out of their defender's way. Make him move around you, or move into him."

The poor kid's eyes widened. "He could *kill* me."

"He won't. Won't even get a scratch. We get it. They're bigger than any of you, but that means you need to work together. Tighten up the space in the center. Force them to skate around you instead of giving them the room and you'll be able to steal the puck. They're big and fast and skilled, but their center has a sloppy dribble. You double-team him and you can get that puck. I'm sure of it."

"All right." Aidan nodded, still looking unsure, but glanced to Ben and Tanner, the other two guys on his line. "We can try that."

Ben held out his fist. "No doubts. Not ever." They fist-pumped. Shaking grins wobbled as they looked to me. "Right, Coach?"

"Damn straight." I clapped my hands together. Goddamn, I was starting to love that kid. He took everything I said and ate it up like gospel.

Let's hope I'd taught him good shit.

"Now, here's what we're going to do. We're going to take Coach Mike's advice...." I pulled out my whiteboard and scribbled a couple plays down for both defense and offense. The kids focused. The buzzer went off and they scrambled back to the ice.

"You're a good coach," Mike said to me as we stood shoulder to shoulder.

"Thanks."

"I mean it. I have a guess of why you ended up doing this, and that first week I wasn't certain you were the guy for this, but you have a gift with these kids that's more than just their hero-worship of you."

My teeth ground together. We'd barely spoken all season when it wasn't about practice, but damn. That felt good.

"Sarah told me she's seen you with Holly after practice. Said you looked close."

At that, I slid my eyes to the side, trying to focus on the kids, but warning him. "And?"

"She's a good woman. From what I hear, Evan didn't do right by her, but Sara has always thought she was sweet even if they're not close."

Irritation pricked into my hands, making my fingers curl into my biceps. "If this is supposed to be a warning—"

"It's not." He shrugged, laidback as he always was, keeping his eyes on the kids still getting creamed, but at least attempting to do what we'd coached. "It just means she's a good woman. I'm guessing there's a lot more to you than what we've all heard about, which means you must be a good guy. Happy for you if something comes from it. That's all."

It shouldn't have meant anything. I didn't know this guy. I doubted after this season I'd ever see him again... unless... unless Ben and Aidan stayed friends and Holly and I stayed together. Then, well, who in the hell knew what would happen then.

"You're right. Holly and Ben are both great. And thanks."

"Although." He smirked, and that laidback look on him turned teasing. "Maybe spread the wealth once in a while with the game tickets, eh?"

I laughed, unable to help myself. "Was that your game this whole time?"

"Doesn't hurt to ask."

"How about I do one better and see if I can get a suite for the kids someday. All the families could come."

"I'm not asking that," he said and we both cringed as Ben and Tanner slid together to stop their center. At the same time, he barreled right into them like they were bowling pins. Both of our kids lost their skates and slid on their asses off to the sides. "Ouch," he groaned.

"Fuck, we're getting creamed."

"Good for them every once in a while. Builds character." The hell it did. That was a lie everyone was told. Losing didn't teach you anything except not to do it again, because it felt like shit.

I stayed quiet and we watched and screamed, and eventually, Mike moved back to me. "I wasn't saying anything about Holly because I want the tickets, but if you're handing them out, I won't say no. I just think you're a good guy. I respect what you've done with the kids, and win or lose, you've given them all a memory that will never die. Especially for Aidan. So thanks."

The buzzer sounded. We lost seven to zero. The kids skated off the ice looking completely dejected, worse than I'd ever seen them.

But somehow, I slapped Mike on the shoulder and squeezed. "Thank you."

Because his words meant more to me than anything. And somehow, as the kids skated off the ice and trudged into the locker room, I didn't give one single shit we lost the game.

I cared that somehow, I was learning I *was* becoming the man my dad had taught me to be... it'd only taken me a while to see it.

"Hey, Mike," I called once we were heading toward the locker room.

"Yeah?"

"I get two tickets to every game. You want them for tomorrow's?"

"Are you kidding? Because really, I wasn't hunting for them or taking advantage."

"Never get to give them out. They'll be at Will Call if you can make it."

"Yeah. Man. Absolutely. Thanks."

"No problem." And it wasn't. After all, it wouldn't hurt to have someone else there I knew, cheering me on.

"LOSING SUCKS," Ben said as we met up with his mom standing with Karly and Blake.

"Yep. But you can't win them all, not ever." I didn't give him platitudes. Losing did suck. Hell, we'd lost to Boston and two other games in the last couple of weeks.

"Yeah. I know."

"Hey, kiddo," Holly sang in that sweet way of hers but this time it was tinged with sadness. "Tough game, huh?"

"Tell me about it," Tanner mumbled. "I spent so much time on the ice my butt is bruised."

Karly rolled her lips together to stop laughing. "We can ice it when we get home."

"No thanks. Spent enough time on the ice today."

"Maybe a warm bath then." She glanced at me, humor in her eyes even while she tried to be compassionate. "Tough loss, Coach."

"It happens." I shrugged. "We'll get them next time."

"We have to play them *again*?" Ben said.

"Probably. Only in playoffs though."

"There goes the trophy," Tanner grumbled. "No way we can beat them."

"Hey." So I didn't mind losing. But a losing attitude was irritating as hell. "You've already lost if that's your thought. We'll practice for them. Be prepared. You never know what can happen."

"Yeah." Ben's eyes lit up. "Maybe they'll all get food poisoning or something beforehand and have to forfeit."

We all laughed. "Not quite what I meant."

"You said anything could happen."

Smart kid. "All right, all right. Next week we'll get ready for the next team, that's all we have to worry about. We'll think about these guys when we have to. Until then, you learn how you can improve and work on that, okay?"

"Yeah, Coach," they grunted and while they talked, I was reminded of the text I got during the game. Coach had given us the day off today to rest after Boston before our game tomorrow. Since there was a day off, of course, the guys were headed out.

"Some of the guys are having dinner at Malley's, that bar Joey owns," I said to Holly. "Want to go with me for a little while? We can take Ben."

It was a bar, but the guys wouldn't care.

"I have a better idea," Karly said, joining the conversation like she usually did. "How about Blake and I take Ben, and he and Tanner have a sleepover? That way, you two can have the *whole night* to yourselves?"

Hell yes.

Next to her, Holly blushed, peered up at me through lashes as she ducked her head.

"Smooth, Karly, real smooth."

Oh, but she wasn't getting out of this. Not with an offer like that on the table and the blatant innuendo in Karly's tone.

"Hell, with an offer like that, I'll pay for dinner to get delivered to your home."

Karly held out her hand. "Deal."

"Woman," Blake growled and shook his head at me. "That's not necessary."

It absolutely was. I'd do anything to finally get another night alone with Holly.

"Yes, it is," Karly cut in. Pretty sure she shoved her elbow into Blake's gut, too. "He offered, I'm taking him up on it."

This woman. She was almost as likable as Gabby.

We both looked to Holly, who was shaking her head, amused and embarrassed in equal measure based on her expression. "Since you've both teamed up on me," she drawled. "Not sure I can say no."

I wouldn't have let her anyway. "Perfect. I'll follow you to your place then."

"Hey, kids!" Karly shouted. "You two are coming home with me, okay?"

Ben looked to his mom for approval and at her nod, he and Tanner slapped hands high in the air. "Awesome!"

I turned to Karly. "Text Holly what you want and your address. I'll take care of the rest."

"That's really nice but you don't have to," Blake said. I didn't know if he was doing it to be polite, or because he was embarrassed, but either way, I'd offered.

"My idea. And trust me, I absolutely do."

"Right," he grunted and held out his hand. I shook it. "I get it."

"So this isn't humiliating at all," Holly mumbled.

"Nonsense," Karly teased and slipped her arm in Holly's as we ushered the kids out of the arena. "You're getting laid tonight. There's nothing humiliating at all about that." She shot me a wicked look. "At least, I *hope* it's not humiliating."

I arched a challenging brow in response.

"Yeah, I doubt that for you," she said back to Holly.

Both women broke out in laughs.

Next to me, Blake shook his head. "You have to excuse my wife. She was raised by wolves."

That may be, but Karly was on my side, so I kind of loved her. "I like her."

"Yeah," Blake said, drawing out the word. "She kicks ass."

25

———

HOLLY

We pulled up to Malley's, Dominick's hand on my thigh, warming my skin through the jeans I still had on from the game earlier. There wasn't a word that existed yet for men who could coach a kid's hockey team without losing their minds in anger when the team didn't play well. I'd sat through a lot of youth sporting events over the years, a lot of hockey, and I'd seen a lot of men who coached kids who made me wonder what they were like in their homes with their families. I figured seeing a man completely lose his cool over a *game* said a lot about their patience as a parent.

Take Evan for example... thank *God* he wasn't at the game today.

But Dominick? He had a gift. For as angry as he could appear, when he coached those boys, it was like there was a different part of him that took over. It wasn't only impressive, it was sexy as hell.

"You're good at that," I told him, out of the blue, so his confusion wasn't surprising.

"What? Parking?" He gestured to where he'd just backed into a spot.

"No. Coaching. You're really good at it. Even from that first day I saw you, and it looked like you didn't want to be there, you were good at it."

"Hm." His brows furrowed. "Mike said the same thing. It's..." He shook his head. "I'm not used to getting compliments, really."

"Well, I think you're great, coaching and playing and as a man." I leaned across the console and kissed him. Something I'd been wanting to do all day and hadn't had the time.

When he followed me to my house, he hadn't even let me go inside. Just told me to get in his car. Based on the look in his eyes, I figured he was worried if we went inside, we wouldn't end up at Malley's, so I'd agreed.

But I, personally, couldn't wait any longer to taste him again. He must have been desperate for it too because as soon as my lips met his, his hand slid to the back of my head. He held me to him, took over the kiss, diving his tongue into my mouth and tangling against mine.

A moan slipped from his throat into mine and I answered in kind, because how could I *not* get lost in the taste and confidence and warmth of this man? Dominick was incredible. In every way and I hated the doubts he occasionally saw, but wanted to do everything necessary to ensure he knew from now on, how great I thought he was.

He slowly pulled back from the kiss, both of us breathing heavy and pressed his forehead to mine. "I don't spend a lot of time with the team, so we're going to have to end this before I throw this car in drive and back to your house."

For a second, I considered agreeing, but there was a slight hint of regret in his voice, like he *wanted* to be with his team. I'd never deny him that.

"Later," I promised him, and gave him a quick peck before pulling away. "I want to see them again."

"And I promise I won't leave you this time."

"That's good." I laughed. I was well beyond the last time that happened. I understood. Opening my door, I flashed him a grin. "Because this time I don't have a ride home if you do."

"Trust me, the only thing you're going to be riding later is me."

Oh, and what a beautiful image that was.

I climbed out of the car and scowled at him. "Play nice. You keep saying things like that to me and you'll learn I don't play fair."

A lie. I always played fair, let someone else set the rules, but when I was around Dominick, there was a whole new game board in front of me. One where I could set the stakes or break the rules, and I figured he'd love every bad move I made.

The way his eyes heated, as he took my hand in his like we'd done it a thousand times before and led me toward the door of Malley's confirmed it.

Let the games begin.

I GOOGLED Malley's after Dominick told me Joey owned it and why he purchased it, so I already knew where it was and what it looked like on the outside. An old brick standalone with standard neon lights highlighting all-American made beers. The outside was completely unassuming. A typical sports bar in a relatively middle-class area of Las Vegas, it was so far off the Strip, there was no way a tourist would ever show up here hoping to get a glimpse of a professional athlete. Even most of the cars outside didn't scream *money* like Dominick's did. There was an Escalade, a Suburban, pickup truck, and a couple of sports cars, but none so out of place it screamed rich people were inside.

The inside, however, was a totally different story and I gasped as we entered.

"Wow. This was not what I was expecting."

Sure, there were all the trappings of a typical bar with booths down one side, a couple pool tables and dartboards at the back with lights that flashed in a circle when they weren't being played. Bar-height tables with tall stools in the other open areas and a bar to the right. But it was the cleanliness of it. The gleaming wood floors looked freshly polished and shined, the wood bar top and brass railing in front brand new. Light fixtures hung, all done in the same brassy color must have been cleaned and polished daily to look so good.

Outside, I'd imagined it dark inside, a little dull and a whole lot old because what guys cared about a nice place to have a few drinks or a meal occasionally, but it was brighter than most bars, giving a lively and happy vibe to the place.

Impressive.

"Yeah. Joey spent some time fixing it up after he bought it. It was in pretty bad shape before, but the guy he bought it from, Jerry, had been sick for a while and fallen down on the job a little bit." He guided me toward the bar where we were handed a couple of menus. We both ordered waters. I wouldn't mind a drink later, but I needed food in me first.

There were calls of hello to Dominick from Max, and a few other guys I didn't know, but he raised his hand in greeting back and we slid into a booth near where some of them were playing pool.

"Who's here?" I asked him.

"Max is the bigger guy. Kane is shooting right now."

I nodded as I took in the guy with hair almost as dark as Dominick's bent over the pool table.

"The blond who barely looks old enough to drink is Arlo, he was called up last season, so this is his first full year in the league and the darker blond with the longer hair is Alix."

"Halvrick?" I asked. Ben talked about him a lot. Almost as much as Dominick or Joey.

"He's the one you know? Out of all of us?"

"Ben's a fan. Used to be his favorite player." I sipped my water.

"And now?" Dom leaned forward, grinning at me.

"I think you might know who he loves the most now."

He shoved his lips to one side. "That means a lot to me."

I couldn't help myself. I reached out and took his hand in mine and squeezed. "What's good here?" I asked, changing the subject, even though I already knew what I wanted. A place like this screamed *excellent burgers,* and I hadn't enjoyed one in a while.

"Anything." He swallowed, and then said, "My dad was my first hockey coach."

"Yeah?" My throat closed. He'd already said how hard it was for him to open up.

"Yeah, Lucy was only one and I only played because my dad liked watching the game so much and that year was all about the baby. I got jealous, wanted attention on me, so I asked my dad to put me in hockey."

"He sounds like a great dad."

"He didn't even hesitate. Signed me up and volunteered to coach. Coached me all the way up until I hit travel leagues, but he never missed a game then." He paused and took a drink of his water. I gave him the time. "He was a good man. The best. I think I've gotten so caught up in taking care of Lucy over the years, I forgot how much he loved watching me play, how much he taught me."

Dear God. I forced a shaky grin and willed back tears clawing at the back of my eyes. "I have no doubt he's so proud of the player and man you've become." I squeezed his hand again, held on tightly, and hoped like hell I could keep my emotions in check.

"I think I forgot some of that until recently."

The guy he called Max appeared and plopped right down next to Dominick, ripping the menu up from the table in front of me. "Sweet, we're eating. I'm starved." He glanced at Dominick, whose emotions were now well-hidden, that familiar scowl in place. "You paying? I'm a bit tight on money this week."

"You make as much as me," Dominick deadpanned.

"Yeah, I know." He scanned the menu, flashing me a wink. I had a feeling Max was the fun-loving goofball. He caught my returning smile and tossed down the menu. "So, Ben's mom." He leaned back and threw both his arms over the back of the booth. "Tell me. What are your intentions with our favorite little all-star here."

"All-star?"

"Yeah. This guy." He tilted his head toward Dominick.

Dominick, who looked exasperated. A slight color to his cheeks. Maybe... embarrassed?

"What do you mean?"

"The all-star break is next weekend. The best of the best are invited. The Taylors always go. Best players from every team, it's a weekend long thing with exhibitions and scrimmages against division, that kind of thing. Dominick here has yet to attend."

"Because I like the rest and don't like people."

"No." Max shook his head, grabbed Dom's water like it was his, and drained it. He popped his lips and sighed.

Dominick glared at the glass still in Max's hand like he wanted to slam it against Max's face, but yet—not really mean it at the same time.

"You like to *pretend* you don't like people. There's a difference. Me, I'm your best friend."

"How in the hell do you figure?"

"Simple." He patted Dominick on the shoulder and slid the empty glass back toward him. "I push your buttons every chance I get, and for all your threats and glares, you haven't hit me yet. Not hard anyway. That means you love me."

"That means I don't want to get suspended from a game or six."

"No." Max shook his head in absolute denial. "It's how my brothers and I treat each other. If you really hated me, you wouldn't put up with it."

I hid my laugh behind my hand. He had a point. My brother

and I drove each other crazy when we were little, but for all our arguing and bickering, we loved each other.

"So you're telling me that if I were to slam your face into this table, you'd finally understand I don't like you?"

"Yep." Max pointed a finger at him that Dominick slapped away. "But you won't. Ergo, you love me."

He shrugged, pushed off the table, and headed toward the bar.

"He has a point," I told Dominick. "At the very least, you don't hate him."

"Yeah. Seems to be a thing lately, me realizing people don't completely suck." He grabbed his water glass, brought it to his lips before remembering where it'd been, and slammed it back down. "Fucking Max. It's probably impossible to hate the guy."

I laughed again. "Tell me more about this all-star thing. Was he serious? The best get invited."

"Yeah, but I don't go." He scratched the side of his neck and flinched. "Heard it's fun though, but I really do like the weekend off. And I figured no one really cared whether or not I went so I never did."

"I think if you gave it a chance, there might be more people who like you and respect you than you think."

"Yeah." Another scratch, another shove of his lips to the side. "I'm beginning to learn that too."

WE BOTH HAD BURGERS, and I was right. Mine was so mammoth I only ate half of it. Fortunately, I was sitting with the human consumption machine who, after he polished off his own burger and fries, he then had two chicken breasts and then finished off my burger, sans the bun. Dominick stuck to water. I had a glass of wine.

Max came back over and for a short time, so did Kane, who shot Dominick a couple of looks I couldn't decipher, but seemed equal parts warning and amused, before Dominick eventually said we were headed out. The bar was only ten minutes away from my house and by the time we pulled up, I'd almost forgotten all about Kane's looks, full from the food, a little bit tired, a whole lot nervous about what was to come.

We climbed out of his car, and I was thankful to see the lights off next door. Hopefully, Evan and Kristi were out of town and another irritating late-night visit wasn't in the cards. If I had room in my garage, I'd have Dominick pull in to be on the safe side, but we were already at my front door and I was unlocking it and letting us in before I decided, screw it.

If Evan still had a problem, we'd deal, and this time I wouldn't let it ruin anything.

"Want a drink? Or anything?" Dominick asked as he locked the door after it closed.

Nerves aside, another drink might knock me out, and I didn't want anything to ruin the rest of the night.

"No." I slid my phone out of my purse, just in case of an emergency, and then hung my purse inside my coat closet. "I want to go upstairs."

My bottom lip found its way between my teeth as Dominick prowled toward me.

"Good. Me too."

He kissed me, hand at my cheek, and this time it was slow. There was passion and desire mixed with a need I couldn't explain. My body understood though, I melted against him as we stood at the bottom of my stairs, kissing, teasing, completely unhurried. Soon, I was breathless, and Dominick's hand was on the railing, guiding us upstairs. I moved, backwards, my hands holding the sides of his neck his shoulders. I scraped my hands through his hair and earned a delicious moan from him in response.

We took the stairs, step by painfully and torturously slow step until we reached the landing and my legs were so warm my knees wobbled.

"I've got you," he said against my mouth and his hands went to my shirt. Unlike last time, when we'd made out on my couch, or the morning after when he'd gone down on me in my entryway, this time there were no nerves as he gripped the bottom of my shirt.

This time, I couldn't think of anything else but *finally.* I finally got to know the feel of Dominick in every way. I helped him, pulling my mouth off his only to whip my shirt off and threw it to the floor. As soon as my shirt hit the floor, my hands went to his. I pushed my hands beneath his shirt, felt the molten heat of his skin and the rapid beat of his heart. I almost didn't want to remove his three-quarter zip-up shirt he always wore when coaching. It fit him like a glove and he looked incredibly sexy in it.

Although... removing it meant I'd get to *finally* see him naked.

I'd admire him in the shirt the next game. Problem solved.

I worked his shirt up his body, reveled in every groove. That hair I'd missed on his muscular body and delighted in the shiver that hit him as I pushed my hands further up his broad, curved chest.

"You're killing me with all this slowness."

I huffed a laugh and leaned in, pressing my lips to the center of his chest, right where the thump of his heart was the strongest. "You'll survive."

He tore off his shirt, cupped my cheeks in his palms and then his mouth seared itself to mine in a kiss that sent fire to my toes that curled to the wood floor beneath our feet.

Oh *dear.* I'd known the first time, but this man could *kiss.* I was dizzy with the taste of him, heated with anticipation of what would come next and then we were moving again, back to my room where he flicked on a light to cast a gentle glow over the space.

"There are so many things I've imagined doing to you in this bed," he murmured, pausing only long enough to tease me with his whispered promises before kissing me again, and guiding me toward my bed.

The backs of my knees hit and then he was leading me down. A hand at my lower back to help me onto the bed and toward the pillows.

"Of all the things I've imagined though," he said and drew his lips down my throat, to my chest and lingered at the center of my bra before crawling off the bed and standing before me. "Is that first moment I slide inside you."

"Yes." I nodded, completely enraptured by the searing heat in his dark, aroused gaze as he pushed down his pants and grabbed his wallet before kicking them to the floor. His boxers immediately followed and there he was.

All of him. Bared to me with no nerves and no hesitation and there was *a lot* of him to appreciate.

Oh my. He was right. We could learn every inch of each other's bodies later. I wanted nothing more than that first moment of connection.

He pulled a string of condoms out of his wallet and tossed them onto the bed.

"You're beautiful," he said on a sigh, and scanned my body while I reached beneath me to unclasp my bra. I tugged it off and threw it. He didn't take his eyes off mine as I wiggled out of my jeans and then he helped me with my underwear. They didn't match my bra and weren't sexy. I hadn't planned for this, but with the way he kept those dark eyes trained on me, I was certain he didn't give a single crap about my lingerie, as simple as it was.

With his hands at my thighs, he spread my legs and climbed onto the bed.

"Are you ready?"

"So ready." I nodded and reached for his hips. Strong thighs. Bricks for abs. Veins curved a map along his forearms I'd taste later with my tongue and then I forgot the rest of my plans because his fingers slipped against me.

"So wet already."

"From the moment you kissed me." I was desperate for him to know how much I enjoyed every piece of beauty he gave me. I'd waited for this moment for *weeks.*

He dipped them inside, gathered moisture and brought them to my clit. He worked me perfectly, quickly. I was already so ready, my breasts heavy and my nipples hardened peaks. Every brush against my sex sent a fissure through me, threatening to break me apart and stitch me back together.

There was the tear of foil. The pause while he covered himself and then Dominick was leaning over me, bracing his weight off me while one hand came to my cheek, pushed hair back and he whispered, "Kiss me, Holly."

I lifted my head and he met me, kissed me and delved his tongue into my mouth while he lowered his body, found my center and slowly pushed inside of me.

"Oh," I whimpered and opened more for him so he could sink between my legs. I wrapped them around his back as he pushed inside, and he kissed away the needy little sounds I made while he slowly moved.

"Shit. Better than I could possibly imagine," he whispered, went back to kissing me until he filled me. I was stretched open for him, *full* of him, and as he began to move, he moved with tenderness and passion. He moved like a man who would wait until I was satisfied and taken care of before reaching his own peak.

He made love to me with his body, his hands, and his mouth, grinding his hips against me, ensuring he pleased me from both the inside and out and every time he hit deep inside of me, a spark of pleasure ignited until I was clinging to him, working with him, fighting to release and hold it back so this didn't end.

Dominick was *marvelous.* Slow and unhurried with deep with hard thrusts that were perfect.

So perfect, everything hit at once and I squeezed my eyes closed, dug fingertips into his hips, and I held on while he grunted, encouraged me to fall with, "Yeah, get there." "So fucking good." "Beautiful like this." A continued stream of commands and praise fell from his full, glistening lips before I couldn't hold back any longer.

I shoved my head into the pillow, clenched my ankles around

his back harder and I cried out my release as it spun me out to sea, tossed me over the waves, sent me into a wild, full-body spin of absolute, wild bliss, before gentle waves brought me back to shore, to Dominick who was buried inside of me, staring down at me.

"You are so damn sexy," he grunted, slammed his mouth to mine at the same time he slammed inside of me and found his own release with a full-body shudder that rolled though him almost as strong as my own had.

He collapsed against me and rolled us to our side, wrapped his arms around me and buried his face in the crook of my neck and shoulder. I clung to him fiercely, let the warmth of his body slowly bring me back to the present.

It was several moments before our breaths settled, before he brushed his thumb over my cheek, tucked it beneath my chin and lifted so he could brush his lips over mine. "I knew it'd be good, but that was incredible."

After our first round, I'd gone to the restroom. Dominick had taken care of the condom and cleaned himself off. When he returned to the bedroom, he'd grabbed my hips, yanked me to the edge of the bed and sank to his knees on the floor.

"Now we play." And play we had, for hours more he took me to the precipice and then over, until I cried out no more, laughed while I pushed him off me.

Now, we were back in my bed. Dominick was on his back, holding me pressed to his side beneath the covers where after getting cleaned up for the last time, I forewent getting re-dressed, only slipping into a pair of clean underwear. My hand was settled at the sparse smattering of hair at his chest. His body was so warm, my personal electric blanket.

My thoughts had drifted back to the night. Perhaps the best I'd had since I could remember.

"What was with the looks from Kane tonight?"

His hand, which had been drifting down my back and up to my shoulders to play with my hair, stopped. "What looks?"

"I don't know. It seemed he kept looking at you funny."

He chuckled, and I pushed up to my elbow only to see his smile in the dim light. "That's just his face."

"That's not what I mean."

"I know." He hugged me to him, pulled me so I was draped over his chest, palmed the back of my head against him, and kissed my temple. A flutter of warmth, but peace, slid through me and I hugged him closer.

"Kane's divorced. Said he lost a good woman. He just told me once if I found a good woman to ensure I did everything I could to take care of her so I didn't end up making his mistakes."

As he spoke, his lips brushed against my skin, warming me in a different way.

"Oh."

"Yeah. I think tonight he was just trying to remind me of that. Also approving of the woman I found."

Oh. That felt nice, but I knew Dominick too well by now. He wouldn't have liked either admitting it, or someone being happy for him. "Not that you need anyone's approval."

"Psh. Of course not." His chest shook with silent laughter. "Except for maybe yours. I don't want to mess this up, and I know we're just still getting to know each other, but I like the way I feel with you. I haven't felt it in a long time, so I'm with Kane, I want to make sure I'm always giving you everything you need."

Damn him.

I pressed a kiss to his chest, his collarbone. "No one's taken care of me in a long time, or really, cared about what was important to me. Trust me, you're already giving me that by simply respecting me."

"You deserve more than the bare minimum."

I closed my eyes, allowed his words to wash over me. He was

absolutely right. I deserved way more than the bare minimum of respect. I fell asleep praying with all my might Dominick could end up being that guy for me in the future, because I was only starting to scratch the surface of his depths, but I was falling for every new layer I discovered.

26

DOMINICK

"Fuck," I groaned into Holly's ear, where I was bent over her from behind. Every damn inch of this woman was perfection. From the way she woke up first this morning, her hand slipping down my stomach. I woke with a start, almost reaching to stop her, so surprised to even be waking up next to a woman.

But once I discovered what she was doing, her fingers gently teasing the band at my boxer briefs before dipping beneath, I'd quickly taken over.

I flipped her, kissed her mouth before sliding down and taking her with mine at her sex, and after she came, hands tugging my hair so hard I was sure I had scalp bruises, maybe lost a chunk of hair I didn't give a shit about, I'd flipped her to her stomach, yanked at her hips.

She'd spread instantly, perfectly, and once I reached around for the spare condoms on the nightstand, I slammed deep inside her, her head shot back, crying out with such extreme pleasure I had to fight against coming before I'd barely slipped inside.

"God. You feel so good taking me like this."

Her hands clawed at the sheets, even as she thrust back against me. This was why I'd just had the best night of sex. She didn't *take* what I gave, she gave back. In everything she did, Holly gave back to me. Sex with her was no different, because even while I was fucking her, she was getting me there too with her lack of inhibition and vivaciousness.

One of her hands slid beneath her and I reached down, slapped her hand away.

"Mine," I all but growled against her shoulder. And what the fuck? But as my fingers felt the slickness of her clit, seeping from her, a possessiveness I didn't know I had in me took over, and soon my fingers were working her there, my dick so deep inside of her as she stretched around me, and she came.

"Dominick." My name was a guttural sound from her throat and hot damn *yes*. Nothing beat this.

As she clenched around me, I kept rubbing her through her orgasm as her walls clamped down around me and I had to grit my teeth to keep from coming, but one more.

Just one more damn time I wanted to hear my name on her lips as she came.

"Can't," she panted, digging into sheets and arching her back.

"You can." I slipped my hand from her front, and brought it back, pushing off her, I grabbed both her hips, spread her cheeks, and as I did, she moaned into the pillows.

"Ohhh... that's..."

I pressed my thumb to her puckered hole.

"Yes."

Hot damn. I knew she'd be up for anything. Using her slickness, I rubbed my fingers against her ass, her whimpers turned more feral with every ounce of pressure I put on her until my finger slipped inside.

As I did, she bucked so hard I almost slid out of her and tightened my grip at her hip.

"You okay?" Because I wanted to pleasure her more than she'd ever felt before, not hurt her or scare her.

"Yes, please. More."

All right then. I pushed my finger into her deeper, relished the sounds that fell from her throat, and as I used both of her holes, one most women would never allow, she came again.

She screamed my name so loud I was damn certain Evan could have heard and *fuck yes* I hoped he did. Knew without a doubt, Holly had never been like this for him.

As her orgasm washed through her, her entire body flushed and trembled, and she whimpered my name, I pulled out and flipped her over.

Hair went in all directions and glazed eyes peered up at me, blinked.

"Wanted to see your face when I came," I said, barely able to hold back for another second. I slid back inside her slick heat and shoved a hand beneath her to lift her hips. My orgasm rushed through me, straight to my balls and the tip of my dick, and I groaned out her name along with a string of cuss words right before I unloaded deep inside of her.

"Shit." My head fell forward and her hands came up, lazily tangling in my hair almost as long as hers. She tugged me down until I brushed my lips over hers.

"I've always wanted to try that, what you did..."

"You liked it."

"Loved it," she agreed, her lips lifting to a grin against mine. "I used a toy there, once."

Oh the visions and ideas that gave me. Me inside of her, her toy in another. Switching them off to figure out what she'd love the most.

"You never trusted Evan enough to ask," I said, and I hated I brought him up, but he was her past. Her only.

"I suppose not." The pleasure dimmed from her eyes for a moment before returning. She slid her hand from my hair to my cheek. "But I trust you."

And hot damn, didn't that feel like winning a playoff game.

"You have a game today at three?"

It was after the best morning sex of my life, after we showered, separately even though I wanted to join her, but she hadn't asked and I didn't know if she'd feel comfortable, so while Holly was showering, I found her coffee pot and coffee downstairs and brought a mug up to her when she was out.

She laughed at the small amount of creamer I put in a bowl along with a spoon and another tiny bowl of sugar. "Just a splash of cream," she'd said, grinning. "For future reference."

"Got it." I'd had my own mug, black, and sipped from it, while she hers, and then I'd kicked her out of the bathroom so I could get to my own shower.

Now, we were dressed, me in the clothes from yesterday, her in a pair of leggings that cupped her ass so perfectly, it was difficult not to stare. She was getting ready to go get Ben from Tanner's and I needed to get things done before my game.

"Yeah, games are always early on Sunday. I have to go see Lucy this morning."

"How is that? For you, I mean, to see her there."

"Better than seeing her outside a rehab center."

Her face fell, and I felt like a dick. She was only trying to get to know me, and I'd just told her last night I wanted to give her everything. That meant, at the very least, honesty. "It sucks and it's hard, but she's doing better. It's just a long road and hard to get my hopes up after all these years."

"I'm sorry." She closed the space and settled her hand at my arm before resting her forehead at my chest. Those two small touches were everything, and so I wrapped her in my arms and held her to me. When had I ever had someone to comfort me when this shit got hard?

Never. Not once had I allowed someone to be there for me.

"You can call me, you know, if you need to talk before your game. I'll just be here with Ben."

I opened my mouth to tell her I wouldn't need it.

Three weeks ago that might have been true, but that was me still believing the lie I didn't need, or care about, anyone.

I squeezed her tighter and kissed the top of her head. I'd always gone for women with long legs and big tits who were my height. Granted, I'd never looked for a woman to date, but I actually really liked Holly's smaller stature. The way she tucked her body up against mine, her head right beneath my chin. Almost like she could curl right into me while I protected her.

She fit. I wanted to keep her.

"I'll call if it's hard. Some days are better than others and there are days where I want to scream at her for still thinking Gloria cares about us."

"I'm sorry you've had to go through all this alone."

A burn heated my chest, sent an ache to my stomach. I probably hadn't *needed* to go it alone. I just chose to.

But I figured finding Holly, opening up to her, was the perfect woman to start that journey with. And hell, even the guys on the team had taken it in stride so far. Too bad I wasted so much time.

But I could do better from here on out.

Learning. Healing.

Dad would be happy about that.

I heaved another sigh, that burn in my chest traveling to my throat, and pressed my lips to her soft hair. She tilted up, rolled to her toes until her lips met mine. I kept the kiss slow despite the desire for more.

I really did need to get going.

"Tell Ben today," I reminded her. "Whatever you think he needs to know or would be okay with, I'll understand."

"You silly man. He already loves you. I tell him we're spending time together and he might explode."

"Well, we wouldn't want that."

She slapped my chest and pulled out of my arms. "Go. See Lucy. Call me if you need to, and then go kick some serious ass at your game later. Ben and I will be watching."

Yeah... I liked hearing that.

THE CHANGE in Lucy over the last week was more than impressive. I almost couldn't believe my eyes when I stepped into her room and she was wearing the standard issued lounge pants, but she had some soft makeup on, hair curled. Her smile was wide as soon as I entered and she'd scrambled off the bed.

"Nicky! You came!" She threw her arms around me and I lifted her, swung her on instinct.

"How's it going, Luce?"

"Great." And she looked it. "I thought we could go for a walk today."

A walk? There were some days I'd have to drag her out of her room. I would definitely take a walk outside, enjoy some fresh air. It'd be good for both of us.

She slipped her arm through mine and we headed out of the building, down her hall to the cafeteria and out the back door. "Where are you taking us?"

"The horses. I want you to meet Nike."

"Nike? Like the shoe?"

She nodded eagerly. Happily. The best part of Lucy was her bubbly personality. It'd been so long since I'd seen this bounce in her step I couldn't remember. "Yes, but before she was a sports brand, she apparently was the goddess of Victory. Penny, my equine therapist, taught me that." We followed the trails, through gardens and covered porticos I knew housed picnic areas and outdoor yoga classes. "I also learned all the horses here came from rescues. Some were racehorses who broke their legs and were given up on, some were abused, beaten. Some were just neglected."

As she spoke, the excitement dimmed. I gave her space. She could be affected by anything, but as we kept walking, she squeezed my arm and rested her head against my shoulder. "Some of them remind me of me."

"Luce..." A claw scratched at my throat.

"It's okay," she said. "They're making me face things. Slowly, but this is the first place that hasn't let me get away with saying I don't want to talk about things. I think they're helping... untwist things in my brain."

Damn. It was so, so damn good to hear that. I tempered my excitement, tried to main realistic hope.

We grew close to the barn, the bright white painted fences, and Lucy strolled right to the barn. "Come on. I get to feed Nike snacks whenever I want unless she's out on a ride. I want you to meet her."

She talked about her like she was her friend. I'd never seen a horse up close and personal, wasn't really an animal person at all. We'd never had pets growing up and the frisky or needy way dogs pawed at you irritated me. The stubborn attitude of cats annoyed me. Lucy led me into the barn, the whole time talking about all the things she'd learned about horses. The trust required, the patience. She taught me about the tack room, how they had to brush and bathe the horses, feed them, and muck out their stalls.

She scrunched her nose. "That's the worst part. Some of the women here won't even sign up for this because of it, but it's been my favorite so far."

It didn't surprise me. Lucy could probably get the meanest, snarliest animal to love her, she was so gentle.

"Yeah. I'd have to side with them." The barn reeked. Animal shit and waste, hay. It was damp and a few windows were open leaving very little airflow, but it was cool, so that was something.

After striding down the long row of stalls, Lucy grabbed my hand and pulled us to a stop.

"She's an Arabian. Apparently she was beaten every day with whips. The owners found her wild and tried to break her, but they never could, so one day, the owner just dumped her on the side of the road. Strangers found her tangled in a barbed wire fence. That's why she has all the cuts on her body and face."

I'd been so lost in her story, the ache in her voice, I hadn't looked at the horse, but the scar she pointed to was obvious. Crooked slash through her eye. Chunks of fur missing from her sides. Angry scar-like marks crisscrossed over and around one of her front legs.

At the sight of us, the horse neighed and stepped back.

"She doesn't like strangers," Lucy said in a voice so soft I'd never heard it before. "And she doesn't really like men, so maybe this wasn't the smartest idea, but if you stay still and calm, I can get her to come to me."

I'd also never heard her sound so certain.

The horse stomped its hooves, backed up farther. Her head swung from Lucy to me, back to Lucy with a shake of her head. Pretty sure that horse was telling Lucy to get me the fuck away from her.

Lucy chuckled, and brushed her hand gently, slowly, over the top of the door. "It's okay, Nike. I've told you all about Nicky, remember? He's always there for me, the best guy. Remember how I told you?"

Damn it. I sniffed and curled my nose. I couldn't even lie to myself and blame the smell of horse shit.

"Stay right there and be still," Lucy said, not looking at me.

Like I could move. This was an entirely new side of my sister.

She stepped away and the horse let out a loud sound, stomped in a circle. The tail swished violently before Lucy came back.

"Hey, Nike. Treats, right? I've got carrots and apples for you." She wiggled a carrot out toward the horse but she was having none of it. The last thing I wanted was Lucy to be disappointed by a horse.

"We can go, Luce."

"No. She'll come to me. She just needs time. The poor girl has been through a lot, you know."

I knew. I knew she wasn't talking about the horse, either.

So we stood there, the carrot slowly moving back and forth, the horse stomping.

For her part, Lucy's smile never wobbled.

"I don't want to see her. Mom," she said. And it was so abrupt, but still in that tone she used with the horse.

She'd also never said it before.

"Yeah?" Because I couldn't push.

"In some of my therapy, I'm learning things. About Mom." She focused on the carrot and looked to Nike. "I don't... I don't think she was nice to me."

She wasn't. She'd been horrific. Did things no mother should do.

Still, I stayed silent. If she was processing, she didn't need my pushing. Part of Lucy's healing needed to be doing the work herself —something I was recently learning.

"She should have been there for me. Taken care of me and protected me. Protected us after Dad died."

"Yup." My throat closed up.

"I don't think I like her for not doing that."

"It's okay to not like her but still love her," I said, only because I knew she needed to hear it. Needed to understand it was okay to be conflicted. Hell, I had been for a long time.

Slowly, her eyes lifted and she blinked. "I want to stay clean this time. For good. I really mean it and I don't think I can do that and be around Mom."

As she said it, the horse stepped closer. She sashayed to the side like she was trying to stay away from me, but as tears fell down Lucy's cheeks, Nike came another step. Then another. I stared, riveted, at how that horse seemed to know exactly what my sister needed. Nike lowered her head, took the carrot straight from Lucy's hand and then nudged that hand with her nose.

"I know, girl, I know. Sometimes people are mean, aren't they?"

Goddamn. I wanted to throw my arms around her, but I was terrified of that horse. She stayed though, let Lucy love on her with long, sweeping brushes up and down her nose, her side, her front flank. Eventually the horse met my eyes, swear that thing stared right at me and then she lowered her head toward me.

"She wants you to pet her. She's trusting you."

I'd rather meet Selkin again on the ice than pet this damn horse. But I rose my hand and touched it anyway.

So we stood there, petting the damn horse that occasionally bumped Lucy's hand in a silent plea for more treats, because Lucy kept feeding her when she did it, and I listened to my sister talk about some of the horror she survived, worse than things I'd known about.

"I will do whatever, absolutely whatever, you need to help you."

"I know," she cried. Hell, we were both sobbing, quietly, so not to spook Nike, but both of our cheeks were soaked with tears. "You've always been there for me, in the way Mom should have been."

Fucking hell. More damn tears. Maybe, just maybe Dad wasn't disappointed in me after all.

"Always," I told her.

"I NEED TO SEE YOU. After my game tonight. Can you come to my place?"

It wasn't nice. It wasn't mean. I was desperate for something good and pure and that was Holly. I needed to unload, and she'd listen.

"I can be there in twenty minutes if you need me now," she said.

No question. No pause.

She knew.

God, I'd love to see her. Almost wished I wouldn't have given those tickets to Mike because I would have loved to play knowing she was there watching. But I could wait. I had to. I'd shove it down and unload it all on her later, and she wouldn't be bothered by it.

In fact, I figured Holly would love to be needed.

"No, it's okay, and... it's all good, really, but is Ben going to his dad's tonight?"

"Yeah. He's getting ready now."

"Will you come to my place?"

I should have already been in the locker room, seeing the massage therapist to loosen up, doing a quick warm-up workout. I should have been at the very least, inside the building, but after I finally pulled myself away from Lucy, I hopped on the interstate and drove. Until I realized I was running late.

But I'd needed a minute. We stood in front of the horse, talking to each other, almost like she needed the horse's strength, comfort, and possibly its own recovery to open up to me. I'd never witnessed her like that, so strong and brave, so *awake* and aware of her life and what she'd experienced, how Mom treated her, and what she wanted to do now.

I'd never been so proud of her.

I'd never cried so hard.

I'd never needed to share it with someone else or have them hold on to hope with me.

"Of course I'll be there," Holly said. "Text me your address."

In addition to everything else, I had a bed I was desperate to see her in. Although compared to her home, mine was anything but a home. It had walls. Lots of them with windows overlooking the city. All white. Furniture I'd dropped a shit ton on, all black. Some glass coffee tables.

I'd walked into a furniture store, found a living room and bedroom set up type thing that didn't have a hint of color, pointed to it, and said, "I want that." No thought. In and out in fifteen minutes and ten of those was the paperwork.

The only picture I had was Lucy, and that was in my bedroom.

I didn't even own a dining room table. Why would I need one when it was always just me?

Holly would probably hate it. Feel bad for me.

I still wanted her to see my place. Spend time in it with me. Maybe this summer Ben and I could hang out in the pool outside. I could grill for them on one of the outdoor decks.

"I will. And Holly?"

"I'm right here." Steady. Probably frowning with worry for me. Who knew what she heard in my voice but it was still raspy.

"Thank you."

27

HOLLY

I left for Dominick's when the game went into intermission before the third period. It was a strange feeling, watching the guy I was dating playing on television and then two minutes later driving to his condo, toward the address of one of the highest condo buildings in Las Vegas. And expensive, because I couldn't stop my curiosity. The smallest studio in the building was currently listed at $750,000.

I doubted Dominick lived in a studio. He didn't strike me as the kind of guy who would do well in a small space.

Still, my fingers tingled around my steering wheel as I followed my GPS toward his building. I was going to his house. His *home*. A place I doubted he invited many. He valued his privacy too much and yet he'd called.

I need to see you.

Of course I'd be there for him. Probably early, before his game was done or before he'd leave the arena and then there'd be the post-game stuff he went through.

Hell, maybe I should have waited. Too late to back out now because his building loomed in the distance, two twin towers which I already knew would have views of the Strip or the mountains, or both, depending on the location. Balconies curved out, some three times as large as others.

Why was I so nervous?

Because it was Dominick, and he wouldn't have admitted to needing anyone.

And he'd called me.

My GPS alerted me I arrived at my destination but I already knew and was pulling into the main parking lot, headed toward the second building and came to a spot in front of the covered doors. The building looked more five-star hotel than condo living and before I even parked there was a doorman at the door.

"Good evening, miss."

"Hi. Holly Byers, here to see Dominick Masters."

"Of course. Mr. Masters said to expect you. Would you like me to park your car or would you prefer the spot in the underground parking he requested for you?"

Wow. Well, heck. I'd just figured I'd park myself, but… "Valet would be wonderful. Thank you." I handed him my keys, waited until he returned with my ticket. "Please, head inside and to the right. Sabrina will be able to help you further."

"Thank you."

This was all… not at all what I was used to and I blew out a breath, brushed my hands down the loose-fitting skirt I'd thrown on. Nothing special, but it was the nicest I'd looked for Dominick. The weather was gorgeous and so my navy skirt with a cream, light-weight sweater felt appropriate earlier.

Now, was it too much? Not enough? Hell, he'd come home from the game and be worn out, both from the game and his time with Lucy, I figured.

Shit. Too late to back out now, the valet was already sliding into my driver's seat and pulling away.

I stepped inside, tucked a chunk of curled hair behind my ear, and adjusted my purse strap. Sabrina, I figured, because she was the only woman behind a large desk with the words Concierge Area in gold in front of it, was already there, smiling at me.

A gorgeous smile with a beautiful face and hair I'd need to spend thousands of dollars on extensions on greeted me as I headed toward her.

"Good evening, how can I help you?"

"I'm a guest of Dominick Masters. Holly. The valet, said..."

"Of course. Mr. Masters called and said he was expecting company. I just need to see your identification please to verify and then you can head up and wait for him."

Wait for him? In his *home*? Oh...

I fumbled with my purse, wallet and sweaty finger slipped from my driver's license three times before I managed to dig it out of the plastic. If Sabrina noticed, she was professional enough not to comment, and with a few taps of her fingers on her keyboard, she was handing me back my license as well as a key card.

"There's a security code for residents, but we don't give those out. This card will get you into Mr. Master's residence, as well, though."

"Thank you."

I took both cards, looked at the blank card I'd hoped would give me further guidance. "Um. What room?"

"2418. Elevators are around the corner there." She pointed behind me, through the marble floored lobby with gorgeous floral plantings on every table surface. "If there's anything you need before Mr. Masters returns, please don't hesitate to call down, although he did request a delivery earlier so everything should be stocked."

Uh... what?

I hid my surprise, thanked Sabrina, and my sandals tapped across the tile as I headed toward the elevators. What kind of delivery had he ordered?

The doors opened immediately and another burst of nerves hit me. There were only twenty-four floors. Of course he'd have the top floor. He wouldn't want anyone on top of him, making noise. That shouldn't have surprised me at all so I tapped the button and was quickly whisked in the open glass elevator giving me a quick view of the city, the Strip, and the red mountains beyond as the elevator zipped me to the top. My stomach flipped once the elevator stopped and I stepped out, the quick rise of the lift giving me a slight waver of motion sickness. The hall was long, much like a hotel with signs on walls pointing the way, so I followed them straight to the end of one hall and again, not surprised.

In fact, outside that Dominick lived on the top floor of this complex, the fact he'd allow himself to have neighbors at all was the only surprising thing so far. I'd almost pictured him on some massive acreage estate, gated and closed off for as much as he claimed he didn't like people in his business.

I slid the card into the slot beneath the keypad Sabrina told me about and then I was opening his door, immediately struck by the glamour of Dominick's home, as well as the starkness of it. Straight ahead of me, through the enormous, curved wall and all marble tile floor was a balcony large enough to host his entire team. Everything gleamed like it was brand new, possibly not at all lived in. There wasn't a single personal effect anywhere. A huge, black leather sectional sat on one wall, facing a television that could have been a movie screen, it was so large, on the opposite wall. Glass tables on both sides and the center of the table. A thick, gray blanket draped over one corner of the couch was the only non-necessity, slight decoration.

No rug.

No artwork.

My feet echoed as I entered and I kicked off my sandals, almost too scared to enter further. He'd obviously known I could arrive before he did, given the care he'd taken to make sure I could enter his home. But this was... well... so much more bare than I'd been expecting.

There wasn't even a jersey of his, framed and hung, and didn't all athletes proudly display their victories or accomplishments. But no—that wasn't Dominick. I prevented myself from snooping further. I could grab my phone and pull up my Kindle app and read on his balcony until he returned. Turning to set my purse on the island, I noticed a single piece of paper and pen. My name at the top.

I reached for it, the pen rolling across the granite surface.

Holly,

If you get here before me, make yourself comfortable, such as it is.

Wine in the fridge for your nerves.

Help yourself.

See you soon

-D.

A CHUCKLE, nervous—as predicted by Dominick—escaped me.

"It's like he knows me," I muttered to the note, brushing my fingers across his writing. It was masculine but neat and legible. Straight lines, no angle or slant. So very much like him—perfect and restrained.

Curious, I skipped around the island and opened the fridge. To my utter shock, next to the fridge were two bottles of red. Inside the fridge, already chilling were two bottles of white.

All four bottles, different brands, all kinds I had in my own home.

My knees wobbled.

I'd never once caught him paying attention to what I drink. What I liked, and yet he'd nailed it all including the vanilla creamer, the brand I had at home set right next to the wine.

My grip on the fridge door tightened. It was such a small thing.

So huge at the same time, and I was in massive trouble. It wasn't the bottles of wine or the brand of creamer.

It was that we'd spent so little time together, and he'd paid so close attention to me. Noticed everything, even knew I'd be nervous being here. He was a man who noticed the small things and then acted on them because the small things were sometimes the most important.

I was pretty sure it was that moment I knew...

I was head over heels, spinning out of control like Ben in starfish mode on the ice, falling for this man.

Dominick entered his home almost thirty minutes later. I'd taken a seat outside, angled a chair on his balcony—surprised at all he had furniture out there based on the emptiness of the rest of the place —so I could see him when he'd entered. I'd propped my feet on another chair and tucked into a book, but I hadn't paid a single attention to the crime thriller I would usually lose myself in.

I'd been too nervous, waiting for him, but that view—I could sit out here forever and never grow bored. If I looked in one direction, the Strat and SkyPod observation tower gleamed in the distance. In the other direction were mountains. The city zipped along beneath me. It was peaceful up there, facing west with the sun slowly descending over the horizon. The slight breeze had sent me inside earlier to grab his blanket, so that was how Dominick saw me as soon as he entered.

Tucked into his blanket on his balcony, phone in one hand, glass of wine in the other.

He brushed his hand over his mouth, down his beard, and then tossed his keys to the island, kicked off his shoes, and before I could move inside to greet him, he was sliding open the doors and stepped out on the balcony. His hands went to the sides of his chair, pinning me in place.

Eyes, dark swirls of emotion, peered down at me. "I don't think I've ever seen a better view, in my entire life, until I walked in and saw you right here."

"Oh..." I breathed out, and then his lips were on mine, firm, seeking, and of course, I opened for him, sinking back into the chair as he followed me, kissing me like he'd been starving for the taste of me.

His hand slid to my neck, held me against him as he kissed me, his chest heaving and his breathing heavy and quick enough to match mine.

I couldn't touch him back without dropping my phone or wine, so I stayed still and let him lead the kiss until he slowly ended it and receded, grinning as I blinked up at him.

"Hey."

He chuckled with a slight grin and brushed his thumb over my cheek. "Hey yourself. I'm glad you're here."

"I got that." I grinned back before remembering why I was here. "Are you okay?"

"Yeah." He drawled the words so quietly, with a deep rumble I felt down to my toes. "We won the game. Need a refill?"

I shouldn't. I needed some food, but Dominick slipped the glass from my hand. "I'll get you some. I need some water and a protein shake and then we'll order food while I tell you about Lucy."

"Okay." I went to stand with him, but he shook his head. "Stay here. I'll be back in a minute."

He returned quickly, a glass of wine and water in one hand, something green and sludgy in another glass.

"That looks like vomit."

"Tastes only half as bad, but it's good for me after a game."

"Congrats on the win."

"Felt good after the loss, played well. Maybe better than usual."

I doubted Dominick ever talked himself up like that. "That's good then."

He took the chair next to me, kicked his feet up, and crossed his ankles on the chair where mine still was, and he fixed the blanket over both our legs.

His free hand settled at my thigh and I stared at his fingers, long and thick, covering and curling over the sides of my leg with a soft grip. "It feels good when I'm out on the ice to be playing and knowing there are people who care about me watching. I haven't had that in a long time."

My throat closed and I took a sip of my wine. I focused on him, the sharp line of his jaw, the crooked bend in his nose I had no doubt was from a fistfight. The full lips with the deep groove in the center of his top one. He stared out to the horizon.

I waited for him to tell me about Lucy, but then I realized, he was *relaxed*. For a man who hadn't had it easy, it warmed my chest to know I gave that to him, so I settled back into the chair, angled toward him so my shoulder was as close to his as I could get and sipped my wine while he drank his smoothie before switching to his water.

"Lucy," he finally said, several minutes later. "I've never seen her doing so well, so early in therapy."

My grip tightened on my wineglass. "That's good, right?"

"It's amazing. And scary. She's never…" He swallowed thickly. "She's always loved our mom, always said even when she was clean that Mom had tried to do right by us after Dad died. She's always thought Mom would someday get clean, then help Lucy. I have no idea how my sister could think such things with all the shit Mom did to her, *made* her do for drug money, but she did."

I couldn't picture his sister, didn't know if she looked like him or the total opposite, but the pain reverberating in his voice *hurt* to listen to.

"Today, she told me she didn't think she liked Gloria all that much and I have to say, I couldn't have been prouder for it."

He turned to me then, eyes wet with unshed tears and a fear in his eyes I couldn't place.

"Does that make me a monster? I'm *glad* my sister doesn't like our mom. What kind of man does that make me?"

"The best kind," I said, no hesitation. He was. He only had to see it. "Your mom was too weak to step up when she needed to. She threw Lucy into this life. She caused the damage. I can see, how maybe for Lucy, while going through the horrors I don't need the specifics of, she needed to hold on to that hope to get her through it, but I think it's okay to hate a woman who'd cause it. Parents are supposed to protect and take care of their children. Anyone who throws them to the wolves is no parent in my book."

I certainly could never fathom my parents or any parent I knew growing up, not fighting to the death to take care of their children.

He ran a hand through his hair. And then he started talking. He told me about Lucy when they were little, how their dad was with them. He told me about growing up with her, never getting annoyed with her like other siblings did with their little brothers or sisters. And then he told me about the first time he learned what was going on in his home, beyond the drugs. The men who'd forced him out of his own home, Lucy crying inside. Calling the cops, Lucy not pressing charges because it'd make her mom upset. Then where would she go. Helping her get clean. He talked until the sun had set, my glass of wine long gone. He talked until my stomach rumbled and then he took me inside.

We ordered dinner.

He kept talking.

And by the time we were exhausted, he took me to his room. We got ready for bed together and I slid into his warm, gray sheets and curled my body around him.

His arm wrapped around me, my head at his chest, I slid my hand over his stomach and squeezed him to me.

"I didn't mean to unload all of that on to you," he admitted. His lips at the top of my head.

"I'm glad you did. Glad you felt like you could trust me enough with it."

"I think I might trust you more than anyone I'd ever met. How did that happen so fast?"

"I don't know. But I feel the same way about you. I've been around shitty men, lived with him. I know a great one when I see it, and it's you. You just need to start seeing what everyone else does."

He was quiet for a while, several moments where it was just our breaths and his air-conditioner the only noise.

"I'm starting to," he finally said, voice raspy. "And in case you don't know, I'm starting to care about you, and Ben, more than I thought possible. Feels good."

My heart leapt and fluttered wildly. "I'm glad," I whispered and placed a soft kiss to his cheek.

In fact, I wasn't sure I'd ever been happier. At least, not in years.

28

HOLLY

The emotion of last night, the sweetness of waking up with Dominick that morning—even with no sex involved, mostly because he had an early practice and needed to get going—I was certain would stay with me all day.

That hope popped like a balloon when I pulled into my driveway and found Kristi, of all people, sitting on my front porch.

"What's wrong?" I jumped out of my SUV, barely throwing it into park. "Is it Ben?"

He should have been dropped off at school an hour ago.

"No. No. Ben's fine. Everything's okay."

She stood to her feet as I rushed toward her, frantic with worry, and then abruptly stopped. My gaze flicked to her home and back to her. She was dressed in leggings and a sweatshirt. Running shoes on her feet. No makeup.

All the markings of a Kristi I rarely saw, even when we were friends.

"Then why are you here?" Because if it wasn't Ben, hell—maybe, even Evan—we had nothing to say to another.

"I came to tell you I'm sorry."

Or... there was that.

"Pardon me?" I crossed my arms over my chest. She'd had over a *year* to say those words to me, to show any remorse for playing her own part in ruining my marriage.

Kristi flinched. "I'm sorry, Holly. For everything. I'm so sorry for everything I did with Evan, for making choices that hurt you and Ben. I..." She shook her head. "I don't know if my excuses would be helpful."

"Oh no," I said. "If we're doing this, we're doing it. You were my friend. I thought a part of our family, and you *fucked* my husband. So yeah... I think I should hear this."

Maybe. Maybe I'd hate myself for it later.

"They all suck. But I was lonely, and Evan was always so good to you and I'd never had that. And yeah, I wanted a shot at feeling like you did and I wasn't finding it dating, because well, men suck and are stupid." She tried for a joke.

It fell flat at the cement drive between us. I'd told her that frequently when we laughed about her crappy dates, or guys who ghosted her, or guys she ditched.

"So you stole mine?"

Not that it was her fault, Evan and his arrogance was obviously amendable to being stolen.

"I'm really sorry. I've felt so guilty for a long time, and I thought I had it, but..."

Ahhh. This was starting to all make sense.

"Let me guess. You learned that even with Evan, men still suck and are stupid."

She rolled her lips together, pressed lips formed a half-smile. She glanced back at their house and then to me. "I'm moving. To Arizona."

"Excuse me?" A small breeze could have knocked me over. "You're... what?"

"I took a job as a travel nurse, and my first assignment is in Phoenix." She stopped and bit her lip. "Evan's not coming with me."

Oh, holy shit... I could not wait to tell Karly *this* news. Right after I told Dominick. This explained *everything* from Evan's behavior in the last few weeks.

"You broke up with him."

She nodded. "I've given him two weeks to find a place and move out. I figured this week with Ben would be hard, so I said he could have next week to be fully out, but yeah. I'm going to list my house in a few weeks. I won't need it, or I don't know, I might rent a studio apartment somewhere when I'm in between assignments." She shrugged. "I haven't figured it out yet, but well, I'm sorry. Again, and I wanted you to know because I know Evan's been talking to you lately..."

"I'm not taking him back," I said, if that was what she was implying.

"Good. I think we both deserve better, I'm just sorry I never saw that earlier, and I was that horrible to you. I've learned, well, a lot about myself in the last year and a lot of it's been ugly things I never wanted to see."

Wow. So much for a light breeze. A feather could have sent me to the ground.

I shook my head, tried to clear it, but there was so much. Evan would be forced to move. I wouldn't have to see him every day. But then Ben couldn't see his dad whenever he wanted. I no longer had to see them make out, or Evan with anyone.

So much of this was such fantastic news I wanted to celebrate.

"Does Ben know?" I asked.

"He heard us fighting this morning. I tried to stop it, but well, I'd told Evan last week. He knew I was going to Phoenix for the interview, one I'd been thinking about for a while. I don't know what he thought—"

That was Evan. He was probably only thinking of himself and his wants. No one else.

"How is he? Ben."

"He was pretty worked up when Evan took him to school. I thought you should know in case Evan will want to switch weeks or, whatever, I don't know and I'm sorry, sorry to say this, but it has nothing to do with me anymore."

Selfish as always. "Right, because you've been in Ben's life since he was four and lived with him, and don't think your absence will do anything to do him."

"I know how bad that sounds, Holly, but we also know it's true. Evan and I have been falling apart since before our Hawaii trip. It was my last hope we could work things out, but I can't be with him and Ben's heard enough and felt enough tension. Trust me, he'll be happy we're not together anymore."

I, for one, was thrilled. Except the part about Ben feeling that between them. He'd never said a word to me.

"Okay. I'll handle it." Because that was what I did. Handled Evan's shitty choices and the fallout of them. "Thanks for telling me, I guess."

"I really did care about you. And again, I'm really sorry."

"I'm not. Not anymore."

"What?" Her brows furrowed.

"You and Evan having an affair. I don't care anymore. It showed me the kind of guy he was, the kind of guy I'd rolled myself into believing he was. It showed me the kind of friend you were. Or weren't. Yeah, it hurt, but truthfully, I'm glad for it now." Because if it hadn't happened, I'd still have my head buried. I'd still be with him, walking on eggshells, bending over backward to please a man who would toss me scraps. I deserved better than that.

"Yeah. He plays the nice guy card really well."

I might have been glad my marriage ended, but I was in no way going to commiserate with his mistress.

"Take care, Kristi," I said and walked past her toward my door. I punched in the code and as the door unlocked, she was halfway across the yard. I called her name. "I hope things work out for you. That you find what you're looking for."

"Thanks. You too."

Funny. I was pretty sure I already had.

"You can come here if you need to," I told Ben through the phone. I'd called him right after school, fought the urge to stomp across the lawns and demand he returned home. "I can talk to your dad if it gets too much."

"It's okay. Kristi's staying with friends, I guess, or something, so it's just Dad and me. It's not bad."

It's not bad. As if that sounded like a great time with his dad. "If you change your mind, it's okay. And I'll talk to your dad about taking you to practice tomorrow, make sure he wasn't planning on it." Not that he usually did, but if his world was again imploding, he might. "And I need to talk to you about something anyway."

"You're dating Dominick?"

"Um. What?"

"Dad already told me. Said if you weren't going to be honest with me, he should be."

"Right." I gritted my teeth. What a fucking dick.

"But it's not like I couldn't tell. He looks at you funny."

As my anger pulsed at Evan's manipulating bullshit, I still smiled. "What do you mean by funny?"

"I dunno. He smiles weird. And I'm ten, not dumb. He pays more attention to me and you than anyone else. I already knew he liked you."

"Okay... how do you feel about that?"

"He's Dominick Masters. You could do worse."

I laughed. This kid. "I love you, kiddo."

"Love you too, Mom."

"Call me if you need me."

"Will do. Bye."

I was still partly fuming, mostly laughing. Screw Evan.

I didn't even care where he ended up as long as it wasn't on this street. Until he learned how to be an adult with real communication skills and a halfway decent heart, he'd always end up alone, miserable, and probably blaming it on everyone else.

Outside of having to deal with him for Ben's sake, I wasn't wasting any more mental space with him.

Except to start planning a party once he officially moved out.

"No shit?" Dom's brows rose on his forehead. I'd just told him the news, waited a whole thirty seconds after he stepped through my front door after he got here. Something I hadn't planned on but when he called while I was eating dinner alone, couldn't fathom saying no to.

As soon as he walked in, I grabbed his hand and pulled him to the couch where we were still sitting, me on my knees facing him, him curled toward me in one corner, knee bent on the cushion, other foot on the floor.

"Yup. Kristi told me herself. It's still her home and she's selling it. Evan has to be out by the end of next week."

"Damn." He scratched his jaw. "I'm glad he's gone, but how big of a dick will he be to you?"

"Time will tell. His office is thirty minutes north of here, in decent traffic. He used to complain a lot about wishing we lived closer, so I'm hoping he does that."

"So, two more weeks, unless he doesn't decide to be an epic ass and buy Kristi's home, and then you don't have to see him daily anymore."

"Oh God. I hadn't thought he'd do that." My eyes widened and Dom laughed. It was this deep rumble, a little rusty, like he was still getting used to doing it. "Enough. He's taken up enough of my day and I haven't even seen him. Tell me about practice. Your week ahead."

"Skate tomorrow, practice with the kids, and then we're gone until Sunday."

"Where to this time?" I should probably print off his schedule. You know, if we were really going to be a *thing* or something.

"Colorado, down to Houston, up to Dallas. We'll fly back Saturday night which means I'll miss the kids' game this weekend, and that sucks after last weekend's loss, and then we play St. Louis at home on Monday."

My heart squeezed as he mentioned the boys. And I still couldn't believe how much traveling he did.

"Ben will be back home Sunday," I said. "Maybe we could do something together then?"

"I'd like that." He grinned and reached toward me. His hands wrapped around my waist and he plucked me off the couch with ease until I was straddling him. "I'd like that a lot. Are you sure he seemed okay with this? Us?"

"He said I could do worse." I laughed again. Ben was hilarious. "But I'm not sure I could do better." I smiled down at Dom and kissed the tip of his nose. "I also think this might be the last night we spend alone for quite some time."

"Hmmm." His hand slid up my back to the base of my neck, up into my hair, and applied pressure. "Whatever shall we do?"

"I think you can think of something."

"Definitely. I have a lot of ideas for you."

I let him guide me to him until we were kissing, and then we were standing. Dominick pushing off the couch as if I weighed nothing and wrapped my ankles around his back.

He took me to my room, stripped me out of my clothes, then his, and proceeded to spend the next several hours showing me at least a half dozen ideas he'd had of us.

All of them leaving me breathless, smiling, and most importantly, happy.

29

———

DOMINICK

The parking lot outside the arena was pure madness. I slowed my car to a crawl to maneuver around news vans and trucks, following behind Joey who'd happened to pull in in front of me.

As soon as we pulled into the private parking ramp and parked, we both climbed out. "What the hell is going on?"

"No clue," he said. "Thought maybe you were arrested again."

"Funny." Not even close. "Have I told you that you suck lately?"

"Nope." His brows tugged in as he beeped the locks on his SUV. "Actually, it's been a while since I've heard you tell anyone that. Are you feeling okay?"

Chuckling, I shoved him into his rear bumper. "You suck."

"Better." He threw his arm around me, and I shoved him off. "But it lacks the angry feeling you used to have."

"Shut up, Joey."

"Things going well with the mom, huh?"

"Holly." Why did everyone keep calling her the mom or Ben's mom? She had a fucking name. "And yeah. They're good."

For the first time in a long time, everything in my life was good. Holly, a woman I'd never had considered starting anything with, was the bright spot after a long day. We talked every night last week when I was out of town. As soon as we were done with our morning skate and film time, I was going to head to her house and spend the rest of the day with her and Ben.

It'd be the first time we spent time together outside of hockey. Just us. And now that he knew we were dating, there was an increasing pressure on me not to screw things up.

"Dominick."

It was Coach, standing in the hallway, and next to him was Brandon Mickelson, our team's main PR representative. I pulled to an abrupt stop right along with Joey.

"What is it?"

"You haven't checked your phone?"

"Should I have?" My phone hadn't made a sound all morning. Hell, I didn't even know if it was charged.

Coach glanced at Brandon. It was Joey who stepped up as a cold ice began coating my veins. "What's going on?"

"We should talk," Brandon said. "There some pretty big rumors swirling we need to address."

"Gloria or Crank?" I asked, because I knew. She'd been quiet for too long.

Coach's hands slid to his hips. "Gloria. And Chad Attler. So yeah."

"Fuck." I dropped my head and stared at the cement floor.

What had I been saying? Things were easy? Good?

Of course, it couldn't stay that way. "All right."

Brandon had a door open to one of the team's offices and I followed him in, dropped my workout bag inside the door as soon as I entered.

Behind me, Coach followed, and to my shock, so did Joey.

For a moment, I considered telling him to go, but his bag landed on the floor right next to mine. "I've got your back." He turned to Brandon. "What's going on?"

"Perhaps I should show you."

"Fuck." I shoved my hands through my hair and groaned.

"Who's Gloria?" Joey asked quietly.

Brandon held a remote in his hands and turned on the television mounted on the wall.

"My mother," I replied and stared at the screen as images of Gloria pulled up.

Dressed in the same ratty clothes she always wore, she'd somehow managed to wash and do her hair, apply some decent makeup. She couldn't hide the scars on her face from meth or the yellowing of her teeth. She looked only mildly horrific instead of the complete waste of space I'd become accustomed to. More surprising, her voice and hands were steady, not shaking from withdrawals as she started speaking.

"Yes, my name is Gloria Masters, and my son is Dominick. We were so proud of the man he's become, until recently anyway. His sister and I are worried about him. His assault on that man... well, I think he really needs some help. I don't even know how he's still allowed to play with anger issues like that."

"You have to be fucking kidding me," I growled. I whipped my head toward Vik.

"Gets worse."

As he said it, images flashed on the screen. Then Crank's beaten face, bruises, and bandages on his cheek. The tread marks of my boot along his ribs.

Fuck. *"Fuck!"*

"How in the hell did this happen?"

They were ruining everything. And using Lucy. Jesus Christ, how was this the first I was hearing about this?

"Far as we know, she was brought to the news station early this morning," Brandon said. "Dropped off, but she and Chad Attler entered together and said they had an interview they wanted to give about your violent history of physical abuse."

"Physical abuse?"

"Lucy," Coach said. "In addition to the charges Attler dropped in

December, she claims you beat your sister in a fit of rage that night and that's why she's in a hospital. Recovering. And you've refused access to allow anyone to see her."

"Holy shit," I rasped and reached for a chair. The blood drained from my face as the reality crashed around me.

"The fuck?" Joey said and reached out to me, but I shook him off.

"Let me see." Of course, the goodness in my life wouldn't last. But this had gone too far. Gloria had gone too far. I almost wanted to make sure Lucy was seeing this just so she could see how truly horrific our mom was.

Together, with Joey by my side, I watched the entire interview. All lies except for Attler describing me beating the shit out of him. He just neglected the part where he was Lucy's pimp and had been trying to force her into a threesome that night.

"Her fucking pimp," I growled beneath my breath so only Joey could hear. "That's who he is. Mom made her do it for drugs."

Because hell, the entire fucking world would soon know twisted lies of my horrific past and life. Might as well tell my side to the guy who'd stood by me since the beginning of this train wreck.

"He's the guy I beat the shit out of Christmas Eve, and Lucy isn't in a hospital, recovering from my beating," I continued, narrowing my eyes on Brandon. "She's in a rehab facility, getting clean from the drugs my *mother* forced her to take because she was too damn weak to handle life after our dad died and couldn't bear being alone, so she had Lucy get high with her."

"Oh fucking hell," Joey groaned next to me.

"She was thirteen."

"Shit."

Brandon, for his part, grew emotional, cheeks burned a dark pink. "This is bad," he murmured, and Gloria's face blurred on the screen behind him.

"What do you want? From this?" the reporter asked.

Gloria turned her twisted smile to the cameras and I felt that look right in my gut. "I want Dominick to get the help he needs, and I want my daughter returned back to me."

"That's enough," Coach said, and Brandon clicked a button to make the screen go black.

I couldn't do this. Couldn't handle it.

It was one thing to tell Holly about my past—and oh shit. Holly. *Ben.* He had Google alerts set up for me. The entire team would hear this. Their parents. Shit.

"Fucking hell." I kicked the chair in front of me, sent it slamming into the table where it bounced off it. My hands slammed to my hair and every muscle in my body coiled with fire racing through me. "What does Pete have to say?"

Vik was the only man in the room not ready to rage, grimaced. "I told him the truth. He knows, but he's obviously not happy. Had *he* known before, had you told anyone, we might have been able to have a story ready to go. We could have used this."

"Don't be a dick now, Vik."

"You knew?" Joey asked, gaping at our coach.

"He coached me in college. You knew that."

"Yeah, but..." He shook his head, and I didn't blame his confusion. How could anyone allow this to happen? Or let it continue.

"It doesn't matter. Get me in front of those cameras. That's what they're out there for, right? Waiting for my statement?"

"I'm not sure that's wise right now," Brandon said. "Not with you ready to murder someone."

"You mean besides *Crank,* my sister's pimp? Yeah. The world would be a better place without him."

"And you can't exactly go accusing him of that without proof. It'll only make it worse."

They were right. Of course they were. But fuck— "Fine," I gritted. "Then I'll tell the entire story."

"Dom—"

"I'll call Lucy. Call her therapists. Make sure she's safe and see what she's okay with saying, but I will not let this woman get away with it."

Fuck. I had the receipts of money I sent her. I had pictures of the trailer she lived in with Lucy. Sure, they were a few years old, taken when I'd gone to find Lucy three years ago and get her clean then. I didn't even know if that was still Gloria's home, but the pictures would show enough.

"I have to make some calls." My lawyer, for one. Lucy. The center.

"What do you need from me?" Joey asked, and the question almost knocked me on my ass.

What could he do for me? Not a damn thing, except what he already gave. "You're here. That's enough."

"All right."

Two hours later, I stood behind the curtains we used occasionally during the season for interviews. The room on the other side was a buzz of voices, a flurry of activity. I'd done all I could, and still, I wasn't ready.

"I think it's wise to wait," Vik said next to me. Maybe it would be. Maybe it'd be smarter to fight this privately, but she'd just smeared my entire reputation and career in one huge lie and I was not letting this stand.

I didn't care if the world now saw my ugly family drama, my waste of space mother. I wouldn't stand still for a moment, while she accused *me* of being the person who destroyed Lucy.

I'd been ensured Lucy was safe. After a quick phone call, where I told her *nothing* just that I wanted to check in on her, I then talked to her doctor who had, of course, heard the news. "We'll make sure she doesn't know anything." Despite the screw up from a few weeks ago, I chose to trust him. There wasn't anything else I could do for her right then, anyway.

"I'll be there as soon as I can." She'd need to hear what was happening. Too many people could tell her or mention it, but I wanted it to come from me, with her therapist in the room. She'd need it. Hell, we both probably did.

My lawyer had the no-contact papers ready to serve. I was waiting on word from him to ensure he'd gotten the cash I requested. Two hundred thousand I was ready to dish out, one hundred to each of those assholes if they promised to stay away forever. I had an extra twenty thousand for one of them to tell me who in the hell took them to the station this morning. There was no way they thought of this all on their own, and someone had to help Gloria get cleaned up enough to look halfway decent.

"All right, then. Do what you need to do."

I took in my coach. The guy who kept me in hockey, encouraged me to stay and then gave me my first decent shot at life where I could make things better for Lucy. He'd done all of that for me, without hesitation. "You know" —I turned to him— "you were the kind of man I needed when I didn't have a dad anymore, and I appreciate that. I don't think I've ever told you that. But I've always wondered, how could you be so good to your team and players, and so shitty to your own family?"

I stomped away before I could see his expression or hear his response. It was true though. He had three daughters. From what I knew, he had no relationship with any of them. He was either a misogynist and never loved them because they weren't going to be hockey players, or he was just a dick. Either way, he had good in him. Somewhere. He just didn't spend it in the right direction.

More shit I was learning.

I stepped out onto the small stage where the microphone was already set up at the lone seat in the center table and all noise from the reporters slashed to nothing.

So did my own heart as I took in the back of the room.

Lined at the back wall was my team. Every single teammate who currently played for the Vipers, including some who had yet to make the travel roster, were lined along the back and the sides. They all had on their jersey, arms crossed at their chest. Every single one was there for me.

To support me.

Damn. Joey worked fast. Or maybe it hadn't been him at all. Kane knew the truth. Max knew. It could have been any of them, but considering I'd been an asshole to a majority of these guys, the fact they'd stand there and show support for me meant more than I could describe.

"Thanks," I murmured into the microphone while I took my seat. Max and Kane and Alix nodded back. Joey shot me a thumbs up.

I glanced at my phone, pulled up the email I'd already drafted, and hit send.

Within seconds, phones around the room began to *ping*.

"What you're about to see, that I didn't have time and don't want to set up, are photos of the home where my mother, Gloria Masters, lived as of two years ago. You will also see pictures of me when I was younger with my sister Lucy, including pictures of my dad, Dennis, before he died in an accident when I was twenty."

As I spoke, the room grew tense. I had the attention of every single person in the room, and I hated it on a good day.

This was torture. Still, I drew on the strength I'd found recently, the comfort Holly had always given me so freely, and continued.

"I was born to Dennis and Gloria Masters in a suburb of Detroit, Michigan. We had a great life. When I was seven, my little sister Lucy was born." I paused and cleared my throat, twisted open the top of a water bottle next to me. I just had to get through this.

"During my sophomore year of college, my dad died in an accident at the auto garage he owned and wanted to someday pass down to me. I didn't only lose my dad that day, my hero and the greatest man I'd ever met, I lost my mom." I pinched the bridge of my nose and inhaled. I just had to get through this part. "Lucy was thirteen the first time my mom put a needle in her arm and forced her to get high with her. She was sixteen the first time my mom made her spend time with an adult male so she could continue getting those drugs..."

A gasp went around the room. Female reporters sniffed, emotion shocking them. Even men in the room cursed. As one, like the team we were, the men at the back of the room, the men who had *my* back, stood tall.

And I continued telling the truth. It might destroy my career. It would definitely put attention onto the team Pete despised. I didn't give a shit. If everything I'd done over the years caused me to lose my spot on the team but helped save my sister, it was worth it.

I explained the pictures they'd see. The drug-filled, disgusting, roach and mice-infested trailer with joints and empty alcohol bottles littered all over the place. Stains on carpets I could only imagine what they entailed.

And when I was done, despite there being few dry eyes in the room, including some from my own teammates, I finished with, "I have *never* laid a hand on my sister. I have fought to protect her and get her help. I will make no apologies for the men who have tried to harm her that I have hurt in the process. Chad Attler being one of those men, in a long line of them. What I have done, is ensure she's safe, away from both our mother who only wants to drag her back to the hell of her own making and make sure she gets every opportunity to get the help she needs to heal from the trauma forced on her.

"You've heard my mother's version. And now you've heard the truth. You can write whatever stories you want, spin whatever tales will get you the most views or ad space or money, I don't give a shit. But no one will ever accuse me of doing anything to *hurt* my sister, least of all the person who's done the worst damage."

I stood, grabbed my water and my phone, and turned back to the quiet room. No one shouted a question. No one demanded more information. If I wasn't mistaken, they were still shell-shocked.

Which I figured was good enough.

I headed toward the back.

I needed an hour in front of a punching bag and an hour on a treadmill at max speed to attempt beginning to calm myself down. Fuck. I'd just spilled every damn secret, every hidden truth, everything about my ugly and nasty life and I did it to reporters. Once I opened my mouth, I hadn't been able to shut it and I'd spewed every disgusting detail without thought or remorse, all but the parts that were Lucy's. But these people could twist this into anything. They could paint me as the hero or villain with a keystroke. The man who helped his sister or the asshole who failed her.

I fell against the wall, my back to it. Scrubbing a hand down my face as the reality of what I shared settled in, I stared at my feet until a shadow fell over me.

"I'm sorry you went through that." To my utter shock, I lifted my head, stared right into Pete's face. "No kid, no matter how old, should have that on his shoulders."

My throat clogged. He *hated* me, but even now, all I saw on his face was genuine sadness. Not pity.

"Thanks," I grunted. My throat still refusing to gather moisture as I swallowed. "My spot on the team, okay?"

His gaze slid toward the room I exited and back to me. "You need time away?"

"No." If I wasn't on the ice, it'd be worse.

"If I asked you to take a couple days, one road trip to stay home, would you?"

"Probably not."

"Then okay."

"That's it?"

"If I benched you or traded you now, it'd make me the most hated man in hockey."

He grinned.

"We can't have that, can we?"

"I'd prefer not to, but I am going to ask you to be honest with

Coach. If the fallout from any of this gets to be too much, think about your team and do what's best for all of us, okay?"

He was giving me the option. What an odd dimension I must have fallen into.

"Will do."

He turned to leave, took a few steps. I waited for him to change his mind but all he said was, "Heard good things about the youth team, too. Dads have told me the kids love you."

Damn him. Emotion rose all over again. It'd be easier if he was a dick to me right now. "It doesn't suck."

"Sounds to me like you take after your own dad, then, and you should be proud of that."

I gaped at him as he left, ducked my head again, and once I figured I wouldn't be bawling my goddamn eyes out, pushed off and went to work out.

Fuck this fucking hellish day.

30

———

HOLLY

He wasn't answering. His phone began going straight to voice mail an hour ago and I had no idea what he was struggling with or how to help, but he needed me. That much I knew.

I heard the news this morning as soon as I turned on the television after I got dressed and ready for the day. I always had the TV on in the background while I worked.

My workday came to a screeching halt as soon as the news reporter mentioned Gloria Masters's name.

Time froze as I sat there, glued to the television. My anger rose and curse words I didn't even know I knew flew from my mouth as she lied straight into the camera with a sad, fake smile on her face.

I'd never wanted to punch a human more, at least not more than Evan, but Gloria won hands down. How could she *do* this to her children? How could she make up such blatant lies about her own son, all because she wanted her daughter with her?

The woman made me sick, and my stomach rolled more than once while she sat in that room, and at the very end when the reporter asked, "What would you like to come from this?"

I'd almost thrown up on my floor as she answered.

"I want my daughter back. With her mama, right where she belongs."

And oh God. Dominick. He had to have seen it. Had to have heard. All of his baggage and history was thrown out there for the world to see, things he'd been so desperate to keep hidden he hadn't opened up to anyone in a decade. And now it was being tossed out there for everyone to dissect. It was twisted, made him look like the evil one.

I dialed his number frantically, unsurprised he didn't answer. And then I texted. Called again.

Hours later, he still hadn't responded or returned a text, and I was desperate with the need to see him. I grabbed my keys and purse. Hell, I knew where he lived. He had to return there at some point. Or he was already there, ignoring the world and who could blame him.

I just needed to see him. Hug him. If he needed space after that I'd give it to him.

Outside, I was opening my door when Evan's truck pulled up.

Ben hopped out of the back seat of his crew cab and ran right to me. "Have you talked to him? Are you going to see him?"

"You heard?" Shit. He'd been at school all day.

"Kids got some alerts on their phones. It sounds... bad."

"Everything that happened to Dominick and Lucy was bad, kiddo. But it's a grown-up thing, and I know you hate hearing it, but let him handle it, okay?"

"Can I come with you?"

"No. But I'll give him a hug for you, okay?"

He opened his mouth to argue when Evan called his name, more like barked it and Ben's head fell.

"Go see your dad. Do your homework. I'll call you when I can, okay?"

"All right. But tell Coach I'm sorry. Sorry he lost his dad and his mom is so mean."

"I will." I hugged Ben and let him go, sent him to his dad's.

As soon as he ran inside, Evan was still in the driveway, hands on his hips, and I swore there was almost a satisfied smirk on his lips. "That's a great, high-caliber man you brought into your kid's life."

There was something ugly about his look. Nastier than I'd seen before and his threat of me regretting not taking him back came back to me. Had he...?

No. Evan wouldn't have a part in something this ugly or spiteful. Would he?

"I suggest you figure out your own life and living situation before you begin commenting on mine. Deal?"

I climbed into my Aviator and slammed the door before he could respond. But seeing that arrogant smirk wiped away?

Priceless.

"HOLLY MYERS, here to see Dominick Masters." It was the same woman, Sabrina, working behind the desk. She had to recognize me except today, she was acting like she didn't. And hell, she and I both knew Dominick didn't get visitors to his place.

"I'm sorry, Miss Myers. I'm currently under orders. Without specific invitation from Mr. Masters, we aren't allowing anyone up to his residence."

"It's 2418. I was here a week ago. You handed me my key."

"I know, but he never put you on an always allowed visitor's list, so I have to follow protocol. I'm sorry."

"Shit." I turned, paced and returned to her. "Can I wait? Here? In the lobby?"

She glanced around, returned my look with a kind smile. "I don't see why not. And I'm sorry, truly."

God. She'd heard. Of course she had. There had been a few police officers outside, no doubt prepared in case media came hunting for him. I should have known.

But where in the hell was he? I'd grown so desperate I'd texted Gabby, having her number from the day I went to their house. She had no clue where he'd be. She'd reached out to Joey, who said he'd left after a grueling workout. Wouldn't let anyone go with him.

No one knew where he was.

I collapsed into a chair in the corner. All the lobby's TVs were off and I hoped like hell they stayed that way. I could only imagine what the local news reports would be saying. Plus all the sports channels. Dominick had dropped no small bomb this morning, followed so quickly on the heels of his mother's lies. If I heard anyone begin to trust his mom, I might break the TV myself, so I'd turned mine off after Dom had stalked off the stage of his own conference.

I called him again, intent on getting his voice mail like I had for the last several hours. Instead, his voice, scratchy and dry came through the line. "I just saw your calls."

"You're okay," I sighed, tears filled my eyes. Relieved ones. Sad ones.

"I wouldn't go that far. I... I meant to call earlier, but..."

"No apologies. Ever. Not for this. I'm actually at your building."

He laughed. "Funny because I was just getting ready to head to your place."

"Well, I'm in your lobby, waiting."

"You can go up."

"They won't let me. It's okay."

"No. I'll call them. I'm only fifteen minutes away."

"If you're sure..."

"Trust me, Holly. After today, the only thing I want to do is feel one of your hugs and see you smile."

A rush of warmth flooded me. I'd almost expected him to run like he had last time. Avoid me. Fear dragging me into his dirt and having me face it with him.

To know he was looking for me? Wanting me after this?

It told me all I needed about him.

"Okay then. I'll see you soon."

"Good."

EXACTLY FIFTEEN MINUTES LATER, his door opened. Dominick walked in and my heart squeezed and my breath stalled.

He looked like utter shit. Like he'd been tossed into a washer on the spin cycle and barely managed to survive.

"Hey," I said, pushing off his couch. I hadn't even made it outside. Hadn't bothered opening a glass of wine.

He kicked off his shoes, tossed his keys to the island, and came straight to me.

His arms wrapped around my back, one sliding up to my shoulders. He hugged me so tightly my back cracked and my ribs were at risk of doing the same.

"Shit. Sorry." He loosened his hold enough so I could breathe, and I buried my face in his chest. The Henley shirt he had on was soft, better it smelled like him. Pine and minty.

"It's okay." I held him back equally tight, wishing I could do more. "Want to talk about it?"

"I'm guessing you saw it all?"

"Yeah." I nodded against his chest. His hand at my shoulders slid up through my hair and then palmed the back of my head.

There was something so comforting when he did this. That large hand, holding me so protectively against him. "It's been a long ass day, but there is some decent news in all the shit."

"Really?"

"Yeah. Need a drink?"

Boy, did I. But I could refrain for now. "I'm good."

He let go of me long enough to take a seat on the couch and he curled up with me. Together, we laid down and I let him put me where he needed me, on our sides on his large couch, facing each other.

"I went and saw Lucy."

My hand was on his side, and as he spoke, I gripped his shirt. "Did you tell her what happened?"

"Had to. She'd hear anyway, but one of her therapists met with us."

"Nike?" I asked, thinking of the horse he said had given her strength.

"No." He chuckled, thankfully. Now probably wasn't the time to crack jokes. "It was a real-life human. But he helped me get out what happened with Gloria and Attler, and then I told her what I did."

"How'd she take it?"

"She got pissed and told us to call the cops. She wanted to file a report."

"What?"

"Yeah." He closed his eyes and pulled me tighter against him. "Surprised the hell out of me too. So we did, or rather the center did. And she filed a report on both of them for sex trafficking."

"What?"

"I wish you could have seen her. She was so strong and it was like a miracle happening in front of me. I'm scared to be hopeful, but she wanted it done, and she knew so much. About who and where Gloria gets her drugs from. Who the main dealer was, how drugs were passed through that bar I found her at on Christmas Eve. She talked to the police for hours, repeating everything, telling her story. Turned out they were alerted after my press conference anyway, had already been watching Attler for drugs but couldn't pin anything on him."

"Wow."

"Tell me about it." His eyes were still closed and he wiped a hand over his face. "Fucking exhausting day. I'd been prepared to pay them off, but Lucy told them where Attler stayed when he wanted to hide and Mom still lived in that trailer, so the cops found them and they've been picked up."

"Dom, that's incredible."

"I know. And Lucy, she didn't hesitate. She just knew Mom lied and hurt me and she went all out for it." He blew out a breath and yawned. "I was so damn proud of her for all of it. You should have seen her. God, I wish you could have. I've never seen her that strong, and it's been years since I've seen her that alert, aware of the truth of everything."

I slid my hand up his arm, to his neck and then his hair. With his eyes closed, he looked like he could fall asleep, and I played with his hair, scraped my nails gently over his scalp until a soft moan left his lips and his eyes slid open.

"There's more, but we're looking into who took them to the news station today."

"Okay."

"I think it might have been Evan."

"What?" I blinked. "Why....?"

"He drives that Silverado?"

"Silver, yeah. He's had it for years."

"I'm pretty sure when I left your house last weekend and went to see Lucy, he followed me. Didn't put it together, but a guy's truck was caught on camera dropping off Gloria when I put my lawyer on it."

"Why would he follow you?" It made no sense, and yet there was that sick smirk on his face earlier. He'd been so damn pleased with himself.

"Why wouldn't he? He made it clear he wanted you. Don't you think he'd do anything possible to get me away from you? He couldn't have known I would have said anything. Hell, for all he knew, once he went digging into my life, he could have believed everything Gloria told him."

"Shit. Why is he such a dick?"

"Because he lost a good woman and regrets it. And he knows he's losing his touch if Kristi left him. Right now he's pissed and he's going to take it out on anyone but looking at himself because he's weak."

"I know, but Ben's there, and he's already been saying stuff to him about us, and he's just... stuck there. So close to me and I can't do anything."

"The hell we can't. Come on." He gently tugged on my hand, bringing us both to sitting and then our feet.

"What are we doing?"

"We're going to your place. I didn't want to be here tonight anyway, I wanted to be at your house where it's comforting and feels like a family and it's warm and smells like you."

My heart squeezed. "Dom—"

"I mean it. I like your home. It feels like love inside, not this cold barren, echo chamber. That was where I wanted to be so that's where we're going. And, we're going to check on Ben, let him see I'm all right. And as a super exciting bonus, I get to show Evan he can't do anything that fucks with what we have."

As much as I'd rather be in my home and see Ben, and that wasn't even thinking about my heart leaping into my throat with the rest of what he said... "I'm not sure pissing him off further is the greatest plan."

"What else can he do?"

I wasn't sure I wanted to tempt fate, but Dom was right. And after the day he had, I'd let him have anything.

BEN TOOK off out of his dad's front door as soon as I pulled into the driveway. Dominick was next to me, holding my thigh like he always seemed to do and I loved, and as soon as Ben saw Dominick sitting in the car next to me, he tripped over his feet, smiling so big his face almost cracked in two.

"Mom! Dominick!"

He raced toward us, slamming right into Dominick as he climbed out of the car.

Dominick, no longer surprised by Ben's hugs, squatted down and hugged him back. "Hey, Ben. How's it going?"

"I was worried about you. I kept waiting for Mom to come home so I could ask her how you were."

The door to Evan's house slammed and Dom stood, me next to him. "Dad's mad," he muttered, and oh boy was he.

"Ben, what did I say?"

I took Ben's shoulder in my hand and kept him with us.

Frankly, I didn't give a crap what he'd said to Ben. He didn't get to continue being an asshole to our son and he certainly wouldn't do it right in front of me.

"He's going to come in and stay with us as long as he wants," I told Evan.

"It's my week. I don't mess with yours."

"The hell you don't, and frankly, I've always allowed Ben to go see you whenever he wants, but today, considering everything..." I stressed *everything*, letting him know exactly what Dom and I believed he did. "He can be with us. At least for a little while."

"If you think you get to start changing custody—"

"Call our lawyers," I stated. I didn't flinch. I hated Ben seeing these arguments, but damn it, I'd kept quiet enough over the last year and I was done. "Call them. Take me to court. You keep making your threats about what the judge would think of me, so do it. But do not think you can get away with *anything* you've done in the recent weeks and I'll allow it."

"I'd choose Mom," Ben said, and his tiny voice shook.

"Ben, kiddo, let's go inside," Dom said, and I had to hand it to him, he was calm despite the rage in his eyes. He truly believed Evan caused today's disaster, but really... had it ended up so bad? Gloria and Attler were arrested. Lucy was stronger. Evan would soon be out of the neighborhood. Really, outside Dominick having his baggage thrown all over the news, the results hadn't been horrific.

"No." Ben shook his head and faced Evan directly. "You're not always nice to me and Mom is. And you don't say nice things about her even though she's the best mom in the world. If you're going to bring up lawyers and judges, I know what that means, and I'll tell them all I don't want anything to do with you."

"You're too young to make that decision."

"I'm ten, not stupid," he retorted, his chin now wobbling. It was the same words he said to me days ago when I brought up dating Dom. Then, they'd been funny. There was nothing funny about watching him tell his dad he didn't want to see him.

"Inside, Ben, he gets it," Dom said. He guided them around me, keeping Ben away from Evan, and I waited until Ben punched in our door code and they went inside.

"Good job, Evan. You've lost your wife, ruined your relationship with Kristi and now you're destroying your relationship with your son. Proud of yourself yet?"

"That man is an asshole with an anger issue and I will not let him be with my son."

"That man used to be your favorite player until he started wanting me. What does that tell you?"

"It means you get to know someone and you realize they weren't all you thought they were. They're worse."

Oh, he had to be joking. I burst out laughing, unable to help it. It was the best comedic relief I needed. "I know, Evan. I lived with you long enough to know you're absolutely right about that." I reined in my laughter. Barely. "Now get the hell off my lawn. I'll send Ben back to you when he's ready to see you. Enjoy your night. Alone."

I looked up, saw Dominick on my porch right where I knew he'd be after getting Ben to safety, and went straight to him. Together, we didn't give Evan the satisfaction of another glance before shutting the door behind us.

"Can we have pizza for dinner?" Ben asked, shouting from the kitchen. "There's nothing good here."

"How can he be hungry after that?" I asked.

"He's a boy. We process our feelings with food."

Really... what normal person didn't?

LATER, after dinner, after I finally caved and had a glass of wine—okay, three, but the day seriously called for it—we turned on a movie. Ben sat between us, so close to Dominick it was like he was either afraid to let Dom out of his sight or he wanted to make sure he was there to feel better. We ignored everything about the day, turned on the old *Mighty Ducks* movie, one Dom claimed was his favorite. Ben fell asleep halfway through it, and I had never had a better night.

"We should get him to bed," I told Dom, whose arm was draped over Ben's shoulders and resting at his hip. Like he'd had a decade to cuddle up with the kid and watch movies with him.

"I kind of like this," he said to me, glancing at Ben and smiling at me. "I like it a lot."

"I'd like it more if we could put him to bed and then you could put *me* to bed."

It was late. Had been a hell of a day, and I doubted tomorrow would be easier.

Dominick arched a brow and smirked. "When you put it like that, I'll take care of Ben."

"Oh, you can just..." He stood, cradled Ben in his arms even though he was ten and weighed over seventy pounds. "Carry him and take care of it."

"He has school tomorrow. I don't want to wake him."

"Do what you think is best," I said and then stood. I gave Ben a soft kiss on his cheek so as not to wake him and once they headed up the stairs, I took our empty glasses to the sink. They could wait until tomorrow. I flipped off lights and locked the doors and followed the guys up the stairs, only to hear soft murmuring coming from Ben's room.

"You like my mom a lot," Ben said groggily.

"A whole lot. She's really nice."

"I like the way you look at her. All funny-like."

"Are you saying I look funny?"

"No." Ben yawned and there was rustling of sheets as he climbed into bed. "It's like you got hearts in your eyes or something. I like it. She's happier now. And I like that too." He yawned again.

"I hope I always make her happy, kiddo."

"Me too. You're cool, too."

My heart squeezed as I eavesdropped, too slow to move before Dom came out of Ben's room.

"Eavesdropping?"

I didn't bother denying it. "You like me. A lot."

"I like both of you a lot. More than I thought possible."

"Good."

He followed me to my room where we both got ready for bed. Gone were my nerves of undressing around him, and I changed while he used the restroom and brushed his teeth. We alternated and by the time I came out of the bathroom, Dominick was in bed, on his side facing me, propped up on an elbow. I hurried to the bed to get close to him, not hide from him like I'd done not so long ago.

But there was something freeing about a man who looked at me the way Dom did. He wasn't cataloging imperfections. He was admiring me the way I was, and every time his eyes slid down my body, I knew he liked what he saw.

"No sex," I stated, and brushed my lips over his. "Not tonight. Not with Ben here." I doubted I needed to tell him, but that was something I wasn't quite ready for.

"I can wait," he said. "I just want to be with you."

He turned only to flip off the lamp on his side of the bed, and I turned to do the same to mine.

"It doesn't matter anyway," he told me, once the room was bathed in darkness and his pine scent. "We have the rest of our lives to have all the sex."

"Oh," I breathed out. "The rest of our lives?" Because it wasn't a declaration of love, but pretty damn close.

"For as long as you'll have me."

Suddenly, the rest of our lives didn't seem nearly long enough.

EPILOGUE

DOMINICK

"Do it again! Do it again!"

Ben's shouts rang across the lake from his spot in the boat.

"I think I'm all worn out," I called back.

"Liar! Do the flip again."

I laughed, shook my hair out like a wet dog, and readjusted the wakeboard on my feet. "Maybe your grandpa needs a break."

"Not that old, son. Hell, all I'm doin' is driving the boat for you hooligans."

Son. Every single damn time Steve called me son, usually with a clap on the shoulder or a fist pump through our weekly FaceTime calls, my heart squeezed. The first day I met Steve and Connie, I'd been wrapped in a hug that almost brought me to my knees.

No wonder Holly was the sweetest, most admirable, and stunning woman I'd ever met. She came from Connie and Steve—two kind and generous people. They were always happy and peaceful with some deep-seated joy in them you couldn't help but love on sight. Holly and I had now been together seven months, if you counted that first meeting in January at Ben's practice—which I for one would never forget—and this was my third time being around her parents. My first vacation to Wisconsin where I was also with her brother Tim's family.

Scared as hell hadn't begun to describe my nerves on the plane ride out.

Didn't help I heard Tim was a rabid Chicago Storm fan and *hated* us Vipers for kicking his beloved Storm out of the playoffs earlier this year.

We hadn't won the Stanley Cup this year. Didn't even make it to the finals. Most guys had been bummed.

But after that loss, I'd been greeted in the hall by Holly and Ben, and any disappointment over losing the game vanished.

I'd won something much larger... and was still winning to this day.

"Don't be such a weenie, Nicky!" I glared at Lucy, suntanned, and smiling—and most importantly—still sober and currently living with me.

"Weenie? Really?" I shouted from where I floated in the water. It didn't matter how many times I flipped over the wake on the wakeboard, Ben kept demanding more. He was convinced the more he saw me do it, the easier it'd get for him to succeed in completing one. "You can't think of a better insult?"

"Not with kids present!"

"It's all right," Ben shouted. "Dominick says *really* bad words. A lot. I've probably heard them all."

In the boat next to Lucy, Holly, and Tim's wife, Ashley, burst out laughing.

"All right, I'll go ahead!" Anything to end the hell of Steve knowing how much I cursed.

Although, given how much I heard him say shit and damn when he watched football or had a bad fishing morning, I figured he understood.

I grabbed the ski rope handle, settled myself, and once Connie and Ashley ensured all the kids were sitting and settled, I lifted and dropped my hand.

"Hit it!" I called out.

The engine of Steve's inboard boat motor revved and then I was up, flying across the air on one of the most gorgeous and clearest lakes I'd ever been on. It took me one day to figure out how to wakeboard, although I hadn't admitted to either Holly or Ben I'd been watching YouTube videos once they told me what they liked to do at their parents' lake house. No way was I showing up looking like a fool.

I'd continue letting Ben think I was a magician and *awesome* and *so incredible* and *amazing*—all his words—for as long as humanly possible.

I flew out of the wake, kept the rope tight in front of my chest. My eyes stayed on Ben, because damn... this kid.

I never knew making a now eleven-year-old boy proud of me would become my greatest accomplishment, but it was. Every time he thought I was awesome, my heart grew three sizes. Coupled with Holly's sassy and fun-spirited and deep love, I was pretty much winning at life.

I cut back toward the wake as Steve started to turn the boat. And as soon as I hit the wave, leaned forward so I was leaning over the front of the board. As soon as we hit air, I flipped my feet, the part of the trick Ben still hadn't mastered—but I blamed the weight of the board and not his effort or skill—and spun in the air. I landed in the flats, outside the opposite wake edge to Ben standing in the boat, hands thrown over his head. Holly's hands were at his waist to keep him safe, and the entire boat cheered.

Damn. This life she gave me.

I'd never be able to repay her for it, but I seriously hoped getting her and Ben to move in with me when we returned to Vegas would be a start.

Holly

. . .

Hot damn, my boyfriend was sexy. I mean, I thought it all the time. When Dominick was skating, even when he was slamming men into boards like they weighed nothing. Every time he ripped off his shirt and showed off those muscles of his.

When he worked out in his gym in his condo and was all sweaty, was a special one. Every time he smiled at me. Every time he made love to me.

Dominick Masters was the sexiest man I'd ever met in my life, but there was nothing... absolutely nothing sexier than sitting on my parents' deck, seeing him laugh so wide I could see the whites of his teeth from thirty yards away while he spent an hour tossing Ben and my nephews into the air, over and over again.

"Damn. I love your brother and all, but that body..."

I clinked my hard seltzer can against hers and we laughed. "He's amazing. Everything about him, but I'm happy to bring the entertainment to Wisconsin for you."

"I'm happy you're here and happy. After everything with Evan..."

"Say no more. Trust me. I get it."

My family had, after all, seen me at my worst, been through the darkest time in my life with me, and while it wasn't like Ashley and I kept in frequent contact, mostly just due to life and she heard everything from my parents anyway, she'd been there for me, too.

"I thought it'd take me longer to trust someone again, you know?" I tilted my head and blocked my eyes from the afternoon sun. "But Dominick made it so easy."

"No ring yet though." She was teasing, but I still glanced at my ring finger. Bare. With no thought of it changing anytime soon.

I shrugged. "We'll get to it eventually, I think. I'm in no hurry, to be honest, and I don't think Dominick ever thought he'd get married, so I doubt he thinks of it."

"No? You don't think he wants you to have his name? Get rid of everything Evan gave you?"

"He's never said, but it's Ben's name too, so…"

We'd actually talked about it a few months back. I was considering going back to my maiden name and Dominick asked me why. I told him I wanted that final tether to Evan cut considering how much I despised the man. It was Dominick who pointed out it was Ben's name too and asked me how I thought he'd feel.

Since then, I'd hadn't gathered the courage to ask Ben. And there was that small part of me that wanted to be Mrs. Masters, even if I wasn't in a hurry to get there.

"Speaking of Evan."

I glared at Ashley. "I wasn't. You keep bringing him up."

"I'm curious. Sue me. How's he doing?"

"Living in Los Angeles. Seeing Ben every other weekend. I do have to give him credit, once he took off I figured he'd cut out Ben, but he calls him every night. I think Evan misses him, but won't return to Vegas because of Dominick."

"Stupid. It's his son."

"Evan's never shown himself to be the brightest or most thoughtful bulb." After Kristi kicked him out, she listed her house. It sold immediately and a young couple, just married with no kids, moved in. They're adorable and loved hanging out with Ben in the yards, playing catch and ball with him. On days Dominick is there, we all hang out. It was like having a little sister, but Hayden was super sweet and her husband Silas was great with Ben. A few weeks later, Evan called and told me he'd taken a job with his company in Los Angeles. It was only four hours away, but I refused to keep our custody so we went to mediation to get it fixed. He now saw Ben every other weekend and we met halfway to make it easier.

We never talked, communicated only through text and only emergencies, which thankfully, had been few and far between. It almost seemed like he was *nicer* to Ben now that he was farther away. At least, if he was still criticizing him, Ben didn't mention it.

It wasn't what I wanted, but it was working.

"Hey, Mom! Come here!"

I looked to Ben on the dock. He was standing next to Dominick, who was holding his phone, pointing out something to Ben.

"You gotta see this!"

"What?"

"Just come here!" I set down my seltzer and groaned. "Mom life, isn't it grand?" I winked at Ashley.

"The best."

Although really, she was right. I had the best life.

I made it down to the dock, tightening my swimsuit wrap at my waist and padded to the guys on bare feet.

"What's going on?"

Dominick was grinning at his phone and then his face fell flat. "Shit." His thumb swiped the screen.

"What is it?"

"We got a—"

"Not now, kiddo," Dom said to Ben, cutting him off, settling a hand on his shoulder. His smile vanished.

Finally, Dom peeled his gaze off his phone.

"What is it?"

"I got bad news. Maybe not so bad, maybe kind of bad."

"What?" I stepped toward him. Ben's excitement was now gone, looking as confused as I felt. "What's wrong?"

"Max is hurt."

My heart flopped and my hand went to my chest. "What happened?"

He shook his head. "He and Alix were rock climbing. That's all I know. Just got a text from Joey. Alix said his shoulder and back are screwed up. They're with the team's surgeon at the hospital."

I'd been to enough games now to know there was always a surgeon from the local hospital at the games, sitting behind their bench in case of an emergency injury. That they were meeting with him, didn't bode good things, but it could also just be the team being cautious.

I'd grown a huge soft spot for the Max. Pretty sure Dom had too over these last few months, even if he wouldn't admit it. "That's horrible, but he'll be fine, right? I mean, it's Max." Big old goof ball who never dropped his smile... I couldn't imagine him frowning, or in pain.

"Of course, he will," Dom said, and he narrowed his eyes in a way that had nothing to do with the sun. "It's Max. As much as he drives me insane, he's a good teammate."

"Do you want to call him?"

"I will. Later." He kissed my cheek and then brushed his nose along my jaw. The soft movement sent a spark of excitement through me, and it was crazy. One brief touch from him and I'd do anything he asked. "Now, there's good news. But I think Ben wants to tell you."

He whispered it in my ear, and I grinned against his cheek as it brushed my mouth.

Then he smiled down at Ben and smiled. The worry for Max was still in his eyes, but now there was a gleam of joy too, and I loved that almost more than his touch. There was something so special seeing Dominick happy.

"Do you want to tell her?" he asked, grinning down at Ben.

Ben, who had stood sullen, mostly because he loved Max too, grinned at Dom. "Can I?"

"It's your show, big man."

Ben turned to me, grinned from ear to ear and then shouted so loud I was certain the folks across the lake heard him. "Dominick bought us a house and it's awesome!"

Holy shit. "What? A house? What house?"

"The one I bought for us, so you and Ben can move in with me."

My knees wobbled and the dock rocked beneath my feet. "What are you talking about?"

He grinned that cocky grin of his that I typically wanted to smack off his face or drop to my knees. "I was going to ask you first, but then I figured, what the hell, you weren't going to say no to me."

"You're kidding."

He shook his head. "Two houses is hard enough during off-season. When I come home from away games starting October, I want it to be to my family." He held out his phone and re-lit his screen. "What do you say? Do you and Ben want to move in?"

"You're crazy."

"About this life we're living. Yeah."

He was insane. Absolutely bonkers. What man just bought a house and *assumed* the woman would want it? Didn't he know anything about aesthetics? My designer choices and preferences? The kind of yard I wanted or schools?

"Dom" —I glanced at the house— "Oh...." It was enormous. Four-car garage. Looked so similar to Gabby and Joey's, I now knew by heart since we spent so much time with them. Had I any say in the house we'd move into together, it would have looked exactly like this. "But... honey. This is a lot."

"Same school Ben goes to, five minutes away from where you live now. It's actually between your current place and Karly's."

I flipped through the photos. He ambushed me into speechless-ness, but as I kept scrolling, the house kept getting more perfect. "The house is huge. And that pool..."

"Pool parties for Ben and his friends and you and Karly, and plenty of room to grow."

"Grow? Dom." I gaped up at him. His back was to the sun, giving him a halo around all his dark, glistening hair. My fallen angel—my forever protector. Damn him. Tears burned my eyes. My voice broke. "You've never said you wanted kids."

"You want more. I can tell."

"Yeah, but if you don't, I have Ben. And you. That's enough."

"My job isn't to make sure you have enough. It's to give you everything."

Silly man. Didn't he know he already did?

"Lucy..." I trailed off as she came down the stairs in my parent's yard toward us.

"What about me? Dom says I get to keep his condo." She flashed me a cheeky grin and waved her hand in the air. "Get out of my house already."

I chuckled. Lucy was the sweetest. Not a single vengeful bone in her body. A lot of healing had occurred in the last several months. She still had a long way to go, but she was doing better than ever. Gloria and Chad Attler had been convicted of multiple accounts of sex trafficking. Add in her history of drugs, the amount they found in her trailer, and she wouldn't be getting out of prison for a long time. Attler even longer. They were gone, hopefully forever, but I knew Dom wouldn't relax for years to come.

Lucy was still doing outpatient weekly and private therapy and had started studying for her GED recently. She now said she wanted to become a therapist at the center where she stayed all those months ago.

I turned back to Dom. "Did everyone know?"

"I talked to Lucy when I saw the house come on the market. I wanted to make sure she felt safe, and I just learned the offer was accepted. Ben was eavesdropping."

"Not *eavesdropping*. I was listening."

Dom ruffled his hair, the blond now almost as long and equally shaggy as Dom's. "Same thing, buddy."

A fist squeezed my heart. "I guess you'll all be mad at me if I say no, huh?"

"Extremely," Ben said. "That pool is so cool."

"You're kind of cramping my high-rise, super-rich condo living lifestyle I've come to love." Lucy grinned at me.

I turned to Dom. "You?"

Who was I kidding? He hadn't been mad at me for a minute. Ever.

"Always on your time."

I shrugged and held out the phone. "Then I guess the time is now. When do we move?"

He plucked the phone from my hand and handed it to Ben.

"Right after we celebrate." He scooped me in his arms and took off running.

"Dominick!" I cried as I realized his intention.

We went airborne, and then splashed, water went up my nose, and I sputtered and coughed as we popped back above the water. "You're a menace." I swiped water off his face and kissed him.

"I'm your menace. Forever. Someday—a wedding, and we're having that even if you don't want one, but I don't give a shit if it's here with only your family and Lucy in your parents' backyard. Hell, on the boat for all I care. And then we're having babies. I want to make sure you have the life you've always wanted."

I wrapped my arms around his neck. Tears mixed with lake water, and I brushed my lips over his before whispering in his ear. "I already do."

THANK you for reading Rule Breaker! For more Las Vegas Vipers, pre-order Shot Taker and watch Max Mikolajczyk have his work cut out for him taking his shot in winning the woman of his dreams.

FOR MORE INFORMATION or news about any of my books, join my mailing list at: www.staceylynnbooks.com

THANK YOU

HUGE thank you to Nina and all the incredible women at Valentine PR for throwing your full enthusiasm and support behind me and these books. I've loved working with you and can't wait to see what the future brings us.

Ellie and Virginia, as always, thanks for putting up with my mess and spit-shining each manuscript until it sparkles. Thank you especially during this crazy time in our world for your flexibility and your extra hard work.

Shannon, you're the best. Always. Forever. Your talent is astounding and I'm thankful I can call you a friend.

To my Sweeties! I love you ladies and your excitement for my books!

To all the bloggers who devote their time and passion into reading books, book tours, release events, leaving reviews, promoting and pimping – you are all rockstars! Thank you for all the love over the years.

My family— I love you all to the moon and back. I don't know what I would do without you in my corner, cheering me on every step of the way. Your support is everything to me and I love you all with all of my heart.

And last but definitely not least – to you the reader. I'm blown away with every release how much you adore my books. You have made my dream a reality and I hope I can cheer you on with yours. Please don't forget to leave reviews on Goodreds or whichever retailer you've purchased this copy from. It helps us so much!

ABOUT THE AUTHOR

Stacey Lynn likes her coffee with a dash of sugar, her heroes with a side of bossy, and her wine a deep shade of red.

The author of over forty romance novels, many of which have been best-selling titles, she loves being able to turn her vivid imagination into a career that brings entertainment and joy to her readers. Focused on sports romance and emotional, small-town romance, she also loves stretching herself in different genres.

Born in Texas and raised in the Midwest, she now makes her home in North Carolina and loves all things Southern. Together with her ultimate tall, dark, and handsome hero, she has four children. Her life is a chaotic mess that fights with her Type-A, list-making, neurotically organized preferences and she wouldn't have it any other way.

Subscribe to her newsletter so you can stay up to date on all her new releases. www.staceylynnbooks.com

OTHER BOOKS BY STACEY LYNN

<u>**Las Vegas Vipers ~hockey romance**</u>

Final Shot (free on all retailers)

Game Changer

Dream Maker

Rule Breaker

Shot Taker – June 2022

<u>**Ice Kings Series ~hockey romance**</u>

Playing With Fire (free on all retailers)

Playing To Win

Scoring Off The Ice

Hooked One Her

Hard Checked

Fighting Dirty

<u>**The Rough Riders Series ~football romance**</u>

Dirty Player

Filthy Player

Wicked Player

Cocky Player

<u>**Love and Lies Duet ~angsty slow burn, romance**</u>

<u>All the Ugly Things</u>

<u>All the Beautiful Things</u>

<u>**Love and Honor Duet ~angsty, romantic suspense**</u>

<u>Twisted Hearts</u>

<u>Unraveled Love</u>

<u>Love In The Heartland ~small town romance</u>

Captivated By You

This Time Around

Long Road Home

Before We Fell

<u>Crazy Love Series ~small town romance</u>

Fake Wife

Knocked Up

28 Dates

Weekend Fling

<u>The Fireside Series ~small town romance</u>

His to Love

His to Protect

His to Cherish

His to Seduce

<u>Tangled Love Series ~erotic romance</u>

Entice

Embrace

Enflame

<u>The Luminous Series ~BDSM romance</u>

Dominate Me

Crave Me

Long For Me

<u>**Just One Series ~rockstar romance**</u>

Just One Song

Just One Week

Just One Regret

Just One Moment

<u>**The Nordic Lords Series ~MC romance**</u>

Point of Return

Point of Redemption

Point of Freedom

Point of Surrender

<u>**Standalones**</u>

Remembering Us

Don't Lie To Me – billionaire romance

Try Me – A Don't Lie To Me Novella